PRAISE FOR VIVIAN AREND

"If you've never read a Vivian Arend book you are missing out on one of the best contemporary authors writing today."
~ *Book Reading Gals*

"A Rancher's Heart was a spectacular start to this new series and I am very excited to see what comes next for the rest of the Heart Falls crew."
~ *Guilty Pleasures Book Review*

"Brilliant, raw, imaginative, irresistible!!"
~ *Avon Romance*

"This story will keep you reading from the first page to the last one. There is never a dull moment…"
~ *Landy Jimenez*

"Arend became a favorite author of mine because not only does she write about sexy cowboys, she gives us families who love and take care of each other."
~ *SmexyBooks*

"This was my first Vivian Arend story, and I know I want more!"
~ *Red Hot Plus Blue Reads*

ALSO BY VIVIAN AREND

The Stones of Heart Falls

A Rancher's Heart

A Rancher's Song

A Rancher's Bride

A Rancher's Love

A Rancher's Vow

The Colemans of Heart Falls

The Cowgirl's Forever Love

The Cowgirl's Secret Love

The Cowgirl's Chosen Love

The Skyes of Heart Falls

A Cowboy's Bride

A Cowboy's Trust

A Cowboy's Claim

Other Heart Falls Series:

Holidays in Heart Falls

Heart Falls Vignette & Novella Collection

A full list of Vivian's print titles is available on her website:
www.vivianarend.com

THE COWBOY'S TRUST

THE SKYES OF HEART FALLS

VIVIAN AREND

This is a work of fiction. Names, characters, places, and incidents either are the product of the author's imagination or are used fictitiously, and any resemblance to any persons, living or dead, business establishments, events, or locales is entirely coincidental.

NO AI TRAINING: Without in any way limiting the author's [and publisher's] exclusive rights under copyright, any use of this publication to "train" generative artificial intelligence (AI) technologies to generate text is expressly prohibited. The author reserves all rights to license uses of this work for generative AI training and development of machine learning language models.

A Cowboy's Trust
Copyright © 2025 by Arend Publishing Inc.
Digital ISBN: 978-1-998508-24-2
Print ISBN: 978-1-998508-25-9
Edited by Angie Ramey
Cover Design © Damonza
Proofed by Linda Levy

All rights reserved. No part of this book may be used or reproduced in any manner whatsoever without written permission except in the case of brief quotations.

1

———

ansy Fields applied the final layer of her lipstick with a delicate touch, fingers steady as a rock. The only signs of the excitement racing through her system were the flush on her cheeks and the delight in her eyes reflected back in the hall mirror.

The end of the year usually involved a lot of thinking back and planning ahead, but tonight seemed extra special. All week she'd been enjoying a series of *one last time* moments, and now she was less than twenty-four hours away from a shiny, clean start.

She rushed through the door of her apartment above the Buns and Roses café, all but skipping along the back passageway to the staircase that led down to the local pub.

Last time to walk this way.

A grin stretched her face as the phrase hit again because it was also the last time she'd be able to do *this*.

Slipping in the side door of Rough Cut pub wasn't a thing that everyone in their row of housing on Main Street did, but Tansy liked using the short cut, and it was the last time and all.

The rest of the pub had rock-solid security in place, but this internal door? Not so much. Not for her at least. She flipped open the lock with a quick slip of the nail she kept handy, plus a hint of pressure and a hip bump in the right spot.

As she slid into the back of the pub, pulsating music wrapped around her and filled her head until her entire body was one big heartbeat.

She headed straight for the gathering spot where her friends and family usually landed, even though it would be a smaller group tonight. Her sister, Rose, and her sister's fiancée, Chance, were out of the county for the holidays. Tansy's doctor pal, Sydney Jerimiah, had volunteered to pull a shift at the emergency room in nearby Diamond Valley, but Petra would be around somewhere.

Rough Cut was rocking. Not only the music, but it seemed everyone who could had come to celebrate and dance away the old year and welcome in the new.

They couldn't possibly be as ready for this as Tansy was, though.

"Hey, girl."

"Tansy. Looking fine."

"Save me a dance," called another local cowboy.

Tansy waved in acknowledgment at them all. Hugging a friend here, offering a high five there. She felt so good she even might toss a bone to Bryce tonight. Nice enough guy, terrible dancer. He somehow managed to put an extra half beat into every other measure.

Tansy had standards when it came to dancing.

It *was* New Year's Eve, though, which meant she was more than willing to be magnanimous and share the bounty that was her with the rest of the world. There was enough of her awesomeness to go around.

A snort escaped as a shot of self-deprivation slipped in. Right. She was not all that special.

"Bullshit. You're a rock star, girl," Tansy offered out loud.

No one here would think anything of her talking to herself, if they heard her in the first place, and there were times she absolutely needed the reminder that she *did* belong. These people weren't pretending to like her—they really did.

Over twenty years later, it was still hard to turn off the voices in her head put there by people whose only agenda had been to take advantage.

Nope, those were not thoughts that were allowed to intrude on a day like today. This momentous, *stepping into the future* kind of day.

"Tansy. Want to dance?" Paul, who rated a seven on the Tansy Dance Scale, smiled at her hopefully.

Tansy generously offered her hand and headed onto the dance floor.

Out among the twirling partners, she got an entirely different perspective of the evening. Quick glimpses slid past of all the local regulars and plenty of visitors as her laughing partner kept up a steady monologue about all the things he had planned for the new year.

Tansy let him rattle on, a smile on her own face plus a nod when it seemed appropriate. But her gaze darted everywhere as her thoughts continued to loop into the future as well.

She was so gosh-darn excited, as she would tell the nieces and nephews. Big sister Ivy wasn't fond of the swearwords her children had already learned prior to being brought into her and her husband Walker's protective embrace. Tansy didn't want to be *that* auntie. Besides, it was fun to make her brother-in-law roll his eyes every time she came up with a new old-fashioned cuss.

Thank God for the internet, that's all Tansy could say.

She twirled out of the arms of one familiar friend into the next, thoroughly enjoying herself in spite of the stepped-on toes and bruised ankles she'd have by tomorrow. Not curating her list like she usually did was physically dangerous.

"Tansy."

This time in the pause between songs, a feminine tone rang out, and Tansy turned and looked into the face of one of her best friends.

Petra Sorenson, brunette hair wild around her shoulders and an enormous grin on her face, slid in beside her.

"I saw you earlier," Tansy said. "But you were moving fast enough to set the globe off-kilter."

Petra's fiancé appeared behind her. Aiden Skye also wore a happy expression. "Trying to keep up with you."

The three of them shuffled their way through the crowd to their usual spot, farther from the speakers so they could hear each other.

"Did I see you dancing with Johnny H?" Aiden shook his head slowly but his blue eyes sparkled with amusement. "That's not the Tansy we know and love."

"Hush," Petra teased. "I'm sure it's part of some grand karma offering to let out the old and bring in the new."

"Makes sense. Although why anyone would want to start the year black and blue, I'm not sure." He winked, tilting his head toward the floor. "Take a spin with me? I promise not to step on you."

Tansy didn't mind one bit.

Aiden expertly danced her off, and she offered a moment of thanks to whatever gods of mischief there were that the man had returned to Heart Falls in time to be there for Petra.

The two of them were perfect together.

Not a bad looking couple either, but then, all the Skye brothers, co-owners of the High Water ranch, were good-looking. All with dark hair and strong jawlines and piercing eyes that made direct contact.

Tansy liked a man who looked her in the eye, and not only because she hated holding a dialogue with anyone who talked to her chest.

"You ready for the coming year?" Aiden asked once they'd whirled their way to slightly more open floor room.

"Ready and waiting." Tansy held her secret to herself, both because it was amusing to know something Aiden didn't, and because it was the right thing to do. She didn't always do the right thing, but in this case it was a good idea.

Besides, tomorrow the secret would be out of the bag.

"Hey, favour to ask," Aiden said, a hint of hesitation slipping in. "I want Petra to have an engagement celebration with her girls. I mentioned it to her in passing, and she mostly waved it off. I don't know if it's because she doesn't want one, or she's not looking forward to planning the details, or if it's too soon."

"I can get to the bottom of that for you, my fine young man. Leave it in Tansy's capable hands, and I'll find out what she wants."

His smile faltered. "Thanks. We do talk, but her reaction seemed...odd," he concluded.

This Tansy could absolutely reassure him on. "Dude, you do not have to justify your relationship. I know you guys talk. Not because Petra gives us a play-by-play or anything, but because she's happy." Tansy offered the update as reassuringly as she could. "And anybody who makes my girl happy gets one hundred percent help. I will report back." She patted his shoulder encouragingly.

The song ended, and Tansy transferred arms again, this time to one of her more consistent dance partners, which meant she once again didn't need to worry about trying to lead without her partner figuring it out.

The crowd was humming and the music loud, and she lost Aiden and Petra to the side of the room where they tucked their heads together and looked so cute and in love it made her heart pump faster with happiness for them.

Did she want that? The head over heels connection with one person? She still wasn't sure—

Which was as good an answer for now as any. Ignoring the question of the distant future, she returned her focus to her dance partner and sank in to enjoy the current moment's good time.

Ten minutes before midnight, Tansy spotted him. Number two in the Skye brother trio. His jaw a little leaner, his eyes a touch more serious. Sometimes he looked as if he'd just lost his puppy, and she always had the irresistible urge to go over and pet him to make him feel better.

Not that he encouraged petting. Oh no, Jake Skye was too independent a man. Plus, he didn't seem to have a funny bone in his body and took himself way too seriously. Maybe that's why she found him intriguing, considering that while she could do serious, she had far more of an *enjoy today, eat dessert first, dance while you can* attitude.

Real or not.

Still, as she was awkwardly guided around the dance floor by her final incompetent dance partner of the year, God rest her shins, Tansy entertained herself by sneaking glances at Jake.

He nursed a beer and never went out on the dance floor, which made her wonder. She knew he could dance. That very first day at the end of summer when Petra and Aidan had been reunited, Tansy had danced with Jake...

Hadn't she?

No. She'd danced with *Declan*, oldest brother and a real sweetheart of a teddy bear. The zero chemistry between her and Declan had been apparent from the get-go, so she'd been telling him about one of the guys who was handsy when they danced who'd started to hang out at the café a little too often. Declan had listened earnestly then offered to delimb the bastard at her convenience, which put Declan firmly in Tansy's good books.

It had been extremely annoying that she'd had spectacularly dirty dreams that night with *Jake* as the main star.

Tansy cringed as she and her partner bounced off another dancing couple.

No, if Jake was intriguing and interesting, it was because the two of them were oil and water, and Tansy got a perverse satisfaction out of sending his knickers into a twist. He used lists and planned and plotted. Hell, he probably had a five and ten year life blueprint organized and posted in triplicate.

She made plans when appropriate, which meant not often.

He'd wanted to set the timer for the hard-boiled eggs she'd made over at their house one day. A timer. *Her.* She never used a timer for anything when she cooked.

An announcement broke in overhead as the music paused. "It's time, folks. Join me as we get ready for the final stroke of midnight and welcome in the new year."

The countdown began.

Ten, nine...

So many people around, all laughing and shifting. Tansy spotted Aiden as he curled Petra close, ignored the clock, and planted a huge kiss on her.

Amused, Tansy twisted a little farther and came face-to-face with Jake. His eyes widened, lips tightened. As if she were the last person he wanted to see.

Fine. Be that way. She pivoted farther.

Four.

Three.

The cowboy she'd been dancing with—Two Left Feet Malone, Tansy had labeled him in her mind—was a nice enough guy, but as he opened his arms for her to join him for the traditional New Year's Kiss, the excitement factor was nil.

Ah well. This too was simply a part of *one last time* before the new year. Because God knew she was *never* inflicting a dance with him on herself again.

From behind her, someone grabbed hold of her wrist and tugged.

She spun away from Malone, caught an instant later against a massive hard body. Tansy's palms splayed over a firm chest as she looked into a set of blue eyes that displayed both wild satisfaction and shock.

Jake Skye.

She was in Jake's arms, and the countdown was done, and she couldn't have planned a better flip from *old to new* if she'd tried.

Especially when he leaned down and pressed their lips together and every *yes* button Tansy possessed clicked on and locked in place. No simple mouth-to-mouth, nearly innocent peck, he dove in wholeheartedly and seared her with heat. A quick nip to her lower lip, a sweep of his tongue. The weight of his big hand on her lower back locking them together so tightly she wanted to purr with satisfaction.

Who knew? The man could *kiss.*

Tansy wrapped her arms around him and joined in enthusiastically. Hell, she wrapped her *legs* around him, pressing closer, trying to connect them at as many points as possible. The firm line of him against her body was sexual temptation incarnate, and if they weren't in the middle of the dance floor, she'd have assumed this was step one toward a very spectacular horizontal dance.

But they *were* on the dance floor, and as the cries of *Happy New Year* around them faded, the other part of why this kiss and embrace were so hilarious kicked in.

She hadn't seen it coming. She'd bet anything neither had Mr. *My Backup Plans Have Backup Plans.*

When they finally broke apart, gasping for breath, Tansy clung on and grinned right into his face. "See? Sometimes spontaneity is fun."

JAKE FOCUSED on staying upright as Tansy shimmied her feet back to the ground. He needed to say something, anything. Maybe even apologize.

Nope, couldn't do it.

"Thanks for the great start to the new year. I'll see you around." Tansy patted his cheek then vanished between one breath and the next.

Jake stood there and tried to figure out what the hell had just happened.

A hand landed on his shoulder. A second later, Aiden hauled him in for a brotherly back pounding. "Happy New Year, bro. Petra and I are headed back to the ranch. Don't call us in the morning."

He said it quietly enough Petra didn't overhear. Instead, she offered Jake a hug and a big smile. "Good things coming this year for us all," she promised before patting his cheek then slipping to Aiden's side.

She curled her arm around his and they wove their way through the crowd.

"I'm headed out as well." Declan stood beside Jake. His

oldest brother laid a hand on his shoulder and squeezed tightly. "Happy New Year. The house will be quiet tonight. Enjoy it while you can."

Declan was gone before Jake could demand to know what that meant.

Instead, he stood there in the noise and chaos of the partiers and wondered why he'd gotten two cheek pats in the past two minutes. As if he was a dog or something.

He'd been ready to head back to High Water himself, but suddenly the empty ranch house and his unfinished room under the art studio was the last place he wanted to be. He lifted a hand to a passing waitress, motioned for another beer, then stood aside as the crowd resumed dancing and flirting and trying to find a partner to take home. Oh yeah, there were plenty of pickups in progress...

The mental image of Tansy staring at him, breathless from his kiss, popped to mind in far too vivid detail. Did he really have to have noticed the way the left side of her mouth quirked up slightly more than the right? Or that her eyes weren't simply light brown, but the faintest hint of gold circled the iris? And her hair. A golden blonde that was soft against his fingertips when he'd cupped the back of her neck and kissed those tempting lips, the taste of her—

"*Fuck.*"

He nursed the beer after it arrived before heading home to toss and turn restlessly for hours.

Which meant the next morning, far later than usual, he stared at the coffee maker and willed it to spit out liquid faster. He felt like shit and still had no idea what had come over him the night before.

Kissing Tansy was not part of any plan. Dirty daydreams, yes, but getting involved with anyone was not on his agenda until High Water was up and running.

He lifted his chin sharply, regretting it instantly. Slow moves were a far better idea. As the coffee trickled into the pot, Jake pulled his focus to the real task at hand.

High Water was ready to kick into gear and start the next stage, which meant he had to get his act together and be ready.

Jake deliberately turned and admired the room and the view out the window, taking in the details of High Water that had already become as familiar as any previous home.

High Water. A place he and his brothers—and now Aiden's fiancée, Petra—were building into the ultimate *pay it forward* location.

The ranch had been a working animal rescue, and would be again. They'd spent the past five months building a retreat house where weekend and weeklong escapes for artists would be held. The retreats would provide income for the ranch to supplement their other sources.

More importantly, running these operations would require work. Cleaning, animal care—all of which provided the real reason for the ranch. A place of short-term employment with no questions asked for people who needed a temporary place of refuge. Women getting away from bad situations. Men trying to escape a life they no longer wanted to be involved in.

Yup, it was really about to happen. Which meant his gut rumbled with unease, his entire system out of kilter since nothing was plannable beyond being ready to open their doors.

He didn't like it when things weren't plannable.

Regretting his New Year's Eve choices more than a little, he stood by the coffee maker and drank an entire cup before refilling and easing his way to the table.

Ten o'clock, and no one else had appeared in the house yet. He figured Aiden and Petra had a good reason to be MIA. Declan was up, but in the barn. Their first High Water arrival, sixteen-year-old Jinx Tremont, no longer considered a short-term ranch hand but part of the family, was sleeping over at the neighbouring ranch with her best friend, Sasha Stone.

Well, to hell with it. It was time to set some goals. That's what people did on New Year's Day, right?

He nabbed his notebook, automatically realigned the envelopes that had slid slightly outside of the hard cover, and turned to a fresh, clean page. He wrote GOALS at the top and a set of numbers to the side, one all the way to ten. He stared at the page for a moment then in the first spot wrote down, crisp and clear...

1. *Learn to be more spontaneous.*

What the fuck?

He all but glared at the journal. *That* was not what he wanted to write. That wasn't what he'd been thinking about at all, and he pressed his hands to his temples, begging for the pounding to die down.

Tansy's fault. It was the word she'd used the night before, and it had bounced in his head most of the night.

He examined the notebook page with disgust. Everyone had their quirks, and he was honest enough to admit this was one of his. Either he crossed it out and left a visible mark of his mistake, or he ripped out the page, neither of which solutions sat well.

He decided to leave the damn sentence for now and let it annoy him.

Someone knocked on the door. Jake was already on his feet even as he checked the time. New Year's Day and they had a visitor?

Oh shit. What if it was Danielle, their contact in youth services? What if somebody needed their help?

He hurried forward and jerked the door open, staring in

shock at a wildly grinning Tansy. She held a plastic container toward him, jamming it into his hands.

"What's this?" he demanded.

"Welcome to High Water brownies," she announced happily, slipping past him and hauling a rolling suitcase after her.

She closed the door then turned back, tugging the container from his fingers. "Thanks. Those are for me."

"You said they were welcome brownies," he repeated.

She nodded eagerly. "They are. You don't know how to bake, and I wanted brownies. Since I'm living here now, they're *welcome home, Tansy* brownies."

She twirled and headed farther into the house.

Jake shook his head, trying to get her words to settle in his brain and make sense. Nope, wasn't working.

He stomped after her into the kitchen. "What do you mean, you're living here?"

She put the brownies on the counter before twisting to face him. She brushed her hands together as if knocking off crumbs then thrust one forward. "Declan and Petra hired me. Hi, I'm your new live-in cook."

2

———

Something was wrong with his hearing. Or his vision.

For sure something was off with his entire morning—the start of a brand-new year, and he was ready to go back to bed.

Jake stared at Tansy. She didn't vanish, and the grin on her face grew wider if that were possible. "Working here?" He stumbled over the words. "You?"

She wiggled her fingers in the air, and he realized he'd completely ignored her offer of a handshake. The cutest nose wrinkle squished her face, probably at his lack of participation, he assumed, as she let her hand fall. "Yup. Let me put my bag away and—"

"Don't move. Don't—" Jake froze.

What was he supposed to tell her? To stand there until he could track down one of his brothers and demand to know what the actual fuck was going on?

Or Petra. Petra was perfect. He might like his future sister-in-law, but she deserved to be woken up right now. He lifted a finger in Tansy's direction even as he hauled out his phone and messaged Petra, New Year's sleep-in be damned.

Jake: Tansy is here.

She responded so quickly she had to have been waiting with phone in hand:

Good. We'll be there in about ten minutes.
Get her settled, will you please?

Jake glanced away from his phone and met Tansy's highly amused gaze. She'd folded her arms over her chest and now raised a single brow in one of the disturbingly easy-to-read expressions she liked to toss his direction. This one clearly said *You are amusing, but slightly annoying.*

"I am so sorry." She waved him back toward the table. "I've distracted you before you had your coffee. I know where I'm going. Sit down, and I'll make myself at home."

The wheels of her suitcase rumbled over the floor into the bedroom section of the house before his motionless stupor registered.

"Wait." He was helpless to stop his feet from rushing him all the way into the primary bedroom after her.

The woman was quick, he had to give her that. She didn't saunter, and she did not loll about. In the approximately three-second lead she'd had, she'd reached the bedroom, hefted her oversized suitcase onto the bed, *and* opened it. Ignoring him, she undid straps and zippered sections then tucked clothing into the dresser beside the bed.

She not only ignored him but began humming. The tune was catchy and bold, and with her shoulders lifting and knees bending, she turned the short trip between the bed and dresser into an ongoing dance.

That's when he noticed. The room, which should have been full of Petra and Aiden's stuff, was completely empty. Except for Tansy, who continued her task without once acknowledging him.

He wasn't sure how long he stood there simply watching her before realizing he must look the fool.

"One question." There. A reasonable tone of voice, he thought.

"Hmmm?" Her suitcase and unpacking seemed to be her only focus in life.

He hesitated. He had way more than one question and wasn't sure where to begin. Out of the all the things he needed to know, what was the most important?

The empty room seemed the best place to start. Petra and Aiden had moved out on the sly. Ergo, they were in on the plan all along.

"When did they hire you?"

Tansy paused, clothes in hand as she twisted to face him. She considered thoughtfully for a moment before answering. "We started talking about it sometime in December, but I signed the contract on Boxing Day."

"You've known for a week that you were coming to work here?"

"Yup." She blinked innocently. "That's how time works. December twenty-sixth to January first is one week."

"Who knew?"

"Me, Petra, Declan." Tansy grinned. "Jinx knows as well. We had to make sure she was comfortable with me being in the house. But that kid can keep her mouth shut."

Incredible. Jake opened his mouth to ask another question when he realized the brightly coloured objects in Tansy's hand were a pile of bras. The lacey kind, not the utilitarian stuff.

Once again, an image popped to mind that was absolutely

out of place and out of line. Tansy naked, except for those bits of pale lavender—

He twisted on his heels and escaped as fast as he could.

Gentle laughter rang on the air behind him all too clearly. The woman was way too observant for his liking.

The open journal on the table mocked him, and he slammed the cover shut on the one damn goal he'd written—

Not a goal, not *really* a goal. Jake tipped back his coffee mug then went to refill it for the fourth time, staring out the window at the slow approach of his younger brother, Aiden, and Petra.

They laughed as they walked hand in hand. Petra stooped and popped up with a handful of snow, and Aiden chased her for a moment before catching her in his arms and kissing her thoroughly.

Jake turned away a moment too late to pretend he hadn't seen them.

Maybe that was a good thing... The sheer joy on their faces and the strong connection between them shoved his own brain into a better direction than thirty seconds earlier.

So what if he hadn't been told about Tansy being hired on? Everyone involved with the High Water ranch, aka, his two brothers, Petra, and Jinx, would expect him to rant and rail about the decision.

Spontaneity and deliberately new behavior were almost the same thing, yes? Jake decided right there and then he wouldn't say a word about Tansy's new position. He would be supportive and positive and focus on other things that needed to be done as soon as possible to make their dream a reality.

Which meant his smile was firmly in place as Petra and Aiden poured in the door with a gust of icy January air.

"Morning, bro." Aiden took the coat from Petra's shoulders

and hung it at the door before placing his own over it. "Ready for a fantastic new year?"

"Of course. Happy New Year, Petra." Jake opened his arms and accepted the massive hug she offered. "Sounds as if we're diving right in. Tansy is in the back room unpacking."

"Perfect." Petra patted Jake's cheek firmly before stepping away. "Excuse me, then. I'll go see if she needs any help."

"Not to be obnoxious, or anything, but find out if she plans to cook starting today," Aiden called after her before turning to Jake with a grin. "Great, huh? Our own on-site resident chef."

"Brilliant." Jake kept the smile in place. No guarantees that it looked natural, but he was proud of the attempt. "Maybe we can take a look at the timelines for the first quarter and make sure we have everything in place for the first bookings."

His brother waved a hand, taking command of the coffee maker and rapidly preparing two cups. "I don't think it's changed in the past three days since we last looked it over. Relax, Jake. Today's a holiday, and we have everything well in hand. Better in hand than before now that Tansy's here."

The door opened in the middle of his sentence, and Declan marched in. "I spotted Tansy's old beater in the parking lot. Glad she made it already."

"Petra told me this morning that you guys had hired Tansy." Aiden stirred sugar into one of the cups. "I can't believe you convinced her it was a good idea, but I, for one, am grateful. My stomach will be grateful, and the time I no longer have to spend cooking for you bottomless pits also makes me grateful."

"We needed help eventually," Declan offered with a shrug. "Seemed like the perfect time." His eyes met Jake's as if expecting him to protest, or question, or make a fuss.

Jake's cheeks ached under the pressure of keeping his expression neutral. "If you've done the math, and I assume you have, I have no objections."

Aiden stopped in his tracks, glancing back at Declan before staring at Jake in shock. "Wait. They didn't tell you, either? I mean, I thought they were keeping me in the dark because I don't need to know everything that goes on around here but you—" His brother hesitated.

Honest amusement snuck in. "But I *do* need to know everything that goes on around here, is that what you're saying?"

"You *are* the details man," Aiden offered reluctantly. He turned to Declan. "Since Jake isn't kicking your ass from one side of the room to the other, I assume he's on board. But we said there would be no secrets between the three of us running this place."

"Wasn't really a secret," Declan said quietly. "Considering how often Jake hired Tansy to cook for him over the past three months, it seemed a fairly natural progression to add her to the payroll instead of him paying out of pocket."

Trapped. Jake made a face. "There is that. Like I said, if we can afford her, we all agree Tansy brings value to the table. Literally. No one in any of the upcoming weekend retreats will complain about what she feeds them."

Aiden eyed him for a moment then dipped his chin. "Still say Declan owes you something for being an ass."

"Petra knew as well," Declan pointed out.

"Yet my fiancée is nothing but sweetness and light, so obviously this was Declan leading her down the path of iniquity." Aiden grinned. "Fine. No punishment except having to eat the delicious food Tansy will undoubtably prepare for us."

The front door opened again, and this time the teenager of the house slid through with Dixie, the golden retriever, on her heels. Jinx paused to wave back at the truck in the driveway then closed the door and turned excitedly to face all three of them. Dixie raced from person to person, offering her own enthusiastic greetings.

"Happy New Year, guys."

Jinx had spent too many years in the foster system, but now with Declan as her official guardian, she'd begun to bloom.

Dark hair pulled back in a braid, she quickly hung up her coat and slipped her feet into her house shoes and marched forward with a smile.

Declan stood as Jinx slipped in and offered a quick hug. He patted her on the shoulder without trapping her in place.

Aiden got the same hello. "Happy New Year. You have a good evening with Sasha?"

"So much fun. We stayed up until two a.m., and then this morning, Mrs. Stone made bacon wrapped sausages for breakfast."

The kid was lucky she still had a teenager's metabolism. "Sounds delicious," Jake offered.

He hesitated. Out of the three of them he was the one who Jinx seemed to feel the most uncomfortable around, so he wasn't about to offer a hug and force her into anything.

Instead, he offered the next best thing. "There's a surprise for you. Well, a surprise you knew about. Tansy's here. She and Petra are in the bedroom. Why don't you go say hi?"

Jinx damn near squealed with excitement. "She's here? Sick."

The girl shot across the floor at high speed and vanished into the bedroom area.

The three brothers exchanged amused glances. "Oh, to have that much energy on five hours of sleep," Declan offered like a prayer. He tilted his chin at Jake. "Don't think I didn't see what you did there. We're getting there. We're making a difference," he promised.

Pay it forward. Make a difference. Do what's right. All the things that their stepfather had not only told them but demonstrated in the years after he'd stepped in when their mom died.

Suddenly, it truly didn't matter that Jake hadn't known about Tansy being hired. Whatever issues he had were his own. Tansy was here for a good reason, not the least of which was it made Jinx happy.

Jake would put up with an awful lot to keep making a difference in that girl's world.

Tansy hadn't brought a lot of things, but organizing her new space was still a treat. She put out the few knickknacks she had stuffed into her suitcase then spent time arranging items in the bathroom.

It had been funny beyond belief to watch Jake stumble until he recovered from his shock. Any arguments that they'd had in the past—and they'd had a few—he'd been unreasonable, not scary. Even today she had to give him credit for how levelheaded he'd stayed. She appreciated that.

She wasn't sure she would've reacted quite as well under the same circumstances. If she'd shown up for work one day and Jake had unexpectedly been dishwashing, she would've given her sister Rose what for.

No. The man had been shocked out of his mind but behaved properly, which said a lot about his character. Maybe she'd even cook his favourite meal this week.

She wouldn't tell him why, but she'd cook it, nevertheless.

"Look who's already getting snug as a bug in a rug."

Tansy whirled. "I'll let you have that saying for its cutesy factor but remind you I usually draw the line at bugs anywhere around my person."

Petra swooped in and tangled Tansy in a hug. "Fine, no bugs. But I am glad you're here. This is the most amazing thing, and I'm so excited that you're going to be part of this with me. I mean with us. I mean with all of High Water."

Laughter bubbled up. "I'm cooking for you, not finding a cure for cancer."

"On a scale of one to ten, you living here is a solid ten. Curing cancer would be a twenty, but I'm not setting my expectations that high." Petra plopped onto the bed, bouncing as she grinned across the space between them. "I know you'll have more details for everybody later, but you obviously figured out a schedule. You're not expected to produce culinary masterpieces three times a day seven days a week."

"That would be a logistical nightmare," Tansy said with a firm nod. "I have done some planning—I can't believe those words just came out of my mouth. I assume it's Jake I should give those details to."

"Probably."

"We signed a contract, but can you really truly afford to be paying me what you are?" When Declan had sent over the contract Tansy had nearly fallen off her chair.

Petra paused. "You'll find out more about the finances of High Water as you go along, since you need to have the ability to order food and the rest of it, but they really can afford you. The boys' stepdad was an amazing man in more ways than one. He left them a healthy inheritance that they didn't touch until coming to Heart Falls. Add in what they make, and what I make doing odd jobs, and the money that will be coming in from the retreat house... We can't be super extravagant, but we can afford you." She snickered. "In fact, it'll cost less than what Jake spent buying meals from you three or four times a week."

"I always appreciated the patronage," Tansy said brightly. "Okay, then I will stop worrying about that, but remember I also want to contribute. Doesn't seem right that I'm the only one putting money in my pocket at the end of the day while all of you pile your resources back into the ranch."

"You'll earn every penny between juggling what you still need to do for Buns and Roses café and cooking and coordinating here. Trust me, you're worth it."

It was nice to hear it, but Tansy would keep her eye out for any signs that she was a burden instead of a help.

"Time to focus on the really important details," Petra said seriously. "First, check your messages. You have your phone on Do Not Disturb, and I know there's a note waiting for you."

Tansy pulled out her phone, curiosity quickly answered as she spotted the message from Sydney, the final member of their friendship trio. She read it with Petra hanging over her shoulder.

> Sydney: Hey, darling. Sorry I can't be there to happy dance in your presence, but trust me, I'm doing one right now for you. Yes, the doctors and nurses around me are giving me the stink eye, but pfft on them.

> Sydney: I'm off to bed once my shift is done, but I wanted to tell you that I think you're going to rock this job, same as you have knocked it out of the park in all previous endeavours. Looking forward to celebrating with you when I can.

> Sydney: Love you lots! Happy New Year and <3 xoxox Get a hug from Petra from me!

Warmth bloomed in Tansy's heart. She really did have the best friends in the world, even if nailing down Sydney was sometimes like catching the wind.

A second later Tansy was enveloped by two strong arms and hugged vigorously.

Petra squeezed her hard then pulled back just far enough to offer a very serious expression. "Now, second most important thing. Do you plan on making more of those fist-sized peanut butter cookies, and can you hide them in a secret cookie stash so that no one but me can get their paws on them?"

A snicker escaped. "I'm about to get requests for secret treats from every one of you. How will I possibly hide them all?"

"You're sneaky, so you'll find a way," Petra offered proudly. "Also, I have a lard container I saved that we can put in the freezer. You can use that for mine."

Laughter mixed with footsteps in the hallway, followed by a loud squeal of excitement. A second later, Jinx slid into the room, a bouncing dog on her heels. She glanced about then made a dive for Tansy. "You're here."

Tansy soaked in the sensation of the unexpected hug, squeezing back even as she met Petra's eyes and saw happiness there. "I'm here. As promised."

Jinx let go, speaking before she was out of arm's reach. She reached down and stroked Dixie's head as words spilled out of her. "Will you teach me to cook?"

"You want to be my sous chef?" Tansy was delighted but figured she'd better make sure that was approved. She glanced at Petra, who shrugged. Jinx waited. Tansy lifted her hands in the air. "Hey, I have zero problem with you helping, which is the best way to learn. But I'm pretty sure you have other things you need to do as well, so we'd better double-check with the powers that be before I promise you the moon and stars."

"I want to make those moon-shaped cookies," Jinx blurted out.

Petra snorted. "And there's the second cookie request."

Jinx looked confused, but Tansy reassured her. "We

absolutely can make crescents. But you get what I mean about helping when it's appropriate?"

"I do, but I don't think it's a problem." Jinx glanced at Petra this time for reassurance. "That's what High Water is about, right? Doing what we can to help others. Making this place work for the people who will start coming through. And since I'm a full-time part of the family, I want to help."

The part inside Tansy's belly that had felt a tingle of *this is right* the minute she had heard what was going on at the ranch —that spot grew warmer.

Jinx had been caught in a bad situation. But even in the short time she'd lived at the ranch, High Water had made a difference in her life. Tansy knew about that. Knew how much her own world had changed when the Fields adopted her.

Petra stepped forward, moisture in her eyes but pride in her expression. She laid a hand on Jinx's shoulder. "You're right. You are part of this family. We'll make sure that you get to help as much as makes sense."

Jinx snuggled into Petra's side, smiling at Tansy. Dixie settled on the girl's feet, offering a picture-perfect moment of clarity. This was the reason why Tansy had arranged to remove herself from her own café and stir up her entire life.

Making a difference. Proving her worth. It was one thing to have been saved by others, but sometimes more was needed.

She held out a hand to Jinx. "I have more boxes in my SUV. Once we bring them in, you and I should talk to Jake and do some planning. After, we'll do some cooking. I think cookies are first on the agenda."

Jinx's smile was a reward in itself.

Followed closely by the thought that showing Jake her plan would be amusing as all get out.

Tansy could do both spontaneity *and* a plan.

Could he?

3

____

The shift to having Tansy on the premises wasn't nearly as difficult as Jake had imaged.

Five days a week, food magically appeared. Hardy, *going to pack on the pounds if I don't watch out* type meals, with a steady supply of treats stacked on the counter of the main ranch house.

The two days when Tansy was officially off-duty, the brothers continued as before, occasionally taking turns working the grill in spite of the temperature dipping well below freezing. None of them were picky eaters as long as the food was plentiful and delivered somewhat on time.

Plus, it was far easier when Tansy left them a well-stocked fridge filled with the ingredients they needed.

No, if anything, Jake had to swallow his pride and give his siblings an award for being smart enough to hire the woman. It was the other component that turned out to be a whole lot more challenging than expected.

Tansy was one huge, enormous distraction.

He grumbled his way along the well-packed snowy trail

that led to the ranch house and tried to figure out exactly what it was about her that got his hackles up.

Maybe it wasn't *her*, but the fact another person now lingered in their space, contributing to what had originally been a plan cooked up by him and his two brothers. They'd always said it was a chance to come back together after moving apart when their stepdad passed.

They needed a fresh start—or at least he and Declan both had. Declan's wife had passed suddenly after a short but intense bout with cancer. Jake had left the police force after becoming completely disheartened by the politics and corruption.

"You look miserable."

Jake glanced up to discover the other full-time occupant of High Water eyeing him with curiosity. Kevin Robb was their on-site psychologist and enthusiastic dog walker for the few beasts currently living in the animal shelter.

Even now he had two of them on leashes, the difference between the giant husky and the small Pomeranian comical as they sniffed eagerly at the full extent of their leads.

"Your dogsled team isn't going to win you any awards," Jake offered dryly.

Kevin grinned. "Wouldn't that be something? Honestly, the big brute is a bit of a lazy butt, so I think Little Princess here would outpull him any day of the week." He eyed Jake closer. "Something on your mind?"

"We hired you for the ranch hands who will be coming through."

Kevin glanced around and raised a hand in the air. "Business is slow, and I've always got my analyst hat on."

Maybe it would be good to talk about it. Jake's commitment to not complain to his brothers had stood firm. Even after two weeks, he hadn't once complained about being left out of the loop with Tansy's hiring.

Talking to Kevin wasn't really complaining—

And there he went, justifying it all over again.

His friend snickered. "The dead-air I just got to my suggestion means you absolutely want to talk about it. So let's do this. I'll take my mismatched oxen here back to the barn, then how about we meet in the art studio?" He considered for a minute. "There's a few final bits of window trim that need to be stained. We can take care of that while we talk."

The man was brilliant. It was somehow easier not to think of it as a therapy session when they were knocking off one of the final things on Jake's checklist.

The art studio absolutely needed to be ready. They had their first weekend visitors arriving Friday night, and while it was only a group of six, it meant High Water was about to officially be open. The public-facing, money-making side of High Water, that was.

Jake filled a thermos with coffee and nabbed a handful of muffins off the counter in the main house, timing it perfectly so Tansy was out of the room when he raided the kitchen.

The woman got up at five a.m. every day. It made it damn near impossible to avoid her when he wanted to grab a quick breakfast.

Of course it also meant that there was fresh baking every morning, so it wasn't as if he really had anything to complain about.

Out in the art studio, the sunshine reflected off the hardwood floors and created a warm honey glow that bounced off the walls. Jake filled a cup and grabbed a muffin, settling into one of the oversized easy chairs arranged to look out over the land to the south.

It was hard to keep that disgruntled feeling inside sharp

when confronted with pristine acres of snow and towering spruce trees against the Rocky Mountains.

He sat and enjoyed his breakfast. Kevin copied him and settled into the chair at his side, munching quietly as he too looked over the endless vista.

"That alone is worth the price of admission," Kevin said. "You know, when you gave me a shout and told me what you were doing here, I thought it was a pretty good idea. Didn't realize how much I'd need it at the time."

Jake took a glance at the friend he'd known for years. The cut that ran through Kevin's brow and down beside his eye had healed, but it left him with a bit of a rakish look. It might be rude, but they'd always spoken bluntly between them. "You have nightmares about getting that scar?"

"Mostly I'm thankful it wasn't worse," Kevin said slowly. "The nightmares I have are regarding the young man who gave it to me. He's exactly the type of person we might see here at High Water."

Ouch. "That's going to make it tough for you."

Kevin shrugged. "Jake, you know this. Doing the right thing isn't always easy. But there's a special sense of pride in doing what's right in spite of how tough it might be. I can't let something that happened to me change the person I am in negative ways."

Jake cringed again, but this time it was for an entirely different reason. He met his friend's gaze straight on. "Yeah, I think that might be my current dilemma. Stuff that happened in the past changed me, and every now and then I get a reminder of how much I don't like it."

His friend leaned back in his chair and crossed his ankles. He sipped his coffee then nodded. "Anything specific?"

Jake wasn't about to bust out Tansy's name, because it was pretty clear she wasn't the problem. Only she came to mind, and he wanted to shake his head to get her out of there.

When he caught Kevin grinning, he realized he was *literally* shaking his head.

Fine. Bite the bullet and spit it out. "I've always been good at organizing things," Jake offered. "With some of the stuff that's happened in my past, I might have gotten too obsessed about it."

"We do like to fall back on habits that give us comfort," Kevin pointed out. "You've had a lot going on over the past years. Your organizational skills have gone a long way to making High Water possible."

It was as if Kevin was giving him an out, but Jake knew there was a difference between a solid plan and paranoia. "Yeah, but I shouldn't feel a sense of panic when somebody changes plans on me."

For a moment, his friend stayed quiet. "Lots to untangle in that sentence," Kevin finally said. "Let's hit the two questions you should start with. First, do you have a reason to panic? I mean, consider the source right at that very moment. Sometimes when we get trained by past experiences, there's a good reason to be wary. We should trust our gut—we earned that knowledge. But if you're talking about situations involving your brothers, or Petra, can you trust them, or should you panic?"

"Good question. That's the part keeping me level. I know where their heads are at, and they're both rock solid. I know what they want in the end is the same thing I want." This was the easy part to answer. "Aidan will do everything he can, even if he puts Petra first now, and that's how it should be. And Declan's pouring his entire life into the place."

Kevin nodded. "Good. That's a solid place to start. Which doesn't mean the panic will go away right away, but it means that you can turn right back on its heels after you ask *Do I need to panic?* No. Feeling uncomfortable is fine, but panic, go away."

"Easier said than done," Jake grumbled.

"Don't I know it," Kevin agreed. "That's where the second question comes in."

"Is it time for a beer?"

His friend laughed. "I don't advocate for self-medicating with alcohol or drugs on a regular basis. No, the question for you is right up your alley because it's action based."

"Drinking beer is an action," Jake complained.

"If you'd said whiskey, I'd be joining you." Kevin finished the last of the coffee in his mug and smiled across the distance between them. "No, the second question is *What should I do right now?*"

Really? "You want the self-confessed excessive planner to make another list?"

Kevin shook his head. "Oh no, the exact opposite. When you get to feeling the way you don't want, I'd like to propose an experiment. You have to find something to do for a short period of time that is absolutely *not* on your list."

For fuck's sake. That damn unfinished goal list in Jake's journal was coming back to haunt him. "You're saying my therapy is to be spontaneous?"

"Yeah, pretty much. Only for fifteen minutes if that's all you can take."

Jake collapsed back in his chair and stared at the ceiling. "This is a new form of hell."

"You might be surprised." Kevin grinned at him, rising to his feet. "Now let's finish our therapy and deal with the window trim. Then we can honestly tell the others we had a productive morning."

Jake washed both their cups and turned on some music.

They spent the next two hours in a comfortable quiet, sanding trim and applying a final layer of varnish.

The place looked great when they stopped to admire their handiwork, and while Jake still wasn't one hundred percent comfortable with the suggestion, Kevin's idea had some merit.

It seemed the universe meant for him to learn some new lessons this year.

THE FIRST WEEKS of working at High Water had been thrilling but frantic.

Tansy had taken on what was essentially a full-time job, but she still had the food element of Buns and Roses café to coordinate. Even with the head baker/chef she'd hired for the café, it took until the middle of January for the woman to fall into a solid routine that meant Tansy only needed to come in once a week for a meeting and to double-check the current food order sheets.

Since she planned to do the food order for High Water then as well, timing for that part of the job balanced out nicely.

"Somebody complained that my cinnamon buns are nowhere near as good as yours," Marina informed her as they met in the early morning on Thursday before the café doors were officially open. The woman had her salt-and-pepper hair tucked under a rainbow-hued headband. The smattering of freckles over her nose and her pale skin hinted that once upon a time she'd been a redhead. Now in her late fifties, she might've gone grey early, but she still moved with amazing speed in the kitchen. "I swear I followed your recipe to the letter."

"Proof them under dishtowels instead of saran wrap," Tansy suggested. "And if people complain after that, tell them we're so sorry, and we'll take them off the menu. I bet they shut up fast."

Marina's amusement was clear. "I can tell this isn't your first rodeo."

"Terrible cinnamon buns are better than no cinnamon buns at all, you know?" Tansy offered a wink then went through the rest of the questions Marina had from the week. When they were done, Tansy nodded her approval. "You're doing a great job. How are you liking the apartment?"

Part of the enticement of getting a trained and experienced chef to move into the area had been to provide instant accommodations. Tansy wasn't using the rooms anymore, so it had made sense.

"I think you're being far too generous, but you can't take it back now." Marina sat back in her chair and sighed happily. "This is a little bit of a dream job for me. You have this place running like clockwork. You haven't gone overboard with too wild and varied of a menu, and other than my inferior cinnamon bun skills, things have been going well. In fact, if you need me to take on any extra baking tasks, I'm ready."

"That is really good news. I'm still okay right now, but over the next three weeks, we start to host events out at High Water." The first people would arrive the next evening, and Tansy had excitement butterflies flipping in her stomach. "When we get to full production, having you deal with some of the breakfast items and baked treats will end up being a lifesaver."

"Not a problem. You know as well as me it's just as easy to cook twelve dozen as six dozen when you have the oven room. Which we do." Marina got to her feet and brushed her hands down the front of her apron, smile brightening. "I need to get back to work before my boss catches me sitting on my butt."

"Fate worse than death. I hear your boss is a real hard-ass," Tansy teased.

She'd just slipped behind the wheel of her clunker when a text message from Sydney arrived.

> Sydney: I truly hate updating qualifications.

> Tansy: Let me guess. They're making you sit through slideshow presentations instead of letting you simply take the test.

> Sydney: Got it in one. What a freakin' waste of my time. Anyway, I wanted to catch up with you. How's the new job? I'm pissed off that I haven't been around to come celebrate with you.

> Tansy: I know you're excited for me. You'll be back in a couple weeks, and we'll get our girls night on then. The job is working out fine. Jinx is a hoot, and you and I need to start planning a wild and woolly bachelorette party for Petra.

> Sydney: It will be a night to remember. Okay, I need to hit the road or I will get the evil eye from the powers that be when I stroll into the lab late. Again—cough, cough. Time to pretend to be a productive member of adult society. Love you. Don't poison anyone.

> Tansy: Love you, too. I wouldn't dream of it unless you were here to help hide the body.

The extra wiggle in the steering wheel and the very creaky brakes of ZenBaby faded to the background as a happy glow wrapped around Tansy on the ride back to the ranch.

Having good friends like Petra and Sydney at her back was amazing. Finding Marina had been a stroke of luck and a stroke of genius. Changing things up at Buns and Roses had been a bit of a risk, but her sister had been fully on board. Knowing that with Marina's help it would work as they'd hoped was an amazing thing.

Which was why it was slightly disconcerting to feel a shot of dissatisfaction wash away her good mood when she bounced into the ranch house and discovered Jake sitting at the table by himself, glaring at his journal.

She'd noticed him withdrawing even more than usual over the past two weeks, and every time it seemed to be triggered by that damn journal and the letters hidden in the pages.

"If they're being mean to you, you could throw them out," Tansy suggested.

He barely moved. Just grunted and glared a little harder.

Whatever. She headed to the kitchen counter and dropped off the tray of inferior cinnamon buns Marina had made—such nonsense. She was sure they were delicious.

Then Tansy bustled around the kitchen and began prepping food for three meals at the same time.

Onions in the crockpot, onions in a pan on the stove to caramelize. Carrots diced into coins for the crockpot, made into sticks for a veggie platter, and grated and left in a bowl to be turned into carrot cake. She expertly disassembled four whole chickens. The breasts were added to the onions on the stove with a shot of stock and the lid put on top to simmer. The thighs were seared and added to the crockpot, and the rest of the bones placed on a cookie sheet and put into the oven to roast so she could pull the cooked meat off to make chicken salad sandwiches.

Every time she glanced at Jake she could've sworn he hadn't moved an inch.

It must be exhausting being that grumpy, she decided.

She scrubbed her hands thoroughly then loaded a plate with the cinnamon buns and poured two cups of coffee.

When she sat down, he blinked as if surprised to find her there.

She shoved the plate with the cinnamon buns toward him. "You must be so hungry you're going catatonic. Eat this. And drink."

He sighed. "I might've had too much coffee already. But thanks for the cinnamon bun. How did your meeting with Marina go this morning at Buns and Roses?"

"Peachy. She's fantastic, and I'm totally replaceable. Exactly what every boss wants, and I'm being serious." Tansy took a big bite of the immense cinnamon roll and hummed happily. "Whoever complained about these was out of their goddamn minds."

Jake took a halfhearted bite then nodded his approval. "They're okay. Not as good as yours."

Tansy snickered. Too funny.

But now was time to poke the bear. "Are you ever going to finish that New Year's goal list?"

He slammed the cover shut on the mostly blank page he'd been staring at. "That was private."

"I wasn't reading over your shoulder. It was right out there in public," Tansy pointed out.

He frowned down at the table and then at where she sat across from him. "You can read upside down?"

He was such an innocent. "I have many skills," she offered with complete sincerity, not about to confess many of them were learned in her misspent and highly illegal childhood.

"I like setting goals," Jake confessed slowly. "But it was recently suggested to me if I feel a little too regimented by all my planning, I should try something different."

Ha. Tansy's brain raced ahead to the final outcome of that situation. "Which means now you don't know if you should make a goal list or if you shouldn't."

He grimaced. "Pretty much."

"Well, indecision is worse than a bad decision in my books." Tansy met his gaze straight on. "I'm pretty good at being spontaneous. Maybe I can help you with that."

Jake muttered softly under his breath, and Tansy laughed. "Yes, I did read that upside down. I think it's a good goal if you're into that sort of thing."

"I suppose you don't set goals." He said it as if she'd confessed to drinking dishwater.

"I set plenty of goals," Tansy insisted. "I try to make them ones I can actively implement. Not things that are dependent on other people. You want to talk about the ultimate goal setter, though, that's what my sister Fern does best. She's been plotting and planning for years—I'm pretty sure you two would get along great."

"We do. I mean, the few times we've done stuff together. Like preparing for this weekend and beyond. Since she works for Chance, she's helping coordinate a lot of the retreat house details."

"I knew you'd met, but I didn't realize you'd had more interactions." Tansy thought for a minute. "Let me help you be spontaneous. I haven't seen my sister Rose since she and Chance got back from Ireland, and we're getting together with the family tonight. Fern will also be there, and my sister Ivy and her family."

A look of horror crossed his face. "I can't drop in unannounced at a family gathering."

Tansy snickered. "Trust me, until you've been to one of my family dinners, you have no idea what you're dropping in on. It'd be good for you."

"That might be a little too spontaneous for me to begin with," he grumbled, and Tansy was once again reminded of trying to move a giant St. Bernard from where he'd settled for a nap.

"You're not a hopeless case. You were spontaneous on New Year's Eve," she generously pointed out.

His jaw hung open as if shocked that she reminded him. His face went red with embarrassment, but he did maintain eye contact. "It was New Year's Eve. Plus, it was only a kiss."

"You should stick to that, then. Stealth kisses. I wouldn't mind—you're a great kisser."

Dear God, she was going to die laughing. Silently, inside, because she didn't want to embarrass him more than simply talking about the kiss was already doing.

Jake alternately opened and closed his mouth in a wonderful imitation of a fish, cheeks completely flushed. "I don't think we should get involved. You're working here, I'm working here. It's not a good idea."

"Who said anything about getting involved?" she asked in all seriousness. "I just said you're a good kisser, and if you need to practice being spontaneous, I'm okay with it."

He pushed back in his chair and folded his arms over his chest. "Yeah, no. Kisses lead to other things. I'm not comfortable going there with you."

"Trust issues?"

"Yes," he stated plainly.

Oh. "All righty. Enough said." Consent was one of those *good for the goose and good for the gander* things. "Forget kissing. I still think you should come to dinner with me. The invitation stands."

She rose from the table and headed to the stove, stirring and seasoning and adjusting temperatures. She grabbed three dozen eggs, put a dozen into a pot to boil then broke the others into the blender to make breakfast bites for anyone who wanted them later.

She twisted at high speed with her hands full of eggshells and smacked right into Jake. The double-handful of stickiness smashed against his rock-solid chest and shattered even farther. "Shit."

He glanced down in annoyance at the broken shards adhering to his shirt, glued on with the remaining bits of egg white that had clung to the shell. A healthy dusting of shells lay at their feet as well—the perfect storm of kitchen disasters.

But his lips twitched slightly as he met her eyes. "Fine. Let's be spontaneous. What time are we heading over to your parents?"

4

———————

*H*e supposed this was some kind of cosmic karma paying him back for being a grump the past two weeks. But even he knew that, when every time he turned around the same thing smacked him in the face, it was time to cave.

Tansy got the meal prepped for High Water—chicken stew with biscuits and apple pie for dessert—then just before five, she nabbed Jake and hustled him out the door.

Sitting in the passenger seat of Tansy's SUV seemed as if they were daring the universe a touch too hard. "You're a far braver woman than I knew, Tansy Fields."

She snickered, head checking as she switched lanes and headed into Heart Falls proper. "Don't think I haven't noticed you white knuckling it over there. I'm not a bad driver."

"No, you're a good driver." He could give her that much. "But even a good driver doesn't stand a chance with bare tires and a brake system that's out of kilter."

She pumped said brakes a couple of times, expertly dealing

with the layer of black ice that coated the entire road at the four-way stop intersection. "ZenBaby might not sound or look pretty, but I am up on his vehicle maintenance, thank you very much."

"ZenBaby?"

She patted the dash fondly. "ZenBaby. He's a little old, but I love him."

Jake locked his jaw together, partly so that if they did get in a crash, he wouldn't bite his tongue off.

Tansy distracted him from his heart palpitations by changing the topic completely. "Okay, heads-up time. Yes, we're joining my parents for dinner. It's not going to be very formal. In fact, chances of us all sitting at the same table at the same time are almost nil."

Thankfully, she kept her gaze firmly fixed on the road as she turned into one of the residential areas.

Jake studied her profile as she spoke. She was every day pretty. Not the sort of woman that made people do a double take, but the kind who the longer you looked at her, the more there was to see.

Another shot of uncalled for interest raced through him, and he shoved it aside. "Explain."

"It might not have been brought up in public, but it's no secret. My oldest sister Ivy, now Ivy Stone, has social anxiety. She also dealt with some pretty big physical issues, but for the most part she's staying healthy these days. But because of her, our family tends to spend more time talking in twos and threes than gathering around and letting one person shoot the breeze or putting one person on the spot."

It was a rather brilliant solution. "And since you've invited me over, are you planning on sticking by my side or tossing me to the wolves?"

A burst of pure amusement escaped her. "My first impulse is to tease you about how shy and retiring you normally are, but after sharing about my sister's issues, I can't be a jerk. You've already stepped outside your comfort zone to come with me. What would make you feel happy tonight? Do you want a wingman?"

It was Jake's turned to snort. "Doesn't that usually mean helping someone find a date? Because I'm not planning on hitting on Fern, who I assume will be the only other single woman there tonight."

Tansy waved a hand briefly before putting both gloved hands back on the steering wheel. "Semantics. Just meant I can stick to your side if you want, or you can go solo. Whatever you think is best."

He certainly didn't need his hand held. The Fields were a highly respected part of the community, and he'd met all of them over the past six months. "Back when I worked for the Winnipeg RCMP, I was a school liaison. I'm okay in groups."

She pulled to a rumbling stop in front of a two-story house that screamed character, full of interesting roof angles and an oversized porch. She put the SUV into Park then focused her attention on him. "Well, if that changes, let me know. Otherwise, come nine o'clock, I'll find you and we'll head home."

"You're a very easy date," Jake teased, sliding out of the SUV and joining her on the sidewalk. He was suddenly shocked by exactly how comfortable this all felt.

Tansy stumbled, and he caught her before she could hit the ground. Only when she turned and tossed a double mittful of snow in his face with a cackling laugh did he realize it was a ploy.

Which meant dropping her unceremoniously into the tall

snow pile at the edge of the walk was the most natural thing in the world.

"Oh, you're nasty." Tansy shot a hand to him for help. "I like that about you."

He grinned as he reached down, totally not expecting for her to take a firm grasp on his wrist then kick her feet into his ankles while she pulled.

He face planted beside her, instantly covered in snow from head to toe.

He rolled, spitting snow.

Tansy laughed so hard she ended up clutching her stomach.

Jake sighed dramatically, shaking his head as he brushed snow off his cheeks.

"Are you bringing him in for supper, or are you planning on killing him out there and hiding the body?" Fern stood, one foot on the porch and one foot in the house, a grin on her face as she eyed them.

"A little snow never hurt anyone," Tansy quipped as she bounced to her feet. When Jake held his hand to her for help to get vertical, she shook her head. "Uh-uh. You're spry enough all on your own. Let's get inside before you start to melt, Mr. Snowman."

Fern waited for them inside the entrance. "Rose isn't here yet. But Ivy and Walker and the kids are around somewhere." She met Jake's gaze. "Carter's the oldest. Prepare for him to latch onto you and not let go. He's suddenly decided some guy out there must know the secret of surviving younger sisters."

"I don't have sisters," Jake reminded her.

"I know that, and you can tell him that. He still thinks that there's something built into grownup men's DNA, and if he hangs around them long enough his little sisters might suddenly vanish. Although he'd miss them a lot if they weren't there." She grinned. "If he's too much of a bother just tell him to go play."

"It's not a problem," Jake insisted. "I like kids. What are his sisters' names?"

Tansy answered this time, grabbing his coat from him and tossing it onto the pile stacked four deep on a preacher's bench. "Chloe is the oldest. Harper is the pixie-faced heartbreaker. If she asks you if you can remove any of your body parts, don't take it personally."

Fern snorted. "It's not my fault."

Jake glanced down at Fern's left arm, which was currently missing the hand and forearm prosthesis he'd seen her wearing before. "Kids like to know stuff. It's not a rude question. Not really."

"Exactly." Fern dipped her chin firmly. Her attention caught on something outside. "Time to vacate the front entrance. Jake, I'll talk to you later."

"Looking forward to it."

Tansy snagged him by the hand and hauled him through the house. It wasn't exactly messy, but the place was filled from top to bottom with interesting things. He wouldn't have minded a slower tour, but suddenly he was pushed through the kitchen and face-to-face with Tansy's older sister.

Pale white hair cut in a bob framed her thin face, and she blinked at him for a moment before offering a smile. "Hello. Did you bring home a stray, Tansy?"

"He's housebroken," Tansy promised. She turned to her sister. "Ivy, this is Jake Skye. One of the owners of High Water ranch, brother-in-law once removed to Jinx Tremont who is now your niece Sasha's bestie."

It was amusing as heck to see that was how Tansy

introduced him. "Nice to meet you," Jake said. "May I offer you my heartiest congratulations on surviving being sister to Tansy." When Ivy's lips twitched, he winked. "I hear you have three children somewhere in the house."

Her smile only widened. "And a husband to go with the three sisters, two parents, and two grandparents. A plethora of blessings." She glanced over her shoulder then pointed to the far corner of the room. "The girls are with their great grandma. Which means my son is outside with his Great Grandpa Ashton."

Tucked in the corner of the room was an oversized recliner. In it sat an older woman with silver white hair and little girl tucked under each arm and a book in her lap. In another one of those interesting twists, Jake knew exactly who she was even though he'd never met her face-to-face.

She and her husband were the previous owners of the animal rescue they'd bought. She read expressively even as her gaze darted over to take in Jake and Tansy.

"Excuse me." Ivy slipped away, headed into the kitchen where she joined her father working at the stove.

Tansy twirled around Jake for a moment, tugging him toward the side wall. "The rule is if somebody leaves suddenly without much of a warning, you didn't do anything wrong."

"Not offended," Jake assured her. He took another glance around the room. "I hear voices at the front door, which I assume would be your sister Rose along with her fiancé. If I'm counting right, there'll be over a dozen people here for dinner."

She considered for a moment then nodded. "Sounds about right."

It was not at all what he was used to. "On a Thursday night, for no special reason."

"Family means there's always a special reason," Tansy

insisted. She frowned for a second and then her face took on that interesting twist. "It's not an official party, but it is Grandpa Ashton's birthday. Also, I hear Chance and Rose's voices, and it sounds as if Chance's brother came along as well. Have you met Cody yet?"

Jake had. Which meant this impulsive evening was turning out to be a whole lot more interesting and less about putting himself into an awkward situation than expected.

The combination of putting himself out there and having a good time seemed to be hitting the nail on the head a little too hard, though. It had to be mostly a coincidence.

Tansy nodded briskly. "Okay, I'm going to go see if anything needs to be done in the kitchen. Wander, make yourself at home. There are drinks on the island, and my brother-in-law Walker is around somewhere."

He was about to reassure her he'd be fine when she patted his cheek, whirling away a second later and leaving him standing there.

Another pat to the cheek. Definitely getting the vibes that he was either being humoured or treated like some sort of overgrown St. Bernard. Either way, right now he didn't mind one bit.

He made his way to the island and found a bucket filled with long neck beer on ice. Across the room he spotted Walker Stone and lifted a beer at him in question. When the other man nodded, he grabbed two, popped off the tops, and took a stroll to join him.

Somewhere in the middle of this evening, Jake might just lose some of the grumpiness that had been plaguing him for the last while. Although it didn't help that the thought kept coming back—

Tansy had been involved with every incident of him having a good time recently.

It was something to be thought over a whole lot harder before he did anything about it.

~

As usual, hanging out with her family was a little slice of heaven. They'd finished stuffing themselves, and now Tansy curled tighter into her sister Rose's side and rested her head on Rose's shoulder.

Her sister linked their fingers together and leaned right back. "You okay?"

"Peachy keen," Tansy informed her. "I mean, I miss you, but at the same time, it's been really neat to wake up in the morning and do something different than I've done for years and years."

"You're still cooking," Rose pointed out. "Although, I suppose there's a big difference between cooking family style and the short-order stuff at Buns and Roses."

Tansy thought for a moment. It wasn't only about the work she was doing. But it wasn't her secret to tell about the underlying mission behind High Water, so she kept her mouth shut on that part.

But somehow knowing that she could make a difference in someone else's life—the potential was there—made her world a whole lot more sparkly.

Six-year-old Harper climbed into Tansy's lap. She pressed her hands to Tansy's cheeks and stared her intently in the eyes. "Auntie Tan."

"Hippie hoppy Harper," Tansy returned.

"Chloe says I'm too little to make a birthday present for Daddy, but I know how I can be big enough."

At her side, Rose sat a little straighter, both of them paying complete attention to their youngest niece.

"Jiminy Cricket. Do you have an idea for a nice present?" Tansy asked.

Harper's eyes widened and she nodded her head seriously. She glanced around the room to double-check where Walker was. He was safely far enough out of earshot, talking to someone out of sight who sat in a wide, upright chair.

She leaned in close and whispered to her aunties. "Daddy wants some afternoon delight."

Tansy bit her lips to keep from laughing out loud.

Rose controlled herself enough to speak—thank goodness because Tansy was not capable. "That's a very interesting present. Two questions for you, sweetie. How do you know that's what your daddy wants, and what do you think that is?"

Tansy snickered, this time a little bit of it escaping. She smiled sweetly at Harper. "You can tell us so we can help you, right?"

Harper was all big eyes and secret whispers. "I was playing under the kitchen table and I heard Mommy and Daddy talking. We tried Turkish Delight one time after we read about it in a story, so I think it's candy." She met Tansy's gaze straight on. "I saved my allowance. I can buy ingredients. Will you help me?"

All amusement got tucked aside because the kid was so stinking cute and earnest, and that needed to be rewarded. Tansy answered the request with a serious nod of her own. "Of course. I'll check all of my cookbooks to find out exactly what we need, and the day before your daddy's birthday, we can cook it up together."

"Although it might have a different name in the cookbooks," Rose pointed out helpfully. "Just so you know, but no matter what it's called, it'll be the perfect thing to give your daddy."

"I love you, Aunties." Harper handed out hugs and kisses as if they were pennies and she was a billionaire.

The instant she crawled off and returned to playing a game with Chloe, Rose and Tansy caught each other's eyes then let themselves enjoy a good hearty laugh.

"God. I can't wait to torment Ivy with this," Tansy offered between snickers.

They were still wiping away tears when Rose nudged Tansy in the shoulder then pointed across the room. "Well, that's rather adorable."

Across the room, the mystery person in the hidden chair was now visible. Jake sat upright with Carter on his knee. A very avid conversation was going on between Walker, Chance, and Ashton Stewart, who had officially joined the family just over two years ago.

Jake was paying attention, but he wasn't saying much. Instead, he rocked slightly as Carter rested his cheek on Jake's chest and his eyes slowly drooped.

"Jake said he was good with kids," Tansy offered. "That's sweet."

Another nudge hit her shoulder. "So. Are you and he..." Rose waggled her eyebrows.

A snort escaped before Tansy could stop it. "Nothing worse than a happily engaged woman. You want everybody to be lined up and tucked away. No, he and I are not...*anything*. Other than exasperating to each other."

Because she was not about to mention *the kiss*. The one that every time she thought about, it ended up in italics or air quotes or all the things that made it more than a simple kiss.

The kiss had power. It had nearly knocked her socks off, and she really, *really* wanted another.

But, since she couldn't always get what she wanted, she smiled sweetly at her sister. "Have you made any decisions about your official wedding day?"

"Nice change of topic, but I'm not done. I could have sworn

every time you talked about Jake Skye in the last six months you were telling me about how very annoying the man was."

"Get your tenses right. How annoying the man *is*, and that hasn't changed. Although I will confess that working in close contact at High Water means I'm immensely grateful that he's easy on the eyes."

"And yet you brought him home with you." Rose lowered her voice and leaned in close. "There is no secret keeping from me. I know all your tells. *You* want to take a nice big bite of that man."

"Maybe I'm on a diet."

"Diet tomorrow, eat pie today. I pretty sure that's your motto," Rose said with a smile, but she brushed her lips over Tansy's cheek and eased away. "Enough teasing. I'm glad you're happy, and so far it seems Buns and Roses isn't falling apart without you. Although for some strange reason I miss you and your mischief, but it is nice to be doing the next thing. Chance is amazing and I'm so very much in love."

"I'm glad." Tansy tapped her sister on the nose and got a laugh. "Now, get your sickeningly sweet engagement cooties away from here because I want none of them."

Chance stepped past, pulled Rose to her feet, and planted a kiss on her that made the little girls clap and squeal. Carter just groaned as if he'd just been handed a sheet of math homework to do over the holidays.

Tansy's dad met her in the kitchen and helped load dirty dishes into the machine. "He seems a solid young man."

"Jake? Oh, yeah. All the Skye brothers are down to earth and trustworthy." Tansy thrust her hands beneath the running water to rinse them clean. "I'm enjoying working for them."

"I heard that tomorrow is the first day with the extra cooking for the retreat house. You ready to roll?"

She considered for a moment then dipped her chin firmly.

"It's funny. I never thought about exactly how many people I cooked for in a single day at the café. But when I did the math, just to be sure, it turns out that catering for a weekend should be a piece of cake. Excuse the cooking humour."

Her father leaned a hip on the counter and folded his arms over his chest as he considered. "You got a bit of butterflies, don't you?"

"You're not only handsome, you're smart as a whip," she teased before shrugging. "Once I've got a few of these events under my belt, it'll be fine. Besides, a little bit of butterflies are sometimes fun."

A laugh escaped him, rolling up, deep and warm. When she'd been twelve years old—the day they'd said that she'd been adopted—she'd heard that laugh, and her world had changed.

Which meant it was completely natural to step forward and curl her arms around her father, hugging him tight. "I don't mind being a little scared these days. I know I've got people at my back, and that makes a difference."

Malachi pressed a kiss to the top of her head. "You've got lots of people. You are loved. Never forget it."

Tansy went and visited with her grandma, then her mom, then her sister Ivy, and when nine o'clock rolled around she went looking for Jake.

He hadn't moved far. In fact, he'd returned to the scene of the crime because he was once again in the big wingback chair. This time he had Harper in his lap, and she was sound asleep.

Tansy swallowed hard. What was that sensation? A tightening between her gut and her throat that made it difficult to breathe for a moment.

He was listening to a conversation again, this time between her mom and Carter. Jake's gaze drifted over the room, but when it landed on Tansy, it froze. They stared at each other, the tickling sensation inside her going off again.

She couldn't ignore that seeing him with the kids was enough to trigger something in her. A level of trust she hadn't had before—maybe it was that.

Something to think about...

She strolled forward. "We should head out. It's starting to snow."

Jake nodded. "You know where your sister is? Where should I put Harper?"

"I'll take her." Tansy's mom offered. Sophie held out her arms, and Jake carefully made the transfer, speaking softly as she offered an approving smile. "I'm glad you came tonight, Jake. You're welcome anytime."

"Thank you, ma'am. It was a very relaxing evening."

Once again, Tansy guided Jake through the house quickly, back to the front door where they grabbed their things and headed outside.

Overhead, light fluffy flakes were falling. Not enough to have accumulated on the windshield yet, so Tansy used the wipers to brush them away, and they were down the road and headed back to High Water.

A comfortable silence fell between them.

Comfortable at least until Tansy couldn't resist asking. "You want kids, don't you?"

"Always said I did. Someday. But in the meantime, it's fun to borrow other people's then give them back. Thanks for giving me a chance to do that tonight."

"Hey, you were the one who was spontaneous," Tansy told him before adding in all seriousness. "I enjoyed having you there. And it was a nice distraction from thinking about tomorrow and all the cooking I'll do over the next three days."

Jake hummed for a minute. "I overheard you talking to your dad," he confessed. "If you need any help, ask."

Tansy snickered. "Because you and I cooking together worked so well the last time we tried?"

"I didn't say I'd be the one who actually *helped*," he said dryly.

They grinned at each other for a minute then Tansy focused back on the road and getting them home safely.

She was headed up the porch steps when she realized Jake was by her side. "You don't have to walk me home."

"Didn't have to, no." Jake shrugged. "Wanted to."

Whatever. Tansy put a hand on the doorknob and got ready to make her way inside. "Well, thanks for coming with me. I'm glad you had a good time."

"Thanks for inviting me."

He swooped. It was the only word that came to mind. One minute he was standing on the top step, and the next he had her bent over his arm and was staring into her eyes as if she were a lady on a historical romance's cover.

"There's only one problem with spontaneity," Jake said. "Consent. But then I realized you already gave me the go-ahead."

He pulled her closer into him, and their lips connected.

Tansy had been thinking maybe she'd been slightly intoxicated on New Year's Eve. Or maybe it had just been so long since she'd been kissed in a seriously hot way that she'd blown *the kiss* up to being better than reality.

Nope. Not her imagination. Not one bit.

He might have started in a rush, but the kiss immediately slowed. He teased his tongue along her upper lip, and the hand on her lower back pressed her even more tightly to him. An invitation to take the kiss deeper, more intimate. A lot of heat, a whole lot of lust, and right when she was ready to slide her fingers into his hair and hold them together for the rest of the night, he straightened.

Stepped back, breathing hard but with a smile on his lips. "Tansy."

He dipped his chin then turned, and whistling, he made his way to his rooms under the art studio.

Tansy stood there in the open doorway, the snow falling and the heat of indoors brushing past her as she tried to reorientate herself.

Okey Dokey. She had not seen that one coming.

5

———

It might have taken a solid two by four to the head for Jake to come to his senses, but now that he had, moving forward would be that much easier. And potentially fun and life altering in all the right ways.

What a night. Score one for spontaneity. Although he was absolutely making a plan of attack going forward.

Jake hurried back to his apartment and removed his winter wear even as his brain tumbled together memories and the itch to accomplish new tasks.

First, there was an important matter he needed to deal with. Tansy had been more right than she'd ever know—God, he could not believe how hard it was to admit that even to himself.

He needed to deal with the letters that made his brain go into a spiral every time he saw them.

Which was often, because ever since the first one had arrived from his ex-wife, he hadn't known what to do with them. Which meant he tucked them into the back of his journal and for the past three years, any time he had a moment to pause, they kicked his butt all over again.

Melissa would be thrilled to find out exactly how much she'd continued to mess with his brain.

No, that was unkind. She hadn't done anything wrong. Truth was, she'd always been good at the card thing. Christmas cards, birthday cards. Even after they'd split up, she'd sent them at regular intervals.

But three years ago, when Declan's wife had died, Melissa had sent an extra card, asking if he'd pass on her condolences to his brother. The entirety of the correspondence had been thoughtful. More than simply *Thinking about you. Hope you're doing okay.*

Considerate good wishes. No one could complain about that, now, could they? So he'd responded.

It meant the next time a letter arrived from Melissa, he'd been a little more willing to open it, and when she started including little tidbits about where she was and what was going on in her life, it didn't seem that strange.

He figured some people stalked their exes on social media and the rest of it. He never had, deliberately. But there was something about getting an actual letter he found impossible to simply throw away.

Every reminder of Melissa he had made him uncomfortable now that he'd begun to have feelings for Tansy.

Straight up, daydreaming about getting down and dirty with Tansy while he carried letters around from Melissa made him feel as if he were somehow cheating. Which was nonsense but still true.

Enough. He was finally ready to do the *turn a new page* part of the new year—almost three weeks too late, but so be it.

Jake pulled all of the cards and envelopes from the back of his journals. He still couldn't toss them, but he could at least put them out of sight and hopefully out of mind. He assembled them in one big stack, bundled them up with an elastic band, then looked around for a good place to stash them.

Somewhere he wouldn't spot too often. Wouldn't accidentally fall back into thinking about the woman who didn't really want him but didn't seem to want to let him go either.

In the end, he shoved the pile to the back of his closet, tucked against the wall behind a pair of dress shoes that he only ever wore to funerals or job interviews. Neither of which he hoped to be doing anytime soon.

Satisfied, he headed to bed, savouring what had been an amazing evening and a spectacular kiss if he did say so himself.

The idea of being able to fluster Tansy made him more than a little pleased.

The entire evening had made him happy, and he couldn't deny the whys of that. The Fields family had something special. Not only the connection between the siblings, but there was a real kindness to them at heart. He'd noticed the glances tossed between him and Tansy, but it hadn't been judgmental. More in the lines of *if you're interested in our Tansy, are you going to treat her right?*

On one level it made him slightly uncomfortable to admit exactly how attractive he found Tansy. But there was no reason for the discomfort. She was a beautiful woman with a good head on her shoulders, and even if she'd didn't do everything the way that he would, she wasn't wrong.

He'd been fighting his attraction and his desires, and while Kevin would have a heyday if he knew everything, Jake was self-aware enough to be able to self-diagnose part of it.

Melissa had done a number on him. While they'd been young and gotten out of the marriage nearly as quickly as they got into it, Jake hadn't really trusted another woman since then.

Trust. Such a little word for such a huge, gigantic, world-altering emotion.

Jake rolled over, the lethargy in his limbs as sleep beckoned closer tangling his thoughts, and yet nearly asleep, his understanding of the big picture seemed clearer. Melissa wasn't the only one who'd broken his trust. His partner on the police force, Sean, had turned out equally deceptive in an entirely different way. Jake had left the RCMP when it was discovered Sean was accepting bribes on the side.

Sean had tried to put the blame on Jake but hadn't succeeded. Still, it was the sort of thing that left a terrible taste in a man's mouth and a chip on his shoulder.

Yet none of those details mattered because both of them were out of his life. Now that the letters were tucked away, hopefully neither Melissa nor Sean could influence Jake's thoughts and he could focus on the here and now.

Focus on what it was he wanted in his world, which meant he needed to make a new list in the morning.

He wouldn't apologize for using his planning skills to try and make good things happen. Like convincing Tansy that while they were oil and water in some ways...

No, oil and *vinegar*. The vinegar was him—a little too sharp, a little too astringent and determined. But combined together the two of them could be delicious on many levels.

He fell asleep amused at trying to woo the woman with food metaphors.

A brisk pounding on his door woke him half an hour before his alarm was supposed to go off at five A.M.. He leapt out of bed, grabbing jeans off the hook on the wall even as he stomped to the door.

When he unlocked it, Declan poked his head in. "We've got a ranch hand arriving sometime in the next half hour. You good to help me get him settled?"

"Hell, yeah. Where are we meeting?"

"Main house. I figured chances are he'll be hungry, and Tansy's already awake, getting set up for this evening."

A momentary flash of concern struck. Jake was glad their first official ranch hand had arrived, but this weekend wasn't the easiest time to slip in someone without being noticed. "You ready to make a judgment call on whether he's out and about this weekend or staying low?"

"I've got it," Declan confirmed with a nod. "I'm headed to the house."

It took under ten minutes before Jake was scrubbed up, teeth brushed, and dressed in his ranching best. Worn blue jeans, an old soft flannel pulled over a plain blue T-shirt, finished with his favourite pair of boots, ones that he'd had for so long his feet slipped into them like a handshake with old friends.

Which meant when he made it to the house he was physically as comfortable as possible. It was all on the mental side that he felt shaky.

But inside the ranch house was warm and homey. Tansy spoke quietly with Declan, never stopping her work as she held an enormous bowl braced on her hip with her left hand and beat batter with the spoon in her right.

Declan offered a chin lift as Jake strode forward. "He's the one who can answer that question," he informed Tansy.

She glanced at him, the faintest hint of pink on her cheeks as she offered a smile. "Morning, Sunshine. I wanted to know which room you're putting the new ranch hand in. I put together a box of snacks for him so he doesn't feel as if he has to come into the house or the common room right away."

"That's a nice idea," Jake said, nodding his head. "I put him in room two. With Kevin in number four, it spaces them out a bit until we have other arrivals."

"Sounds good. I have a couple more things I want to tuck in the box, and I can do that as soon as I've got these cupcakes in the oven."

"We can take the box with us when we show him the room," Declan offered.

"Perfect. Now excuse me, I need to finish my arm exercises for the morning." Tansy turned her back to focus on expertly pouring from the enormous bowl into prepared tins lined with rows and rows of paper muffin cups.

Declan filled a cup of coffee and offered it to Jake. "Our guest hopes to stay less than a month. He gave some information to the authorities that put him in trouble with past employers. He's got somewhere to go out on the East Coast as soon as he can get in touch with them."

Past employers was code word for gangs or other criminal operation.

Jake focused on the short-term part. Well, it was where they thought they'd start. "He have a name?"

"He's going by Chris. For our purposes, Chris Smith."

Behind them at the counter, Tansy snorted. "Sorry. Just realized there's going to be a whole lot of that around here. Smith and Choi and Turner and Singh. Such imaginative names."

"This from the woman whose last name is *Fields*?" Jake teased.

This time she outright snickered, still working away.

Declan frowned momentarily at Jake, confusion in his eyes, but he didn't say anything as they headed to the table to finalize plans.

Yeah. His poke at Tansy had come out a whole lot more friendly than most of his interactions with her over the past days. Weeks.

Hell, he'd been an ass for nearly as long as they'd been in Heart Falls. After the bullshit he'd handed her, it was a wonder that she talked to him at all, let alone invited him to her family's for dinner.

Or let him kiss her.

Jake sat with Declan and hashed out details until a knock on the door sent them both rushing to their feet.

But while he concentrated hard on the man entering the house, his eyes dark with worry and evidence of sleepless nights on his face, Jake didn't forget about the beautiful blonde woman moving silently in the background.

His plan wasn't quite complete, but he had a few good ideas of where to start.

WITH A MILLION TASKS TO juggle mentally, Tansy had to pay attention to the job at hand. The group of six and their instructor taking over the art studio would arrive after six, so she'd planned a snack-type dinner for Friday night. But all day Saturday, and Sunday until noon, she was responsible for feeding them plus the regular High Water crew.

Thank goodness everyone involved at High Water had understood the need for serving food family style. Buffet at the counter, continental-type grab-it-yourself breakfasts. Trying to do plated dinners would take more time and hands than Tansy possessed.

Working quickly and steadily, her current curiosity had to be satisfied with listening hard and some quick glances back at the table where the new ranch hand sat nodding seriously as Declan explained the rules.

Chris looked pretty ordinary, which was a good thing, she supposed. It wasn't as if everybody who was hiding from the authorities or the bad guys out there should have signs on their foreheads announcing what they'd been up to.

She knew that getting to put the past behind them was vitally important.

She brought toasted bagels already smeared with cream cheese to the table, with muffins and egg bites stacked high on the plate. "I'll make you a real breakfast in a minute, but this should take the edge off."

Declan nodded seriously as Chris scrambled to his feet, dipping his head in Tansy's direction. "This is Tansy. She's part of the family, and if there's anything you need food-wise, you need to let her know."

Chris took a quick glance over her before fixing his gaze firmly on his hands. "Nothing special. But I am hungry, so thank you."

"I'm glad you're here." Tansy said it simply but honestly before meeting Declan's gaze. "I'm frying up some eggs for Chris. Do you two want breakfast now or later?"

"I'll grab something later," Jake said. "Can I help with anything?"

She held back the snappy remark about how helpful he was suddenly being after kissing her stupid. "I'll have food to carry to the studio later in the day. If someone shows up to help, that will save me from having to make multiple trips."

"I'll make sure it happens," Jake promised.

Declan offered his brother an odd stare for a moment before continuing to talk to Chris. "We have paying guests in the art studio this weekend. There are some animal chores you could help with while you're here at the ranch, but we'll also need a hand washing dishes and doing other household chores."

"Dishes, push broom. I'll do whatever. I'm thankful for the place to stay. I should hear from my brother soon, though, so I won't be a burden for long," Chris promised.

"You're not a burden," Jake assured him. "Let that go and get your feet under you."

Tansy was back at the stove, making breakfast for Chris and beginning to work on the fruit platters she'd need for the late-night snack.

"Just so we're clear, Tansy, my brother's fiancée, Petra, and my ward, Jinx, all live on the ranch. The ladies are all family and are to be treated with respect." Declan's tone of voice remained matter of fact but brutally firm.

"Got a sister myself who I'd want to be treated properly," Chris returned. "They'll get no trouble from me."

The smallest bit of tension that had hovered at the back of Tansy's mind eased. Of course, the man could be lying, but the fact he responded quickly meant she'd only sleep with one eye open.

She fell into the rhythm of preparing food for the family as well as what was necessary for the weekend. She dropped a plate of food in front of Chris, was thanked profusely, then went back to her tasks, satisfied at having done something simple but meaningful.

Maybe twenty minutes later, she whirled, blinking in surprise when she found Jake waiting patiently in front of her. "Whoa. Didn't see you there."

He grinned. "Next time, should I warn you? Then you can get the eggshells ready."

Tansy stuck out her tongue.

His smile shifted to something far more needy as he stared at her mouth. The kind of look a man gives a woman when they're interested in getting down and dirty. Which...

The temptation to lick her lips was so great.

His gaze snapped back to hers, and the moment passed. "We'll get Chris settled, then work some chores. I expect the man will take a few days to get caught up on his sleep. I think he's been awake twenty-four seven for nearly a week to keep ahead of trouble."

"Poor guy. I'll make sure there's always a plate of leftovers in the fridge he can warm if he misses a meal."

"Nice. I'll let him know." Jake hesitated for a moment then nodded firmly. "After this weekend, you'll need a break."

"After this weekend, I'm going to celebrate," Tansy informed him.

"I can see why. Let's plan on celebrating." He spoke fast enough he had to have preplanned his next suggestion. "You're off on Monday. How about we head into Diamond Valley and hit that Korean restaurant you were telling Petra about?"

"That's playing dirty," Tansy said even as she smiled. "Enticing the cook with the restaurant she wants to go check out? How could I possibly say no?"

"You obviously can't," he agreed.

The rice cooker beeped at that moment, and Tansy turned to deal with it. When she looked up again, Jake was gone. Which was fine since she had a ton to do.

Still, having something to look forward to on Monday was a great idea. She'd find out what time Petra wanted to go— Aiden would be ready whenever they told him to be. Jinx usually went home with Sasha on Monday nights to study and to hang out. They could pick her up on the way home from dinner. Declan was the only unknown—he seemed to disappear at times, and Tansy had no idea where he went. Plus, he might want to stick around with Chris for the time being.

Unsolved mysteries would have to wait—she had work to do.

The day passed in a blur. Tansy laid out sandwich fixings on the counter at lunch—chicken salad and thick beef slices from the enormous roast earlier in the week—plus a huge pot of lentil soup. She'd baked buns first thing, so that part was simple.

She loaded trays with the food for the studio on the dining room table. As promised, around four o'clock, Jake showed up with Kevin and Aiden in tow to help her carry them.

Kevin sniffed appreciatively as he accepted the oversized box she pressed into his arms. "It smells amazing in here."

"Nothing fancy," Tansy insisted. "I went super easy for family supper tonight and made pans of lasagna with garlic bread and a Caesar salad. If you guys can all be in here by five, though, that would help. I want to be out in the studio when everyone arrives to go over the details with them."

"We'll be here," Jake promised. "I'll let the others know."

Out in the studio, she tucked the cold food into the fridge and the hot into the ovens, satisfaction welling up at the sight of so much tastiness created by her own hands. All ready to be laid out in their chafing dishes or set out on the tiered serving stands.

She hurried back to the house and found the table already set for eight. Jinx and Jake were at the counter, prepping iced tea and water in the pitchers they used for the family setting. Dixie was curled up in her dog bed at the side of the couch, chin resting on her paws, but her gaze open enough to keep an eye on Jinx.

"This is a nice surprise," Tansy said.

Jinx made a face. "The fact you sound so shocked means Jake was right—I'm sorry. I should have been helping you more over the past couple of weeks with the simple things I can do."

Tansy paused. "You're okay. You're not here every night. And you have homework and stuff."

"I do. But I also need to help. The days I'm home, you need to let me know if it's plates or bowls, but I'll make sure the table is set." Jinx nodded firmly then all but pushed Tansy toward the oven. "You have the important job of getting that lasagna out because it smells so good I'm drooling."

"Yes, ma'am. But thank you. One thing off my to-do list." Tansy slipped on oven mitts, pausing to hip check Jake who had studiously stayed out of the conversation by staring at the pitcher as it filled. "Thank you, as well," she offered quietly. "I appreciate that you noticed something that will make my job simpler."

He shrugged. "You're working hard, and with the retreat house starting up and ranch hands arriving, your job just got bigger. We need to make it easier where we can."

She wasn't about to argue. She put the piping hot lasagna on the table, then while Jinx transferred the two loaves of savoury garlic bread from their foil wrappers to serving bowls, Tansy tossed the salad one last time.

Minutes later when she sat at the head of the table, staring down the row at seven very appreciative dinner companions, Tansy worked hard to keep from bouncing in her chair.

So far, working for High Water had been everything she'd hoped for.

Let's hope nothing goes wrong.

God, she hated that little voice of doom. It always showed up at the most inconvenient and unwelcome moments. As her sister Rose had told her time and time again—she needed to shove that voice off a bridge.

Go away, melancholy. I have a home here and I'm valuable.

Then she mentally stuck her tongue out at the thoughts from the past that said when things were going well, that's when everything would go wrong. Those terrible days were in the past. The far, far distant past, and gloomy thoughts had no place messing with her here and now.

She scooped up a hearty serving of her own cooking and dove in.

6

"I agree. I consider the entire weekend a smashing success." Aiden pushed back from the breakfast table on Monday, grabbing his plate and coffee cup and giving Jinx a nod. "We need to get going if we plan to pick up Sasha before heading to school."

"I need to grab my stuff for drama class." Jinx snatched up her dishes as well, pausing to nab a hug from Petra as she passed. "I won't be late tonight. Sasha has to train after supper."

"Someone will come for you. Weather report says it'll be really cold, and I don't want you walking back in the dark." Petra shooed her out of the room. "I'll load the dishwasher. Go get ready. You don't want to keep Sasha waiting."

"Tansy and I will grab you," Jake offered. "Text me when you're ready."

"Okay." Jinx left the room at a run, Dixie bouncing on her heels, barking with excitement.

Petra leaned back in her chair. "It doesn't seem right that after working so hard all weekend, Tansy still got up at the crack of dawn and headed over to Buns and Roses. It's her day off. She should be sleeping in and celebrating how well things went with the food services this weekend."

"She said before the shop opened was the easiest time to meet with Marina." Declan topped up his coffee cup and sat back down at the table. He glanced over at the ranch hand who was sitting quietly but seemed to enjoy being included in their group gatherings. "It's too cold to do much outside. Chris, I was thinking of taking a drive today. I have to grab a feed order, but not much else. Want to come along?"

The man hesitated. "I don't think going into any stores in the city is a good idea."

"Nah." Declan shook his head. "We'll drive south to the Pincher Creek area and maybe beyond. It's cold out there, but it's pretty. Sometimes days like this are the best time to look at the scenery and think about the future."

Chris's lips twitched. "I seem to have done a lot of that lately, but yeah. I'll head out with you."

"I also know a great hole-in-the-wall pub about an hour from here. We'll hit it for supper at the end of the day. It'll be safe and a chance to listen to some music and play some pool."

"Sounding better and better." Chris smiled this time.

"Which means you two are on your own for supper," Petra announced, glancing between Kevin and Jake. "Aiden and I are having dinner at my brother and sister-in-law's."

Kevin raised a brow. "I notice you seem to accept invitations to eat there at least one night of every two that Tansy has off."

Petra pressed a hand to her chest. "Us? Contrive not to cook? Absolutely."

From the front door where he was pulling on his winter gear, Aiden laughed. "If the rest of Petra's enormous family lived closer, we'd be dining away both nights Tansy doesn't cook."

"Sorry to desert you, Kev, but I have plans for tonight as well." Jake had debated all weekend whether he should tell the rest of them about his interest in Tansy. The final pro/con checklist had ended up five to four in favour of waiting until after their first date.

Just make sure she didn't cut him off at the knees.

Kevin raised his hands in the air. "I will entertain myself, then. And try to keep up with Dixie. She's always a great companion."

Jinx rushed past, offering high-fives to everyone on the outer side of the table as she passed. She jerked on her coat and slammed a toque over her head. She barely had her feet into her boots before reaching for the door.

"Slow down there, girl. Zip your coat and tie your boots before you set yourself up to freeze in the first ten seconds of being outside." As Aiden waited for Jinx to finished dressing, he bent and patted the top of Dixie's head. "Such a good girl. You take care of Petra. And Kevin. Kevin's going to spoil you rotten, yes, he is."

Once Aiden and Jinx were gone, Dixie wandered sadly back to her dog bed where she lay down and let out a long, mournful sigh. Everyone else scattered, and suddenly the room was down to Jake and Petra, clearing the table and preparing for their days.

"What are you doing today?" he asked. "Other than being a mooching moocher and nabbing dinner off your brother?"

"You're so funny. You're jealous that we'll be eating something far more edible than I could cook. Or you, for that matter."

"I'm not jealous at all. I'm going out for dinner, remember?" Too late it dawned on him that he hadn't specifically mentioned that.

She eyed him, stacking the remaining plates in the

industrial-sized dishwasher. "You said you were going out, but nothing more. From that guilty look you're wearing, I'd say it's time to share the details."

Shit. He'd walked into this one. "If you must know, I happen to agree that Tansy deserves to celebrate how well everything went with her first catering gig for High Water. I'm taking her out so that she doesn't have to cook tonight, not even for herself."

Petra turned on the spot, jaw dropping. "You?"

He folded his arms over his chest. "Don't you think that Tansy deserves to have a day off and something to cheer on how well things went?"

"Absolutely, but..." Petra frowned. "Are you like dropping her off and letting her eat by herself?"

Jake snorted. "Because I'm such terrible company you don't think she'd want to eat with me?"

"Because the two of you have been bickering like cats and dogs ever since you laid eyes on each other last September." Only her frown deepened. "Wait. No. That's wrong. You haven't been fighting lately..."

"And now you sound more concerned than before." Jake rinsed a washcloth and went to the table. "We're getting along fine these days. Tansy is a talented woman. It was helpful when you pointed out that while we might do things differently, she wasn't doing anything wrong."

He finished wiping the table with a flourish and turned to discover Petra right behind him.

Her fists were planted firmly on her hips. "You're up to something." She eyed him with suspicion. "Tell me, or do I have to break out the big guns and get Sydney to stick you with some truth serum?"

"It's only dinner," he said calmly.

A lot more calmly than he felt inside.

Why had he forgotten that any hopes of getting involved with Tansy meant running the gauntlet? Not only with her own family, but with a far more deadly group—her best friends.

Petra examined him for another moment. Then she took a big breath and shrugged. "So. If it's only dinner, I hope you have a nice time. And if it's anything more than that?" Her chin lowered the slightest bit, meaning if her eyes were laser beams, he'd have been burned to a crisp. "Then you better treat my girl nicely. Or else."

Thank God her phone rang at that moment.

Petra answered it, the cheer in her voice miles away from the death threat she'd just offered.

Jake got the dishwasher going then hightailed it from the main house before Petra finished her call.

He didn't see Tansy during the day. When he came in to grab lunch, she was out in the barn doing something. Come five thirty, though, he got himself dressed and headed into the house.

Damn butterflies in his stomach—he hadn't been this nervous since tenth grade, which was before he'd had a driver's license, and his stepdad Jeff had to drive him and his date.

He slipped into the house and was greeted enthusiastically by Dixie.

He scratched her head. "Hey there. Had a good day?"

"Pretty good."

He jumped a little at the answer from the living room.

Tansy waved at him from where she was curled up on one side of the loveseat, the blanket that usually lived over the back of the chair wrapped around her shoulders and a book resting in her lap. "Only I was a butterfingers right after I got back from Buns and Roses. I dropped my cell phone into the watering trough in the barn."

"Drat. Stick it in a bag of rice?"

"Of course. The universal solution to watery disasters." Her grin was evil. "I just have to decide whether I throw the rice away afterward or use it."

He shuddered.

Tansy outright laughed. "Sorry. I'm kidding. I promise to put the rice in the compost. But in the meantime, I've been having a tech-free day."

"Sometimes that's not a bad idea." He tipped his head toward the door. "If you're ready to go, we can head out now."

She shot to her feet and threw off the soft beige blanket, revealing a crimson red sweater over formfitting black pants. "I am not yet starving, but I will be by the time we get there. Is everyone else meeting us at the restaurant?"

Jake froze in the middle of reaching for her coat.

He turned back to her. "Everyone else?"

"Petra and Aiden. Kevin. Declan. You know." She slid her feet into a pair of high-top leather boots then stood, frowning back at him. "They're not here. I assumed that they had things to do and were going straight to the restaurant."

He hadn't seen this one coming. "There's no one else headed to the restaurant. Just us. Well, I assume there will be other people *at* the restaurant, but nobody from High Water."

It was her turn to freeze. She blinked, confusion slipping over her face before her cheeks flushed slightly. "Oh."

If she'd said it with any sort of disgust, he would've changed tactics right then and there. But that single word, combined with her body language, were less about being uncomfortable that she was getting stuck alone with him for the night. More about being a little off balance in a good way about them being alone.

A sentiment he could understand completely because, again, he was far too old for the nerves kicking up a riot along his spine right now.

"I think we had a bit of a misunderstanding, but that's okay. Let's start again." May as well do it the right way. Jake cleared his throat. "Tansy, I want to take you out on a *date* to celebrate your first successful weekend as head chef at the High Water Artists' Retreat. Would you like to go to dinner with me?"

He stepped forward and held out a hand. Tansy stared at it for the longest time. His heart pounded so hard he was worried she'd be able to hear it.

"Okay. I'd like that." She placed her fingers in his, lifted her gaze, and offered a sheepish smile. "How about that new Korean restaurant in Diamond Valley?"

For a guy she'd thought was pretty easy to read and far too regimented, Jake Skye was zigzagging often enough to keep her on her toes.

He walked her to his truck and opened the passenger door. Tansy climbed in and got settled, running a hand over the soft leather interior. He started it, glancing over when she reached down beside the door to play with the *adjust the seat back* and *distance from the dash* buttons.

"Make yourself at home," he said with amusement.

"I usually do." Nice, automated controls. A newer vehicle than her's, that's for sure. Now she wondered. She leaned forward and checked the dashboard more closely. "Sweet."

She stabbed the heated seat button for both of them, easing back into her chair and sighing as the cushioning beneath her butt warmed.

"Heated steering wheel as well," Jake informed her. "In case your hands are cold."

"You're my chauffeur today. I have other ways of keeping my fingers toasty." She raised her hands in front of her and showed them off. Mickey and Minnie Mouse grinned from the back of her mittens.

"Very chic."

She examined him a little closer. "Not my usual style," she confessed. "But Fern won them for me, so that makes them perfect."

"She won them for you? Like at a fair ball toss? Which is totally rad except if she's got some sort of guided missile program on her prosthesis that I don't know about."

A snort escaped before Tansy could stop it. "She's right-handed, most of the time. And she would never dream of using mechanical advantage when it's inappropriate. No, she won these beauties by knowing what was special about the word *screeched*."

She didn't have to wait long. Jake raised a brow at her as he took a quick glance. "And what is special about the word *screeched*?"

"Longest single syllable word in the English language."

He chuckled softly, easing around a slow driver on the highway. "Is this the sort of thing that your sister knows automatically, or is she a word geek?"

"Not a word geek, but she definitely knows bits and pieces about an awful lot of things." Tansy peered out the window, admiring the way the approaching car lights glittered off the fresh snow, turning the fields around them into sparkling wonderlands. "If you're ever playing a trivia game, she's a good one to have on your side."

"Good to know. What about you?"

Tansy shook her head, readjusting position until she could admire him more thoroughly. "I do really well in a few categories, and really badly in a lot of others."

"I'd still pick you for my team." Jake cleared his throat.

"Although we better make sure Fern plays with us, because I too have my strengths and weaknesses."

"What categories would you kill it in?"

"Security, sports, gardening, and R&B songs."

Too funny. But also a little too practiced a response. Tansy watched him for a minute. "Sounds as if you had that list ready to go. Did you preplan a set of topics for us to discuss this evening?"

Jake swore softly then made a face. "I can't stop myself. The being prepared bit."

"We're not helping you with your spontaneity goal. Not if we follow a predetermined conversation list."

He nodded, far too serious. "It's a habit. And it's my fallback when I want to make a good impression on somebody."

There they were, finally at the biggest item that had been ringing bells in Tansy's brain since the moment he'd announced he wanted to take her on a date. "Maybe we need to talk about that part, just a little bit."

"The fact that I fall back on making lists?"

"The idea that you want to impress me." Tansy shrugged. "I mean, I like it that we're getting along, and I'm no longer dreaming up ways to make your head explode. But I—"

A loud laugh burst from Jake. "You *were* deliberately tormenting me."

"Torment is such an extreme word. But yes, I'd go with deliberate in a heartbeat." Tansy took a deep breath and let it out slowly. "Why did you ask me out?"

"Why did you let me kiss you on New Year's Eve?"

That was easy. "Because you are one hot number and infinitely better than the dude who was kicking my ankles every other step."

His amusement was not dying down, judging by the assorted chuckles and snorts escaping him. "You're top notch at delivering compliments that then whack my feet out from under me and leave me sitting on my ass."

"We all have to be good at something."

He pulled to a stop in a free spot half a block from the restaurant then twisted toward her. "I asked you out because, while we might've gotten off on the wrong foot in the beginning, the longer I'm around you the more I'm intrigued. I'd like to get to know you better. I hope, as annoying as I am with my lists and unnecessary preplanning, that you like me too."

Tansy examined his face. Such earnestness there, and yet as he dipped his chin slightly, a flash of mischievousness hit her as well. Maybe he could be somebody she could enjoy more than just dirty dreams about.

"I wasn't planning on getting serious with anyone," she started.

"Me neither," he agreed. "I was married once, briefly. It didn't go well, and since then I've pretty much only dated casually."

May as well shock the hell out of him. "Let me finish that sentence. I *wasn't* planning on getting serious with anyone, but then Rose found Chance. Ever since, I've been thinking that maybe I'm okay with risking the idea of one guy forever."

Jake dipped his head slowly. "It does feel like a risk, doesn't it?"

"Absolutely." Going for broke. "So, the whole getting to know me better, and being intrigued by me—are you serious about maybe getting serious?"

Jake laughed, shaking his head slightly. "Every time I think I've got things under control, you come out of left field and make me have to reopen my eyes and man up. Yes, Tansy. The reason why I asked you out was because I'm ready to take some risks and go looking for something like what Aiden and Petra have. I don't know if that's going to be with you, but I feel as if there's a chance. So this isn't casual, and I'm not just looking for a good time. This is honest-to-God dating. Finding out about each other and seeing if what we want in the future makes us a good match. A good fit."

"How spicy do you eat your food?" Tansy asked.

His lips twitched. "Try me."

She grinned back. "Just to be clear, yes, I heard your answer. We're both willing to risk to see if there's a chance for more. And while you're not just looking for a good time, I hope we can have some. Sex, that is."

It looked as if he wanted to swear but mostly his lips moved without any sound coming out.

Finally, Jake cleared his throat. "Blunt."

"I tend to be. I'm not talking about jumping into bed with you tonight. I enjoy teasing my sister Rose too much that she had a one night stand with Chance. I can't go and basically do the same thing, or I lose the moral high ground. Plus, it would remove any chance to poke Petra and Aiden that they did it the first time they met. But I am interested—"

"Hang on." Jake's eyes were wide. "What the hell? I mean, the part about my brother and Petra."

"Really? You haven't heard this one?" It absolutely was not a secret. "Petra was teasing Aiden about it in the living room a few nights ago, and you and Declan were right there."

Jake shook his head. He opened his door and came around to the other side of the truck, the cold air sweeping in, making Tansy all the more eager to take his hand and head toward the restaurant. "Let's order the food, medium to hot, then you can tell me more about the gossip right under my nose that I was unaware of."

Which is how they ended up with six dishes on the table in front of them, one a little too spicy even for Tansy's tastebuds.

After spilling the dirt on Petra and Aiden, conversation continued to flow about food and their long-ago high school classes, of all things.

It was as if both of them were very deliberately keeping away from serious topics, at least for tonight, and just appreciating each other for who they were. Two people feeling out the future and seeing if there was more than the physical attraction bubbling between them.

Although the attraction was there. Absolutely.

At the end of the meal, as they stepped outside, Jake slid his hand around hers. A shock wave rolled through Tansy from fingertip to toes.

So weird. They were just holding hands for heaven's sake.

Outside the truck, Jake tugged her to a stop. "We have to nab Jinx at the Stones on our way home. Which means we should conclude our first date here. If that's okay with you?"

Tansy slid her hands up his chest until she could curl her arms around his neck. "Considering how cold it is outside, we will obviously not be getting beyond first base."

She really liked his snicker. She liked it even better when he leaned down and pressed his lips to hers. A slow, delicate kiss. A gentle nibble at her lower lip followed by a sweep of his tongue. Nothing demanding, and yet from the way his arms wrapped around her torso, holding her against him, she was not getting away anytime soon.

Which was more than fine. She didn't want to get away.

They stood there as the icy cold air around them heated a few degrees and a low rumble of need built in her belly.

When he broke the kiss, she smiled into his eyes. "Would it be really terrible to tell you that I plan to use my vibrator tonight and think about you?"

A look of utter pain crossed his face, and Jake squeezed his eyes shut briefly. When he opened them again they were filled with heat and amusement. "You are one ball of trouble."

"Think of me when you stroke one off," she suggested.

Jake swore. "Get in the damn truck."

She leaned in and gave him a final quick kiss then scurried into the passenger seat. When he settled in the driver's seat, she slid into the center, hip tight against his, and left hand resting gently on his thigh.

He glanced at her in surprise.

Tansy shrugged. "Jinx will need room to sit. And if we're doing this dating thing for real, it's not as if we're keeping a secret." She eyed him, narrowing her gaze. "You weren't thinking about keeping it a secret?"

"Absolutely not. In fact, only the fact that your phone went for a swim kept Petra from informing you that she knew I was taking you out tonight alone. She threatened me, as any good best friend would, but didn't actually hurt me."

Huh. Tansy thought that one over as Jake got them back on the highway, headed toward Silver Stone. "It'll be okay. Petra and Sydney like you. Mostly."

He laughed again and draped his arm around her shoulders as he drove. "This is going to be quite the adventure."

"Should be fun."

A shiver stole over her. Was it possible to have one more dream come true? Too soon to tell, but in spite of herself, a tiny flame lit in Tansy's chest and refused to be extinguished.

Pulsing a small steady beat in time with her hopeful heart.

7

———

Outside, the wind howled, rattling the windows and loud enough to be heard over the music playing softly in the background. But inside what was now Marina's apartment over Buns and Roses, the smell of popcorn, chocolate, and cheesy goodness hung on the air.

It was the sort of cold January night that made staying indoors feel like a luxury.

Tonight, a nice combination had gathered, and while Tansy was considered the host, she'd had the brilliant brainwave of asking Marina if she wanted to join them and Marina had instantly offered her apartment for them to gather in. She'd added thick blankets to the backs of the couches, and as everyone settled, the soft covers were eagerly grabbed and draped over legs and shoulders. Candles were lit and snack plates filled.

"It's been forever since our last girls' night out." Petra made a face. "Or it feels like forever."

"You've been too busy with your guy and being Mom-ish to Jinx to notice we're constantly underfoot. Tansy more so than usual." Petra's sister-in-law Julia Sorenson pointed out. Her hand rested lightly on her belly, stroking the small bulge.

Petra looked thoughtful. "I suppose. Although I don't know how I feel about that Mom-ish moniker."

"We do need to come up with something snappier, but it's true." Tansy dropped onto the couch next to her. She glanced at the other ladies settling around the coffee table that all but groaned under the weight of all the goodies on it. "Jinx seems to have settled on Aiden and Petra as her surrogate parental figures. She asked Aiden to come to the father/daughter game night at the school."

Marina frowned for a moment. "I thought Declan was Jinx's official guardian while she's going to school here."

Tansy waved a hand. "He is, but Jinx seems to consider Declan a combination of superhero and idol to be kept on a pedestal. If she needs some parental-type cuddling or advice, look no farther than Petra and Aiden."

"Awww, that's sweet," Marina said as a series of nods set off around the room, like cooperative bobble heads.

"As long as she's got someone, that's what counts," Sydney offered approvingly.

With seven of them tucked around the table, it was a little tight, but it still seemed perfect to Tansy. Like most girls' night out gatherings in recent years, whoever hosted sent the time and place out to the universe, and those who could make it, did.

Of course, these days that meant less of certain ladies at sometimes, or in far different combinations, as work, children, and life in general interfered. So far their girl gang had stayed tight, though, which was a joy all in itself Tansy liked to take some credit for.

She and Rose were the founding members of the group, after all.

Tansy scooped up a cheesy jalapeño onto a cracker and

popped it in her mouth, as she counted heads, somewhat amused to realize that in spite of Rose being missing, the ladies were a near perfect mix of old to new residents.

Petra, Sydney, and Marina were definitely on the new list. Petra's sister-in-law Julia, and the very mischievous Lisa Ryder —now married to the local veterinarian with a three-year-old and five-month-old baby—had both been around long enough that they qualified right in the middle.

Finally there were Tansy, and Kelli Stone, a ranch hand at the local Silver Stone ranch and married to Sasha Stone's uncle Luke. They'd both lived in Heart Falls for years.

As a fifteen-year-old runaway, Kelli had walked into Silver Stone ranch as if she owned the place and been accepted. Tansy had held Kelli's secret tightly all those years. Just like Kelli was the only one who knew all the details of Tansy's past, pre-Fields adoption.

They were the Fort Knox of secret keepers for each other, they'd always teased.

Now as Kelli wiggled to the front of her chair, expertly manoeuvering in spite of the baby belly rounding in front of her, so many memories tangled in Tansy's mind.

In spite of her past, Kelli was now loved beyond measure by not only Luke, but the entire Stone family. She was about to start a family of her own—

Maybe, just maybe, big, beautiful changes were possible for Tansy as well.

Thankfully, before she could spend more time being hyper-contemplative, Petra pointed at Kelli's belly. "Is that not supposed to be bigger by now? It's the end of January, and you're due in four weeks."

Kelli filled a bowl with chips then eased back in her chair. She stretched her legs out in front of her displaying fuzzy socks that didn't quite match. Somehow it totally worked. "The baby is healthy. I just have a long torso, I guess."

Julia sighed. "What do you want to guess that *I'm* going to swell up and look as if I swallowed a watermelon patch?"

"You'll look adorable," Petra assured her. "Oh, and I found something for you that I think is appropriate for this moment." She reached under the couch and pulled out a paper bag.

Suspicion on her face, Julia wiggled the present. "Is it safe to open this in public?"

"Of course. I'm always public approved," Petra assured her sister-in-law before glancing at the candle on the table she'd brought that said *So Fucking Zen*. "Well, mostly public approved."

The gift was safe to open but also hilarious. Petra had made a T-shirt that had an image of a flag planted right where Julia's belly would eventually push out the fabric. The flag was emblazoned with *This territory claimed by baby Sorenson. Touch at your own risk.*

"I need one," Kelli muttered. "I never realized exactly how many people assume it's okay to come in too close and pat my belly."

"Are they still doing that?" Lisa asked in amazement. "I thought they would've stopped after you accidentally slugged Mrs. Wilson."

A burst of laughter danced around the room. Marina eyed Kelli with admiration. "Good for you. I want to know how to accidentally slug someone. Sounds like a skill we need to learn."

"Twirl rapidly and lift your elbows, and that's all I'll say about that," Kelli offered with a wink.

"Wonderful advice." Lisa cleared her throat. "This seems an appropriate moment to announce I'm on the baby brigade again."

Everyone paused for a moment, then a cheer went up.

"Congratulations," Julia said. "When's your due date? I'm April fourth, which means cousins who are close together in age."

"August fifteenth, so I'm past the first trimester. Which means I am no longer waiting in dread for the moment my sister Tamara always threatened would come. You know, the vomiting your guts out twenty-four seven."

Tansy snickered. Too funny. Poor Tamara had dealt with morning sickness that lasted until she gave birth. "Did you get away scot-free *again?*"

"Except from the wrath of Tamara, yes," Lisa said with a smirk. "Although, I don't know if the fact I don't get morning sickness but do have the labour from hell is a trade-off win."

The only one of the ladies not leaning forward and offering their heartfelt congratulations was Sydney. She eyed Lisa. "You really okay with the barefoot and pregnant for years on end routine? Or do I need to suggest a little snipping to a certain obviously viral male?"

"It's hardly been years on end. That's my cousin Jaxi, although it looks as if she's finally stopped at six kiddos." Lisa settled back in the couch, lifting her soft drink in the air. "I know, it shocks me too. Not the fact that I'm pregnant again, because I do know how that happens. And the happy cause of getting me pregnant occurs often, with great enthusiasm, thank you." She leered at Tansy, who couldn't help but grin in return. "But Zoe and Mason are so much fun, and Josiah's like the dad of the century with them. I always wanted three or four kids, so these two will be spaced out like dominoes, one year after the other."

"As long as it's your plan, I'll celebrate," Sydney assured her. She took a glance around the room. "Onward from babies. Because as awesome a topic as they are, it's time to discuss what's keeping all of us busy these days, including the ones who haven't bred."

"Busy, or entertained." Petra grabbed a wine bottle off the table and topped up her glass. "The busy for me is High Water, and entertained is Tansy and all *her* excitement."

What the hell? Tansy shot Petra a look. "You make me sound like a walking circus."

"If the clown shoes fit," Petra teased.

Tansy threw popcorn at her.

Across the coffee table, Julia smirked. "I think what Petra means is that you seem a little distracted lately."

Kelli raised a brow. "Do tell. Luke and I just got back into town after visiting my grandfather for most of January. I've obviously missed some exciting news."

This time Marina lifted a hand as if an eager student. "Oh, oh. Pick me. Pick me." She leaned forward on her elbows. "Tansy's smitten."

A snicker escaped Kelli. "Tansy's always smitten. She's always got a flavour of the week or two lined up for dancing and other enjoyment."

"Oh, no. This is totally different." Petra ignored the evil glare Tansy shot her way, lips twitching into a grin. "Tansy is serious about someone."

"Wait—serious?" Kelli sat up, suddenly very interested. "I was gone for three weeks, and I missed a serious Tansy?"

Tansy groaned and buried her face in her hands. "Why do I hang out with you people?"

"Because we're your best friends, *and* we're fascinated by this rare phenomenon." Lisa jerked the bowl of popcorn away from Tansy's hands to avoid getting showered with it. "Now spill. What's going on with you and Jake?"

"Yes, details. I thought you'd be done with him by now," Julia added. "According to everybody, two weeks is your max."

"Then everybody is wrong."

Lisa leaned toward Marina, dipping her chin knowledgeably. "The sex must be out of this world."

Before she could stop herself, Tansy shot that idea down. "We haven't had sex."

She could have heard a pin drop.

Tansy was tempted to buried her face in her hands again, but instead she glared at Lisa, cheeks burning hot.

Lisa faked a gasp. "You haven't had sex? Who are you, and what have you done with Tansy?"

"Stop it," Tansy whined even though she grinned through the embarrassment. "It's not as if I'm sitting around not working. We're both killer busy these days. Plus..." She considered how much to say but decided this was worth mentioning. "He and I are polar opposites, so it's a good idea to take it slow. Making sure that we—at least on my part—don't give up what makes us unique just to try and be together."

Which got a chorus of *awww*s from the group.

Marina sighed heavily. "Well, I'm glad *someone* is having fun in the dating world. The last guy I went out with spent the entire date talking about his fantasy football league."

Petra snorted into her wineglass. "You're kidding."

"Sadly, no. I know more about his imaginary team than I do about his real-life."

At which point the topic drifted, and Tansy no longer found herself the center of attention. Which was nice, since she hadn't really wanted to be there in the first place. This whole thing with Jake was new and odd and yet still somehow shiny.

When Kelli took the opportunity and slipped onto the couch beside her to chat, Tansy welcomed the distraction. They spoke softly, separated enough that no one could overhear.

Kelli eyed her for a moment. "You happy?"

"I think so." Tansy laid her head against the back of the couch. "I don't know where this is going, Kell, but I feel hopeful. It's a nice sensation."

Her friend nodded slowly. "You had any serious talks with him yet?"

A shiver went through her. Tansy shook her head.

"Okay. I get it. There's no rule that you have to tell him everything, but—speaking from experience—when I finally got to tell Luke the truth about my past, it felt good. Really good, like I'd been carrying a giant box around my entire life, and suddenly I didn't have to anymore. Not with him." Kelli grabbed her fingers. "Your secrets are *yours*, and I will never share them."

"But you think maybe I need to share them with Jake?" The really scary part was the thought didn't make Tansy go into an instant panic.

Kelli took a moment and breathed out slowly. "You're not that person anymore, but what you went through, what you did, make you who you are today. Which is a wonderful, loving, amazing person. I see it, and I think maybe Jake sees it too."

Which was a wonderful thought, but the opposite could be true as well. "He could decide he wants nothing more to do with me."

Kelli lifted a shoulder. "Might be better to know that sooner than later, but if you're feeling deep Tansy-feelings for him, I doubt that's something you have to worry about. Trust yourself, sweetie. You're smart, and you're kind, and you're amazing. You need to believe that."

Tansy offered Kelli a giant hug. "You're so kickass."

"Takes one to know one." Kelli squeezed her tight before letting her go as they rejoined the general party.

But it gave Tansy a lot to think about as she and Petra returned to High Water. Petra gave her a hug then took off to the apartment she shared with Aiden. Tansy slipped into the house quietly.

It was nearly midnight, but the light in the living room shone clearly on Jake as he rose to his feet and approached.

"You're up late," she teased.

"Not that late." He took her coat from her. "Besides, I had lists to make."

She snickered. "Of course you did."

In spite of the whirling in her brain, she didn't protest as he pulled her into his arms. A good, long kiss was followed by another, and Tansy pressed her hands to his torso, caressing as she slid her palms around to his back. The firm muscles under his soft flannel shirt made her sigh happily, and it was tempting to tug him down the hall to her room so they could get rid of their clothes and increase the skin contact.

Before she could act on the impulse, Jake eased away. "We'd better stop now."

"Really?" She couldn't imagine why that was a good idea. Tansy dug her fingertips into his chest a little harder, scratching slowly, and he groaned.

A second later, dog nails sounded on the floor. Dixie came dancing up to them, and Tansy separated herself to stand at Jake's side a second before Jinx rounded the corner, blinking sleepily.

"Oh, hi. Sorry, I thought I heard something. Dixie was excited—happy excited, not upset excited, if you know what I mean. I figured it was you." Jinx yawned. "Have a good time with your girls?"

"The best. Sorry we woke you," Tansy said.

"Just wanted to make sure Tansy got home safe. I'll see you ladies in the morning." Jake squeezed Tansy's fingers then snatched his coat from the wall and was out the door before she could protest.

Jinx made a face as Tansy strolled toward her. "I really am sorry."

Tansy frowned at her. "For what?"

"Interrupting."

This time it was easy to laugh. Tansy slipped her arm around Jinx's shoulders and guided her back toward the bedroom area. "Here's a fun thing to know about grownups. If they want to kiss, they're allowed to find a place to kiss. If they decide to kiss in public, interruptions are fair game. But now you need to get back to bed."

"Okay." Jinx paused at the door, Dixie weaving in and out of her legs as the young woman examined Tansy thoughtfully. "I like Jake. He's a little too serious sometimes, but you can tell he's got a good heart."

"Go to bed," Tansy said firmly.

A soft snicker escaped the younger woman. "Good night."

Now she had the teenager of the house selling her on how good Jake was. Problem was, she already believed the bill of sale.

It was just that Kelli's suggestion of telling Jake more of her past was both a great idea and a huge sticking point. It would take a little longer for Tansy to wrap her brain around that particular suggestion.

She took herself off to bed and hoped for a dreamless sleep where she didn't need to make any decisions.

8

The end of January and beginning of February blurred together, filled with the usual bustle of ranch life and putting the finishing touches on the apartments for Declan and himself.

Bookings for the art studio began in earnest. Tansy cooked for another weekend event at the start of February and then made plans for the biggest booking yet—a seven-day event over the reading week break running from Sunday to the following Saturday.

Which meant Jake's hopes of enticing her away for another official date were nil. Especially when Tansy announced she was taking her two days off early since she'd have to work the Monday and Tuesday of the booking.

"Rose, Fern, and I are headed to Calgary tomorrow for a getaway," she informed them at breakfast on Wednesday. "I'll be back on Saturday in plenty of time to get things ready for Sunday and the rest of the week. And Marina is booked to help with the baking."

"You need to take your time off," Declan agreed. "I'll cook Thursday. Jake can do Friday."

"Looking forward to it," Jake said as cheerfully as possible. "Hope you guys have a great time."

Petra outright laughed at him. "You have a shitty poker face. And that's saying something considering how bad mine is, or so I've been told."

Tansy eyed him curiously but said nothing.

At least not until she caught him alone later in the day. He was barely in the door, hanging up his coat, when she slipped her arms around his waist from behind and hugged him tightly. "We're not having a good time figuring out this dating thing, are we?"

"It's fine. He twisted on the spot and caught hold of her, loving how soft and warm she felt in his arms and how delicious she smelled. "I think it feels different since we eat together most days. Seems as if we should move faster, but really, we're doing okay. We talk, we share moments here and there."

"We get totally frustrated because we'd like to get naked?"

He laughed. "Yeah, there's a hell of a lot of that as well." Her eyes sparkled as she grinned at him. Suddenly, it didn't feel as if he was pushing the truth at all. "But it's okay. We'll do the next thing soon enough."

Still, the hum of activity over the weekend held a different energy. Maybe it was the cold snap that arrived. Or the unspoken tension from preparing to bring strangers into their space, even ones paying for the privilege of using the art studio, but for some reason, the weight of responsibility pressed down on Jake more than usual.

Not even the kisses he stole on the sly from Tansy once she got back could chase away the sensation inside that something was about to go wrong.

Chris was still in residence, but he had a bus ticket booked to move to his brother's on the East Coast the following week. In the meantime, the man had dove in full force. The extra help was invaluable, especially when two pregnant terriers were found abandoned on the edge of the property. Jake and Chris spent Saturday afternoon building makeshift shelters and setting up warm spots for the dogs in the barn, preparing for the pups that would likely arrive any day.

Jake tried to balance his time between the ranch, helping with the art studio, and the animal rescue, yet everything he did felt incomplete or somehow lacking, and his nerves were stretched to the breaking point.

Sunday evening, as the sun set behind the mountains and a bitter chill settled over the ranch, Jake gathered in the living room with the others. The nightly tradition they'd begun was one of the only things that gave him a sense of peace.

The fire crackled warmly in the hearth, filling the room with a comforting glow.

Kevin sat quietly in one corner, thumbing slowly through a thick book, his brow furrowed in concentration. Chris had declined to join them, claiming he wanted an early evening. Aiden plucked at the strings of his guitar, filling the air with a soft, classical melody that wrapped around everyone with a calming stroke.

Petra and Jinx sat together, crocheting. Petra's hands moved with practiced ease, creating delicate patterns from brightly colored yarn. Jinx muttered under her breath when the unfamiliar motion caused her to slip. Or maybe it was because Jinx spent more time watching Declan than her own fingers.

Jake's oldest brother sat nearby leafing through an old catalog.

"Very high tech, Declan," Jinx teased, eyes twinkling with mischief. "I didn't know they even printed those anymore."

Declan's lip barely moved, unfazed by the ribbing. "Old-fashioned doesn't mean outdated, kid. I find treasures in these." He held up a page featuring a pair of carved bear statues, one perched high in a tree. "What do you think? Which one would look better by the barn?"

Jinx pretended to scrutinize the page. "Definitely the one on the left," she finally said, nodding sagely. "The other one looks too grumpy."

"Kind of like Declan?" Aiden pondered out loud.

"I'm not grumpy. I'm dignified," Declan deadpanned.

Jake chuckled at their exchange, feeling the tension of the day slowly slip away.

These were the moments he loved most—the simple, quiet evenings spent together as a family. No chaos, no emergencies, just the warmth of the fire and the easy comfort of being surrounded by the people who mattered most.

The main reason for his current happiness, though, was that Tansy sat beside him on the couch, flipping through a colouring book. She'd convinced him to try his hand at it earlier, passing him a set of coloured pencils and coaxing him into filling in one of the pages. He wasn't much for art, but he'd done it anyway, mostly because he couldn't resist that it gave him a chance to sit beside her and share the pencils.

"Means you can't make lists tonight," she whispered quietly.

Which only tempted him to write on the edge of the colouring page. In fact...

It was tough to do on the sly, but he managed. As he shaded in a section of the page, Tansy leaned against him, her body warm and soft. She handed him another pencil, her fingers brushing his.

"Here, try this one for the sky," she suggested, her voice soft. "It's the perfect shade of blue."

Jake took the pencil from her with a nod, though the truth

was he didn't care much if the sky was pink. The best part of the evening was the way she'd curled up beside him, head resting on his shoulder at times, sharing the quiet.

He could get used to this. Maybe the worrying sensation was him being an overprotective ass.

"Hey. What's that?" She tugged the page out of his hands and lifted it to her nose. When she twisted the page ninety degrees, then snickered, Jake knew she'd found his list.

All around the outside of the picture he'd written in the smallest letters possible:

1. Kiss Tansy
2. Kiss Tansy
3. Kiss Tansy
4. Kiss Tansy

"You're a goof," she whispered.

Jake tucked his arm tighter around her and soaked in the sweetness of having her close and getting to maybe learn how to be more optimistic as well as spontaneous.

That idea flew out the window the next day when a new ranch hand showed up. The bruised eye the man sported was spectacular shades of green and purple and looked as if it hurt like hell, but when he quietly asked to speak to Declan, there was nothing belligerent in his actions.

But something seemed off. Jake and Aiden kept at their chores even as they both observed silently.

Not even fifteen minutes later, Declan brought the man to Room 1 in the bunkhouse area then motioned for Aiden and Jake to meet him inside the barn where they could talk privately.

"New hand?" Aiden leaned back on the stall railing, eyeing Declan.

"He got our address from my contact with the McCloud Corrections Institution." Declan said it quietly, but there was an edge to his tone.

"Something not right?" Jake demanded.

"Yeah, with me," Declan confessed.

Jake and Aiden exchanged shocked glances.

"What do you mean?" Aiden asked.

Declan stared at the ground for a moment before lifting his head. "We talked about this when we discussed High Water. Would we accept felons? And the answer was of course. In some ways, they need the hand up the most as a ton of people will see nothing but a criminal record and turn them down immediately for any job."

"So, what's the issue?" Aiden asked again.

Jake kept his mouth shut because he had a feeling where this was going, and if he was right, he was guilty as well.

Declan cleared his throat. "Now that Don is here, I'm finding it harder to be generous. He said all the right things, but..." An enormous sigh escaped Declan. "How much of what I'm currently feeling is because of society, and how much is because something really is not right?"

Aiden shook his head. "I hear you, and trust me, I get it. Thinking about protecting Petra and Jinx, and now Tansy—I don't want to endanger them in any way. But..."

The churning in Jake's gut didn't die down, but one thing he remembered helped. "You're right, Deck. We did talk about this. We researched and made a list of dos and don'ts that covered every angle. Let me find it, and we'll see what we're not thinking of right now that might help."

Declan's expression lightened considerably. "Thank God, I remember that now. You're right. We had some really good checkpoints to put in place. Between the four of us, including

Kevin, we can keep High Water a safe haven for our precious family and even the rougher guys."

That's what the *pay it forward* policy meant. Not everyone would look as if they deserved a second chance. They had to give people the benefit of the doubt and trust that they'd live up to the ideals.

Jake found the list, and they sat down with Don, outlining exactly where he was allowed on the property, and when, and other expectations.

The man seemed to take his restrictions in stride. "I just need a couple of weeks. That's all I'm asking."

Which made both Aiden and Declan kick their own butts again for being suspicious.

Jake? He didn't say anything but silently vowed to keep a close eye on Don. He could deal with having a guilty conscience over thinking less of the man if it ultimately meant keeping the women safe.

Two days later, another man arrived. This one was even quieter. He introduced himself as Tony, accepted their help with a nod, and then disappeared into his room unless called upon to help with chores. He didn't cause any trouble, but his presence added to the growing tension in Jake's gut.

By midway through the weeklong booking, Jake had gotten used to knowing the only way he'd catch a glimpse of Tansy was to join her in the kitchen or help with setup in the studio. Both of which he did, but it wasn't the same.

He dropped Chris off at the bus station on Thursday. "Good luck," Jake offered, extending his hand.

Chris took it and shook it firmly then pulled Jake in and bro-hugged him, accompanied by extensive back pounding. 'Thanks. For everything. You guys were lifesavers. And I mean that."

"Glad we could be there," Jake offered sincerely.

The man stepped back and shouldered his duffle. Chris hesitated then lifted his chin. "You guys have a great situation. Not just the ranch, but all of it. Your family. Hold on tight to that."

"We mean to."

Chris struggled to say something more, then shook his head. "Gotta go."

He walked away, and both pride and worry smacked Jake upside the head. They'd made a difference in one more life.

Balancing act. Always with the balancing act.

It didn't help that the feeling something was brewing returned. It wasn't anything specific, but the air felt charged, like a storm waiting to break.

The sensation only intensified when Jinx tracked him down on Friday, her face unusually serious. She caught him brushing down one of the horses.

"Can I ask you something?"

He glanced around to see what had spooked her. "What's going on?"

Jinx hesitated. "I need a favour," she said finally. "Would you move into the house? Please?"

Jake's hand stilled on the horse's flank, surprise flickering in. "Move into the house?" he repeated. "Why?"

Jinx shifted from foot to foot, clearly uncomfortable. "It's nothing specific, really. I just... That new guy, Don. He reminds me of someone I ran away from. I don't like him. I figured I was being overly sensitive, but Sasha and I were talking about something else and she reminded me that I'm allowed to be picky about what happens in my world."

"No more explanation needed." He trusted Jinx's instincts. She'd been through more than most, and if something about the new guy set her off, that was reason enough to take her seriously.

But still, it surprised him that she'd ask *him* to move in, especially since she and Declan were close.

"You sure you want me in the house?" he asked gently, not wanting to push but needing to understand. "We can ask Declan. He won't mind either."

Jinx flushed slightly, looking away. "No," she mumbled. "I'd feel better if it was you, that's all."

Jake studied her for a moment then nodded. He wasn't about to press for more. If she needed him to stay in the house, then that's what he'd do. "No problem," he said. "I'll move in tonight."

Relief washed over her face, and she gave him a small, grateful smile. "Thanks, Jake."

"No thanks needed." He nodded at her. "I'm glad you have a good friend like Sasha."

"Me too."

He didn't ask any more questions. It wasn't his place to pry into Jinx's reasons. If she had secrets, that was her right. His job, as he read it, was to keep everyone safe—and if moving into the house helped with that, then so be it.

Right after supper, he and Declan went out to the old barn at the edge of the property and worked with the ranch hands.

"Sorry for the late night, but I have an order of extra feed coming in early, and with the possible weather, it can't sit outside. If we prep tonight, we'll be ready for tomorrow." Declan pointed to the pile of lumber that arrived late that afternoon. "That was supposed to be here five days ago."

"Can't be helped." Don shrugged. "I know which end of the hammer to use if someone else cuts and measures."

Tony mostly looked at the floor, but he nodded his agreement and followed orders.

They put up multiple rows of shelves for pellets and feed along the inside wall of the animal rescue. It wasn't hard physical labour, but finicky as they fit the shelves against a crooked vertical wall and under a staircase.

Sacrificing their family time and the time with Tansy was hard, but in the end, Tony spoke a bit, and even Don seemed to lighten up and crack a smile.

After they said good night to the guys and headed to their own apartments, Declan laid a hand on Jake's shoulder and squeezed firmly. "It wasn't what I wanted to be doing, but you know what I kept thinking? I bet Jeff didn't always want to listen to me tell him everything about horses that I knew, every single night."

Jake laughed. "Yeah, you were pretty one tone at one point in your life."

"I'm much more rounded now," Declan said without a hint of amusement. "Now I can talk about horses *and* the price of hay."

Which meant Jake was snickering softly and in a much better mood when he slipped into his small apartment to pack a few things. Declan was right. It had been worthwhile, and for once, Don hadn't acted odd.

Didn't change the fact Jake was moving into the house. Jinx had asked, Jinx would get.

It didn't take long—a duffel bag of clothes and a bunch of odds and ends he wanted. Those he shoved into the nearest half-empty box he found in his closet. He ignored most of the rest—

The stack of letters tipped over into view when he grabbed the box.

I wonder where Melissa is these days?

Then he kicked his own ass. "Brilliant, Einstein."

That's why he'd gotten rid of the letters in the first place. Or mostly gotten rid of them. Maybe he should toss the entire batch.

He stared at the bundle for a good two minutes before deciding he didn't have the bandwidth to deal with them right then and shoved them back into the closet.

Everything else, including the letters, he'd leave where they were. He'd be back in the apartment soon enough once these particular ranch hands had moved on and Jinx felt comfortable again.

He hoisted the duffle bag over his shoulder and carried the box into the house, navigating through the darkened living room. He should've been paying more attention, but his mind was elsewhere, daydreaming about Tansy, wondering what it would be like to share more than just a couch and a colouring book. First chance he got he was going to—

His foot caught on the edge of the living room rug, and before he knew it, he headed for the floor. The duffle bag slammed into him and the box tumbled from his grasp.

Its contents spilled everywhere.

"Damn it," Jake muttered under his breath, dropping to his knees to gather everything. He stuffed his belongings back into the box, his thoughts still wandering. So much closer to Tansy now that he was here in the house.

Only distance didn't matter. It was what they were trying to establish. Right speed, right motivations.

Once he'd collected everything, he headed down the hallway to the room Jinx had set up for him. The one right across from Tansy's.

Jake paused outside her door, his heart thudding in his chest. The faint sounds of her getting ready for bed carried on the air and for a moment, he let himself imagine what it would be like to join her. To fall asleep with her in his arms, to wake beside her. To be with her completely.

He shook his head, forcing the thought away. No use in rushing. She had another full day of work tomorrow, and so did he. Whatever was building between them would have to stay slow.

With a sigh, he stepped into his new room, setting the box on the chest of drawers. He ran a hand through his hair, looking around. It wasn't much—a simple space with a bed, a dresser, and a window that looked out over the back pasture. But it was where he was supposed to be.

For now.

9

—————

With the mad rush of the weeklong cooking spree over, Tansy woke late on Monday—six thirty was late in her books—to the familiar scent of fresh coffee drifting through the house.

Which was lovely. Coffee she didn't have to make was always a treat, at least once she'd trained them to make it properly.

But more, there was that *something else* that was different— her senses tingled with an awareness that she wasn't alone.

Tansy snickered. She was never alone, not in the bustling ranch house that was High Water, but *this* was different.

Jake was here now. *Living* here.

She stared at the ceiling, trying to process the shift. Jake had moved in. Not forever, she reminded herself. Just for a little while to make sure things stayed running smoothly and to help Jinx feel safe. But it did mean he was right there, across the hall from her.

One quiet midnight walk away...

Tansy groaned and threw off the blankets, swinging her

feet out of bed. "Temptation does not need to be answered," she muttered. "It needs to be resisted."

The pep talk didn't do much to quiet the butterflies in her stomach or the vivid images flashing through her brain. How did Jake sleep? Naked, or did he...

"Creeper," she scolded herself. Definitely veering into creeper territory. Shoving a facecloth under cold water was barely a punishment—her cheeks grew hot thinking of the man stretched out naked in bed.

When she finally made her way to the kitchen, Jake was there, sitting at the table with a half-empty mug of coffee and his phone in his hand. He glanced up and offered a lazy smile that did nothing to calm her.

"Morning, Sunshine," he greeted. "You're finally up."

Amusement hit hard. "Didn't realize you were an early riser."

"Didn't realize you were one to sleep in."

She smirked but didn't reply. Grabbing her own mug of coffee, she leaned against the counter, trying not to stare for too long. He always looked so at ease, as if he belonged.

The easy confidence both irritated and attracted her. She'd bet the man could walk into any room and instantly feel as if he was home. For her, pretending to belong was a long practiced deception.

Which made staring at him all the more necessary and dangerous. She headed to the counter and made herself breakfast.

After a few minutes of comfortable silence, the house started to come to life as the rest of the family filtered in. It was the usual chaos—Aiden discussed the ranch chores planned for the day with Don and Tony. Declan tried to coax Jinx into eating more than just toast and peanut butter. Petra and Kevin debated about the layout for the next artists' event. And then, as quickly as it began, everyone else was gone, off to tackle the day.

As Tansy rinsed her coffee mug, Jake lingered in the kitchen, watching her with an amused glint in his eye.

"So." He settled a hip on the table. "Remember what I said about taking you out for a real date?"

Tansy raised a brow. "As opposed to a fake date?"

Jake shrugged. "I don't want you to miss out on the benefits of planning. I want to put my skills to the test and show you how amazing a real, thought-out date can be."

A snort escaped, and she shook her head. "We're supposed to be working on your spontaneity. You have no idea how wonderful go-with-the-flow can be."

"I'll get there," he said, lowering his voice as he stepped closer. "But that's why I think you'll be surprised. A little planning can go a long way."

A terrible thought slipped in. "How much planning, Jake? Please tell me you're not one of *those* guys."

A crease formed between his eyes. "Which guys?"

Tansy held up a hand, lifting a finger with each comment. "Accidental arm bump. Fingers touch. Holding hands. Hand caress over cheek. Curl hand around back of neck and stare into eyes, then kiss."

If anything, he looked more confused.

She lifted her other hand. "After kissing, hands over body. Move to torso—linger if you're a breast man, but otherwise head south rapidly. The occasional shiny unicorn will repeat the same path with mouth. Progress to penetration as quickly as possible."

She stood with both hands in the air, fingers spread wide.

Shock and outrage battled on Jake's face. "What the fuck was that?" he demanded.

"The steps to get from random meetup to sex."

Horror won over all the other emotions flitting over his expression. "Guys *do* that?"

A snort escaped her, and she folded her arms over her chest. "They shake it up a little, but yeah. I mean, I get it. Foreplay is a thing some people don't seem to need."

"Sex is not a checklist."

"My point exactly, which is why I always baled on any date that started feeling like sex by the numbers. Which is to reassure you that *I'm* not here with an agenda or expectations. If it'll help you learn important life lessons, kiss me out of the blue." Her lips twitched, but she kept a blank expression. "And then show me that day's page in your planner so I can check it doesn't say 'Kiss Tansy.'"

He laughed. "So much for getting points for my colouring page."

Too funny.

"No, Tansy. I'm not one of those guys." Jake offered his best smolder. "Sex is one area where I can guarantee that I'm very spontaneous."

The shiver that took her was delicious and dangerous.

"Time to get back on track." Tansy crossed her arms, feeling the spark of a challenge. "Fine. You get to plan one date, but I'll *plan* one as well, whatever that means. Then we'll vote to see which one was better."

He raised a brow. "Oh, it's a competition now?"

"Everything is a competition," she replied with a smirk. "Besides, I do want to see what you think constitutes a 'real' date. Considering we already went out for dinner."

Jake grinned, his eyes glinting with mischief. "All right. I'll take that challenge." He paused, tilting his head. "But since I need time to plan, why don't you go first? How about tonight or tomorrow?"

Tansy considered for a moment, scrambling for ideas. She

could wing this. No problem. "Fine. Tomorrow right after lunch," she said without blinking. "Pack a swimsuit."

His eyebrows shot up. "You're not about to chop a hole in the ice of the nearest frozen lake, are you?"

She laughed. "Trust me, it'll be fun. You're not a stick-in-the-mud, right?"

His hesitation only made her grin wider. She did have a plan forming, such as she ever did, and it didn't involve icy dips. It would definitely take him out of his comfort zone, and it would help deal with one of their biggest issues.

The need for some *hands-on* time.

"ONLY US FIVE FOR LUNCH?" Petra asked Jake.

Aiden stood at the counter, plating sandwiches for himself and Petra. Kevin and Tansy were already seated as Jake brought the iced tea pitcher to the table.

"Declan took the hands out riding this morning. They won't be back until late," Jake told Petra.

"*Brrr.*" Tansy wrapped her arms around herself. "It's far too cold to spend the entire day outside."

"Agreed." Petra took the plate Aiden handed her with a thanks then eyed Tansy hard. "What are you up to?"

Jake turned immediately to make sure he had a prime view of whatever followed. He hadn't been about to say anything, but Tansy had basically spent all morning wearing a smirk that was somehow simultaneously adorable and annoying.

Thank goodness someone else had finally noticed and called her on it.

"Tell me," Petra demanded. "I see mischief written all over your face."

"Mischief? Moi? *Never.*" Tansy's snort of amusement

landed the same moment as Petra's *ha!*. "Fine. I'm taking Jake out this afternoon for a date I planned."

Across the table from them, Aiden and Kevin both froze. Aiden's lips twitched, but Kevin looked confused. "You *planned?* What does that even mean?" he asked.

"That Jake isn't going to know what hit him," Petra muttered into her glass.

"Sounds about right," Tansy agreed far too quickly, and between Aiden's snicker and Petra's grin, suddenly Jake was a whole lot more uncertain about surviving his afternoon.

He sat, turning to Kevin. "If I need an emergency extraction, I have you on speed dial, agreed?"

Kevin raised his hands in the air in protest. "Hey, I'm booked this afternoon. You're on your own."

Interesting. Distracted for a moment, Jake examined Kevin closer. "Who are you meeting with? The hands are all out riding."

Their resident psychologist shrugged, focusing on his plate. "Never said I had a work meeting."

Now Jake was really curious. "You have a date?"

"Well, that would make sense, wouldn't it?" Kevin lifted his sandwich to his mouth and took a big bite, ensuring his mouth was too full to answer nosy questions.

Petra was delighted. "You can try to keep it a secret, but it's doubtful that will last long. Life would be much simpler if you simply told us."

The man nodded but kept silently chewing.

Which meant the rest of the meal was dedicated to tormenting Kevin and not teasing Tansy for more details. A far better use of their time, Jake decided.

Still, when the meal was over and Tansy all but hauled him toward the door, Jake had to laugh. "You safe to drive? You're bouncing pretty hard."

"Of course. Just ready for fun and games." Mischief sparkled in her eyes. "You?"

"More ready than I thought I'd be."

He swung both their bags over his shoulder then took her hand and walked beside her to her SUV.

He waited until they were on the highway to speak again. "You plan to give me any hints about what's happening on this date?"

"You're going to enjoy yourself, that's what. And it won't involve freezing your ass off riding country highways with your brother and the ranch hands."

Tansy's smile was so bright Jake couldn't look away. "Okay. I trust you." He settled back in his seat and watched out his window so he didn't try to guess where they were going.

The winter day was made colder by the grey clouds overhead. Jake was glad he wasn't out on horseback at the moment. They sat in a comfortable silence, the SUV making odd noises at times, until Tansy pulled in at the long drive beside the decorative wooden sign that declared *Red Boot Ranch*.

"We're headed to Petra's brother's place?" Jake asked.

"Sort of, but not really. Patience is a virtue," Tansy teased.

He had no idea what was going on as she guided the van down a twisting road, all the way past the small rental cabins and the barns.

When she finally pulled into a parking space outside a not-quite-finished building, Jake's suspicions flared. "That sign says *spa*."

"Don't worry, it's not open yet. I'm not making you do a mani-pedi or anything." Tansy cut off the engine then waggled her brows at him. "Although, speaking of spontaneity, you might decide you like having a pedicure."

"That's someone touching my feet?" Jake made a face then

joined her at the cleared path that led to the oversized cabin. "Unlikely."

"Ticklish?"

He didn't offer an answer, although, hell yeah.

Thankfully, she stepped forward, pushed through the unlocked door, and entered the spa. The inside lit up as she hit a panel of lights, and Jake glanced around, expecting to see...

Well, someone, to be honest. But the foyer with a pristine white front counter topped with a cedar plank was empty. Peaceful yet upbeat art hung on the walls—images of wide open lakes and wheat fields and sunflowers made of multiple layers of fabric and paint.

Tansy tapped at her phone for a moment, and soft music began playing. She finally turned and caught his eye. "Ta-da. Here we are."

"Here we are, indeed." Jake stepped in a slow circle, trying his best to be a good date for Tansy. Someone who embraced spontaneity instead of desperately attempting to figure out what happened in closed spas.

Laughter spilled toward him, and he turned away from what looked to be a massage room to take in Tansy in all her glory. Brown eyes bright, the gold in the core flashing at him in amusement as she pulled her hair into a ponytail high on the top of her head and secured it with a purple thing off her wrist.

"Time to put you out of your misery." She nodded, the top fluff of blonde hair sticking upright bouncing with the motion. "I'm ready if you are."

"Me too."

An instant later, he was tugged down the hall, Tansy sweeping him up in her wake. "Here's the first thing you need to know. The spa is not officially open. Red Boot is adding services for their dude ranch guests, but not until the spring. We're testing the place out for them."

"Since there's no official staff, does that mean I get to give you a massage?" The suggestion came out an octave lower than usual, need colouring his voice.

She jerked to a stop, twirling against him. Heated palms pressed to his chest as she smiled. "Better. Get your swimsuit on and meet me in that room."

After a quick point across the hall, she tucked him into a small changing room and vanished.

Jake stripped at the speed of light. His board shorts didn't do much to hide his hardening dick. Empty rooms to themselves with showers and massage tables available? Swimsuits might mean a hot tub...

Yeah, he was already enjoying this.

He slipped across the hall, shocked to discover Tansy had beaten him there. The room was about the size of High Water's main living space, the air extra warm as it swirled around his bare shoulders. The faintest hint of coconut and fresh clean wood ash filled his nose.

Recessed lighting turned low created a golden glow that danced over Tansy's bare legs and torso as she leaned over and placed a couple of pots beside what looked like a sunken, half-full wading pool.

Flickering sparkles danced back at him from the teeny square of yellow fabric barely covering her mighty fine ass. He could cup one cheek in his hand, and his fingers would easily slip under the edge of the fabric and stroke and tease until she was panting his name. And that's just where he'd start. Next he'd dive in on her breasts before returning to that addictive mouth of hers...

Of course, Tansy being Tansy, she would probably kill him if she knew exactly how dirty the thoughts racing through his head were.

Scratch that. She'd kill him for making a list.

She stood and turned, and damn if he could stop his gaze from dropping to her breasts. The sweet, soft swells were covered with equally tiny triangles that matched her briefs.

Briefs? His gaze dropped farther, stuttering to a stop over her mound. It too was a golden-wrapped present he wanted to open this instant, preferably with his teeth.

God. Jake swallowed hard to stop from drooling as every inch of her seemed to glisten.

"You seem onboard with our date." Tansy waited until he met her eyes then deliberately dropped her own gaze to the tenting in his trunks. "If *that's* any indication."

His cock hardened even farther. "I have a whole lot of ideas. Really *good* ideas."

She grinned. "Hold that thought. Here's the second thing you need to know. We're sharing a mud bath."

Images of her naked under his hands vanished...replaced with confusion. Not enough to completely make his erection flag, but clarification would help. "That stuff ladies put on their faces?"

"Sometimes." She held a hand to him, and he took it willingly, stepping into the wading pool thing with her. "Third thing. We are not having sex today."

He stroked a hand up her forearm and over the curve of her bare shoulder. "That's okay. I mean, I'd like to, but going slow is fine."

"No, going slow sucks," Tansy complained. "Turns out spontaneity is good for some things, but not the timing of sexy-time dates with period schedules. And while sex is not always off-limits when I'm on my period, that's not what I want for our first time."

Jake laughed. "Okay. Does that mean the planner in this relationship gets a bonus point for being able to time our next date during a period-free time frame?"

"You get a point for not freaking out when I mentioned my period."

Yeah. He knew what she was talking about. He shrugged. "Our stepdad knocked the embarrassment out of us good when we were teens, explaining more than the health videos in biology class. Jeff said if we didn't know how females were built, including the day to day reality of menses, hormones, and societal expectations, we had no right going near the enticing parts for fun."

She guided him to the lower edge of the pool, laughing the entire time. "Your dad was a rock star."

"He really was."

Jake's feet to his knees were immersed in warm water. Not hot enough to make him sweat, but enough to be aware the water was there. It was like sitting in an upside down layer cake. His feet on the bottom, hips resting on the middle layer. The pots rested on the top layer, about rib height on him.

Tansy crawled over his lap, knees resting on the tiles on either side of his hips. "Thanks for being understanding."

"Screw that." Jake cupped her face in his hands. "You're here. I'm here. We're both barely dressed, and I'm about to touch your gorgeous body. I'm already having a fucking great time."

She stroked her hands over his shoulders, gaze following the tickling caress as a mischievous smile twisted her lips. "The mud bath needs explaining because we got in this afternoon as guinea pigs. Petra's brother Zach and his bestie are the thinker types. Turns out when they went excavating for some new building here on the ranch, they found ashes from a volcanic eruption that happened over seven thousand years ago."

"Ah, the plot thickens. Literally. The mud involves these ashes?" Jake asked, slowly smoothing his hands down her waist.

"Mount Mazama is about to be all over you," Tansy agreed.

"We'll have to report back in twenty-four hours if we had any adverse reactions, but so far, they've tested and tried it a bunch on themselves and had no problems."

Jake teased his fingers along her bikini bra straps. "I have one concern. This bikini is *make my jaw drop* pretty. I'd hate to see it get stained from ancient volcanic muck."

Her grin widened. "Breast man, are you?"

"All of you, every inch. That's my current obsession," he corrected, tugging gently on the strings. "I won't go near your pussy if that's off-limits but give me these."

She took a long slow breath as if considering hard before nestling in closer and breathing her answer in his ear. "When you have the time, you're welcome to strip me naked."

Which meant ASAP as far as he—

Tansy kissed him, and all plans and agendas except her lips on his went out the window. With warm skin under his palms, Jake stroked and petted the smooth skin on her back as he tangled his tongue with hers. The weight of her in his lap was barely there, yet everything. He sucked her tongue, and she gasped. He tugged at her bikini top ties, and the fabric scraps hung between them as he held her torso so tight to his her every breath rose and fell against him.

"Jake?"

She murmured his name against his lips, and he pulled back far enough to see her eyes, liquid with lust. "Yeah?"

"Mud bath time."

Something hot and wet and sticky smeared as she guided her open fingers over his chest. The scent of ash and coconut grew stronger, and his lips twitched as Tansy reached into the nearest pot and scooped up a second handful of the rich, black-brown gunk.

He let her work in silence for a few minutes, loving the heated touches and how she teasingly rocked along his erection over and over as she reloaded with more ammunition. She traced the lines of his abdomen, outlining squares as her lips curled. "Six pack. Happy trail. It's like sexy algebra."

When she stroked her fingers to the very edge of his trunks and lingered there, even he had a limit.

"My turn." It came out a half growl, half curse.

Tansy eased back on his thighs, lifting her chin. Her perfect breasts aimed straight at him.

Jake shifted the pot to beside his hip so he wouldn't have to interrupt his explorations. Carefully, he dipped one finger into the moist mess then lifted his hand toward her torso.

She took a deep breath, and her breasts rose tantalizingly.

Jake redirected and drew a muddy line down Tansy's nose.

Laughter burst free. "*Jake.*"

"Being spontaneous," he told her proudly. "Also, I'm not mudding up your tits until I've had a chance to do this."

He wrapped his hands around her hips and hefted her upward to line up properly. Leaning close, he curled his lips over the peak of her right breast and sucked the tight tip into his mouth.

10

———

ansy's vision of what would happen that afternoon had been foggy, but she had hoped, after experiencing Jake's kisses, that the chemistry between them would continue to flare brightly.

Oh hell, yes. Bright. Dazzlingly bright. Super-nova, earth-shatteringly, blindness-inducing bright.

Jake's torso was covered with stripes of mud, but his hands were still mostly clean. He held her with his right arm and cupped a breast with his left hand, squeezing and kneading as he made happy sounds and kept sucking. The edge of his teeth rasping over her tender skin sent a shot of pure lust directly between her legs.

"God, I don't know if I want to haul you off so I can kiss you or keep you right where you are." Tansy gulped as Jake switched sides, nipping and pinching and driving her wild. "Both," she decided. "Somehow both would be good."

He laughed, which sadly moved him off her body. The heat in his eyes was worth it, though. "We have time, Tansy. Don't be blue. Or should I say yellow?"

Ignoring the fact her action streaked him with mud, she caught his face in her hands and tilted until they made eye contact. "You looked up what a tansy is." Laughter bubbled at the back of her throat.

"On a naturalist blog." He looked far too pleased with himself. "Don't tell me that's what you're thinking about right now, though. Seems I have to up my game."

Huge smile in place, he stroked his way down her breasts again, one hand drifting away to dip briefly into the mud pot. When he held up his thoroughly coated fingers for her approval, Tansy took another deep breath.

Time to go for it. "Do your worst."

His worst was torment. One caressing touch after another, he painted. Lines on her ribs, circles around her breasts, zigzags on her sides.

When he meticulously drew a triangle around her belly button, Tansy growled at him. "*Jake.*"

"Art class was never my favourite, but maybe I didn't have the right canvas," he said with amusement.

Torn between laughing and crying, Tansy went for hugging the stuffing out of him, which slicked them both with mud.

Jake chuckled, but he curled his arms around her and reciprocated the embrace. "You're a nut," he told her.

"You agreed to this, so, ditto."

She kissed him then, slow and deep and hot, rocking over the thick length of his cock. Tongues and teeth and lips and heated breaths mingling, Jake caught her hips and added to the rhythm. Dragging her higher, harder, until gasps and grunts carried on the air with an animalistic soundtrack.

Tansy ground down hard and found that final kick she needed, an orgasm breaking over her with a hot, quick burst of pleasure. Gloating satisfaction followed a second later as Jake groaned, shaking under her as he too found release.

They stared at each other, grins stretching from ear to ear.

"I guess I'm sort of a stick-in-the-mud, aren't I?" Jake asked.

Tansy leaned her forehead on his and stared into his shining blue eyes. "Pogo stick, maybe. Thanks for the ride."

Laughter continued through their clean up showers and the shared ride home.

Thinking back on the afternoon a couple days later made Tansy beam. The aroma of garlic and curry filled the small, cozy kitchen, mingling with the scent of fresh baked bread cooling on the counter.

The ranch hands had changed the previous day. Don and Tony had been joined by two more men, Aaron and Brett, which meant with Kevin, the five rooms under the art studio for short-term visitors were officially full. It also meant cooking meals for eleven on a daily basis.

Not a problem. Her hands moved mechanically—chopping, seasoning, stirring—but her mind was elsewhere.

Jake. She'd admit it. After their time together at the spa, she wanted more. With him just across the hall, once her period was over, she was planning on walking in her sleep.

But more than sex, she was ready to keep upping their game in terms of growing closer. Which meant at some point she would have to venture into that scary territory Kelli had referenced. The wicked, nasty past.

Sharing was the right thing, no matter how hard.

Hmmm, *hard*.

Damn her brain for going back to Jake in those shorts and bemoaning the fact she never got to see him fully naked. Maybe she could convince him to do a sexy striptease for her...

The spoon in her fingers slipped. She scrambled and somehow smacked it in mid-air. The spoon flew away from her and hit the floor with a moist *plop*.

"Poetry in motion, Tans," she poked at herself, stepping

quickly across the room to pick it up. With incredibly bad timing, she kicked the handle, sending sauce splattering farther across the tile floor as the spoon made a break for it and vanished under the couch.

"Oh, for crying out loud," she muttered. "Get it together."

Amused at her Jake-induced clumsiness, she knelt beside the couch to find the spoon. Sweeping her fingers under the edge, she brushed against something cold and metallic, but not a spoon. Confused, she put her head all the way to the floor and used her phone to peer into the dark space.

Something glittered back at her.

She pulled it out, resting on her knees as she examined the piece of jewelry in her hand. The bracelet was beautiful—delicate yet sturdy, with intricate links of silver interwoven with small, sparkling gems. The design was elegant, and far too expensive to belong to anyone in her circle of friends.

Her mind raced as she turned it over in her fingers. Who did it belong to, and how on earth had it ended up under the couch?

She thumbed her phone on to message Petra, jerking upright as the front door burst open and slammed against the wall with a loud bang.

"Tansy!" Sasha Stone stood in the doorway, panic in her voice. "Where are you? We need you."

Tansy reacted to the tone more than anything. In all the years she had known the girl, Sasha had never sounded this scared.

The bracelet was shoved into her pocket as Tansy shot to her feet and rushed toward the door, the cold winter air biting at her skin. "Hey kiddo, what's wrong? Is Jinx okay?"

"She's good, but we found someone," Sasha panted, leaning forward and clutching her sides as if she'd sprinted to the house. "He's hurt. You need to come quick."

Tansy's pulse shot up as she grabbed her jacket from its hook on the wall. "Where?"

"Behind the old haybarn on the edge of the property near our place," Sasha informed her as they hurried out the door and into the cold of winter twilight. "Jinx stayed with him. She tried calling Aiden, but her phone is dead and I didn't bring mine. I was just walking her back from my house after we finished our homework."

"You lead, I'll call for backup." Tansy dialed Jake's number as she rushed after Sasha.

He answered on the second ring. "What's up, gorgeous?"

"The girls found a stranger by the old barn, and Sasha says he's hurt. You anywhere nearby, or do I call the shots on getting him help?"

"I'm less than ten minutes out but do what you think is right." Jake spoke without a tremour of doubt, and Tansy appreciated his calm response. "You got this, sweetheart. I'll be there as soon as I can."

Tansy and Sasha struggled forward, the howling wind biting at their faces as they hurried through the swirling snow. The sky loomed dark above them, but Sasha led the way without hesitation. Tansy followed closely, questions darting through her mind. Who was this man? Had he somehow heard High Water was a refuge, or was him showing up here simply a coincidence?

After what felt like an eternity, and just as Tansy's thighs were ready to give out, they reached the edge of the property where the old barn stood. The silhouette of someone crouching in the snow came into view, and Tansy's stomach clenched.

Jinx knelt beside a figure lying very still on the ground. As they approached, the man came into focus. Young, maybe early twenties, his head resting awkwardly on a hunk of fabric, his blond hair streaked with blood. He was unconscious and covered with Jinx's winter coat.

Tansy swore inside. Jinx would be frozen through.

Jinx glanced up as they approached, her face tight with worry. She had her arms wrapped around herself, shaking from fear and the icy cold. "He's been like this for a while. He was shaking so hard I thought he needed to be covered up, but I didn't think it was safe to lie down beside him. I didn't know what else to do."

"You did the right thing, but now you're heading home, stat," Tansy said quickly, kneeling beside the man and checking his pulse. It was faint but steady. "Jake's on his way. He and I will get him back to the house. Sasha, take Jinx back to High Water. Jinx, hot shower right away. Sasha, Make hot chocolate, okay?"

"I can do that." Sasha wrapped her arms around Jinx. "Will you be okay?"

As if on cue, headlights cut through the darkness, and Jake's truck rumbled up the narrow road toward them.

"Yup. Now get."

By the time the girls vanished around the corner and Jake had pulled to a stop and jumped from the vehicle, Tansy had dropped to her knees and done a quick scan on the injured man.

Jake's breath puffed into the cold air. "What happened?" he asked, his gaze scanning the scene as he joined her on the ground.

"Don't know," Tansy admitted. "But he's hurt. Other than the head wound, I don't see any major injuries. I think getting him out of the cold is the most important thing."

Jake nodded. He crouched then gently lifted the young man into his arms. "I've got him. Let's move."

The fastest way back with the least jostling was for Jake to settle into the truck bed still holding the injured man. Tansy drove as carefully as possible, but every second of the journey was tense until she pulled to a stop outside the main house.

"Put him in the guest room," Tansy suggested. "We can get him cleaned up a bit, but first, we should call Sydney."

Jake hummed his approval. "She did offer to help us out in situations like this."

"She'll keep things quiet," Tansy assured him, hurrying ahead to get the door for him. It swung open before she could touch the knob.

Sasha stepped back. Her eyes widened as Jake rushed past her with his burden. "Is he okay?"

"Don't know yet," Tansy offered truthfully. Another person who they'd need to discuss keeping things quiet with. "Take care of Jinx and stay out of the way for now, got it?"

"Yes, ma'am."

Down the hall, Jake shouldered the guest room door open then laid the injured man carefully on the bed. "Help me get this coat off him. It's soaked through and only making him colder."

They worked quickly then Tansy pulled out her phone and dialed Sydney's number. When her friend picked up immediately, Tansy explained the situation quietly.

"I just hit the highway after a house call, so I can be there in under twenty minutes." The sound of a turn indicator clicked in the background. Sydney's no nonsense directions helped ease some of Tansy's panic. "Take off his boots, but other than that, worry more about piling on the blankets. If the head wound starts bleeding again, gently press a facecloth to it, but otherwise, wait for me."

"We got it." Tansy met Jake's gaze, and he nodded. "Come straight in when you get here. Sasha might be in the kitchen."

"Well, shit. That's a complication." Sydney made a rude

noise. "She's a smart kid, though. Not a huge problem if you ask me. See you soon."

Tansy slipped her phone away. "Extra blankets are in the hall closet."

"You get them. I'm staying close in case he wakes up swinging." Jake went to work on the laces of the man's worn boots.

Ten minutes later, quilts were piled three deep on the shivering man who looked even younger now than before, his face pale against the white pillow. His head wound looked worse up close—a deep gash above his temple that had bled profusely before freezing in the cold.

"I should go wash my hands then check on the girls," Tansy said.

Jake slipped an arm around her shoulders and squeezed tight. "He's going to be okay. You did well. All of you."

She leaned into him for one more second then escaped the room. This was part of what she'd wanted—to be a helper.

Shocking how terrifying it was in reality. Helping meant another person hurting first, and as logical as that was, right now it felt as if the bottom had dropped out of Tansy's world.

Struggling to find her mental balance, she soaked a face cloth and washed her face and hands. She smoothed down the front of her shirt and pants and hit the bulge of the forgotten bracelet in her pocket.

She pulled it out, turning it over in her hand. The gems caught the light from the bathroom mirror and turned it into a miniature light show. Another unreal moment. Another thing that didn't make sense.

How had something so valuable ended up under their couch?

However it had happened, now wasn't the time to ask those

questions. With a small sigh, Tansy dropped the bracelet into her bathroom drawer to deal with later.

JAKE STOOD beside the bed watching Sydney work. Every time she motioned, he eased forward, using a warm washcloth to help clean the dirt and blood from the young man.

Bullshit on that—the body sprawled in the bed belonged to someone barely more than a kid. If the stranger had reached twenty years old yet, Jake would eat his hat.

In spite of Sydney's poking and prodding and Jake's manhandling, their guest lay quiet. Shallow breaths, the faintest pulse at his neck. He looked as if he'd been worked over from top to bottom, and once again Jake was slammed with one of those delicate balancing acts.

This was what the ranch was all about, wasn't it? Helping those who needed it. Offering shelter to anyone lost or desperate for safety. It felt right to be helping the kid, yet Jake couldn't shake the gnawing feeling at the back of his mind. It wasn't only the battered body lying unconscious before him—

The fact people out there were willing to inflict pain on a fellow human made Jake sick to his soul. He would never understand how that was possible, and his instinct to protect grew stronger.

She would smack him upside the head if she knew, but worry rushed in for Tansy, and Jinx, and Sasha.

Hell, Sydney was right here. Her petite frame would be no match for an agitated patient who had clearly been in some sort of fight.

"Jake?"

Sydney's summons pulled him from his thoughts. She'd moved the blankets away to access the young man's legs, and

Jake hurried to clean away the grime that clung to their patient's bruised skin.

"See these marks?" Sydney spoke quietly as she gestured toward crisscrossing bruises and scars. "These aren't from a single fall or accident. These are old. He's been hurt before—lots of times."

Jake's concern shot skyward again. "You think he's been in constant trouble? Like street fights?"

"I'd say they're more likely beatings," Sydney offered reluctantly. "Look at the patterns. Those are defensive wounds. He's been trying to protect himself."

Jake swore under his breath. The kid hadn't only been hurt—he'd been running from something. Or someone. "What the hell did he get himself into?"

"We'll figure that out once he wakes up," Sydney said her tone soft but firm. "For now, he needs rest."

Jake stood, running a hand through his hair as he paced the room. Tansy had promised to get the word out to his brothers, but until he had a chance to talk to them, he planned to stay on guard duty. "That's fine. He can—"

The young man groaned, stirring slightly. His head shifted uncomfortably from side to side.

Sydney rested a hand on his chest, soothing him. "Stay still. You shouldn't be moving a lot right now."

The kid's eyes fluttered open, unfocused at first then narrowing as he took in his unfamiliar surroundings. He tensed, arms flailing instinctively.

"Shit." Jake ducked forward, getting a fist in the face for his troubles. He cursed softly even as he held the kid down to keep him from hitting Sydney. "Stop. You're safe. We won't hurt you."

"I'm a doctor," Sydney said quickly. "And your doctor says you need to lie still."

The young man blinked a few times, his gaze shifting between Jake and Sydney. Confusion etched his face, followed quickly by a wave of panic. "Who... Where..."

"It's okay," Jake said, ignoring the urge to press a hand to his throbbing eye. He kept his words as calm and steady as possible. "You're at High Water ranch. My niece Jinx found you then got help. You're safe now."

The young man relaxed slightly, though tension lingered in his face. He met Jake's eyes. "I'm sorry. I didn't mean to cause trouble."

"It's okay, we understand," Sydney assured him, patting his shoulder gently. "You didn't know that this is a safe place, but we'll take care of you."

"I can't stay. I need to go."

Sydney raised a brow. "Nope." She eased away, placed her hands on her hips, and gave the kid a doctor glare that didn't invite argument. "You're not going anywhere. You've got injuries that need tending to. If you push yourself too hard, you'll make them worse. You'll be taking it easy for at least a week."

The kid's jaw tightened, but this time he didn't argue, exhaustion weighing him down. The kid was too tired to fight—physically and mentally.

Still, it'd be good to get some information before the kid crashed. "I'm Jake, and this is Sydney. You'll meet my two brothers soon enough, and the rest of us who live here on the ranch." The young man met his gaze straight on. Jake nodded his approval. "You got a name?"

"Logan." He hesitated, probably debating whether he should include his last name or lie and make something up.

"You don't need to rush to tell us much more. This place is safe. Nobody's going to hurt you here."

Logan's eyes flickered, a hesitation in their depths. The kid was still holding something back—something that had him ready to bolt the moment he got a chance.

"You in trouble with the authorities?" Jake asked carefully.

Panic flashed across the young man's face. He shook his head quickly—too quickly. His face contorted with pain, and Sydney snapped out a chastisement.

"Easy there, bucko," she said. "No quick movements. Or that week I gave you will become longer. He's not asking because we're about to kick you out, but we need to know what to expect. Trust me, I will lie my ass off to keep you safe."

"I'm not running from the cops," Logan said, his voice week but sincere. "But I am running. There are people I don't want to find me."

Jake exchanged a glance with Sydney. That alone confirmed what they'd expected.

The door behind them opened, and Declan walked in. He scanned the scene and instantly moved to stand beside Sydney. He took a thorough look over Logan then met Jake's gaze. He stared for a moment at the eye the kid had smacked, silently asking if everything was okay.

Jake gave him a reassuring nod, but the tension in the room was thick.

"Look, Logan." Jake kept his voice steady. "Even if you are in trouble, you're staying for now. We won't let anyone hurt you. This is my brother Declan, and he'll vouch for that as well."

Instantly, his brother backed his play. Declan dipped his chin. "Jake's right. This is a place of refuge for people who need it. We'll help you if you let us."

Logan glanced between the two brothers, uncertainty in his eyes even as fatigue rapidly slid in. For a moment, it seemed as if he might try to argue, but then he relaxed into the bed and let out a long, weary sigh.

"Thank you," he whispered. His eyes drooped, exhaustion finally catching up. He muttered under his breath, barely audible. "Found by an angel."

Sydney checked him over once again then pulled the blanket under the kid's chin. She tilted her head toward the door.

"He'll need a lot of rest," Sydney offered as they paused in the hallway outside the door. "I'll come back tomorrow to check on him, but you'll need to wake him every few hours tonight to check for signs of a concussion. Watch for dizziness, confusion, anything out of the ordinary."

Jake nodded, absorbing her instructions. "We can do that."

Sydney took one last glance back into the room, gaze softening as she took in the sleeping figure. "He's been through a lot," she said. "Whatever he's running from, I hope he finds peace here."

Declan rested a hand on her shoulder and squeezed. "That's our goal. Thanks for being part of it."

Her lips curled up at the corners. "Now you get to feed me. I talked to Tansy on my way in, and she said supper would be on the table once we were done. I'll get washed, then we can figure out what comes next."

11

There was more than enough to keep Tansy distracted from the activity going on in the back room. She went to check on Jinx first, found her out of the shower and in her bedroom, wrapped in a cozy blanket. Sasha was nestled beside her on the bed, and both of them had their hands wrapped around large cups that smelled amazing.

Dixie lay across both their feet, curled to face the door as if guarding precious treasure.

"I can tell by the scent in here you found the good chocolate," Tansy teased, sliding forward to rest a hip on the bed beside the girls. She scratched Dixie's head as a *well done.*

Jinx smacked her lips then placed her cup on the headboard. "I'm warming up from the inside out."

Tansy glanced over her, but Jinx didn't seem any worse for wear. She turned her attention to Sasha. "Did you talk to your parents?"

A slow nod in return, given with extra wide eyes. "I told them I was staying for supper. I didn't say anything other than that. Jinx asked me to wait until we talked to Declan."

"Good thinking." Tansy offered both the girls an approving nod. "You guys did well, but you're right. Declan will help figure out what happens next."

A second later, Jinx was cuddled against Tansy, hugging her tightly. "Is the guy we found okay?"

"So far, so good," Tansy assured her, squeezing hard. She lifted her eyes to meet Sasha's. "You were pretty scared, weren't you?"

A quiver sounded in Sasha's voice as she answered. "We thought he was dead."

"Come here." Tansy opened her other arm and Sasha immediately slipped in.

The three of them huddled together for comfort as Dixie headbutted them, worried at the high intensity emotion filling the air. "I bet it was scary, but other than Jinx putting herself at risk of hypothermia, you guys reacted quickly. You probably saved his life."

A ragged sob escaped Jinx, and she burrowed in closer for a moment. Tansy held the girls and let them find their equilibrium, happy for a chance to take comfort from them, as well.

When Jinx's breathing settled out, Tansy gave one last squeeze then let go. "We'll wait to talk to Declan, but one thing I know that has to happen next is supper. I had things mostly under control, but let's go finish."

Having a tangible task to do helped. By the time Petra and Aiden rushed into the house followed by Kevin and the hands, the girls had the table set, including salads, chutney, and rice. Tansy had the pot full of Massaman beef ready to bring out.

Jake and Declan stepped in front of the fire, and Tansy jerked upright in a moment of panic. Jake's right eye was decidedly red.

Before she could rush across the room, Sydney reappeared

from the back of the house. She joined Tansy, leaning against the counter beside her. "I used your bathroom to freshen up. Figured you wouldn't mind."

"Never a problem. What happened to Jake?"

"Jake got hit by an accidental swing from Logan. The kid felt terrible about it. He's resting now, but he'll wake up starving. If you have any broth, that's the best thing for him for a while."

Taking one final peek at Jake's face, Tansy mentally went through what she had in the freezer. "I can warm something whenever it's needed." She caught Sydney's fingers in hers. "Thank you for being close by."

"Glad I could help." Sydney lifted her chin at Petra, striding determinedly across the room as Aiden darted past to join his brothers in front of the fire. "There's one curious cat coming our direction."

"Logan's arrival isn't dinner conversation, privacy reasons and all the rest," Tansy said quietly as she held her hand to Petra and pulled her in for a hug. "I'm okay, the girls are okay, and now you need to pretend you're okay and make sure dinner conversation keeps flowing."

For a good solid fifteen seconds, Petra squeezed the stuffing out of her before pulling back and examining her. "I hate it when you're right."

"Yet it happens so very often."

Sydney snickered, pulling to vertical and sniffing appreciatively. She raised her volume to be heard clearly by the entire room. "I hope the smell means that supper is nearly ready. I'm starving."

Across the room, Declan raised a brow even as everyone headed to the table. "Starving? Really? That means you'll be eating three tablespoons tonight instead of your usual two?"

Aiden frowned at his brother. "The fact you watch how much we all eat on a regular basis is creepy, bro."

"Agreed. Also, I eat as much as I need to. More than I need to when it's Tansy's curry." Sydney got ready to pull out the chair at the head of the table, and both Kevin and Declan jumped in ahead of her to help. She rolled her eyes then smiled sweetly, glancing down the table to where Jinx and Sasha sat side by side. "Is Declan still hassling you over breakfast, Jinx?"

"Not since I showed him the nutritional analysis you gave me comparing what I was eating to what he eats."

Soft laughter rose around the table as everybody settled and the bowls and plates were passed.

"Try growing up with a nurse for a mother," Petra complained. "One who is blunt, knowledgeable, and far too willing to talk about the important effect of fiber on our systems."

Just like that, things were under control. Tansy was pretty sure that the ranch hands had no idea someone lay injured at the other end of the house. They'd get to meet him soon enough, she supposed. But right now, Logan deserved his privacy.

The end of the meal rolled around, and through some wordless magic, Kevin took charge of the hands. "All right guys, enough smack talk about who's the best pool shark. Tournament starts now in the common room. Winner declared before chores."

The minute they were out the door, Declan motioned to Sasha to get ready. "I'll take you home."

Sasha nodded, her fingers linked with Jinx's for a minute before she lifted her chin. "I know something's going on here, more than the art studio and the animal rescue, but I won't tell anybody. I promise."

Unexpectedly, Jake stepped forward, the gentle smile on

his face contrasting with the rising swell of his eye. "We trust that you can keep secrets, Sasha, but you're young enough that your parents need to be a part of the important ones."

The tension seemed to drain out of her, and this time when she nodded, her eyes had filled. "Yeah. I'd like it if they knew."

"We'll talk to your parents together," Declan assured her.

Jinx slipped her arms around Sasha and squeezed her tight, then Sasha headed to the door where Declan held her coat ready for her.

"I'll peek in on our guest, then I should head home," Sydney said after the door closed on the wintry night.

"Take a look, but why don't you stay?" Petra suggested. "The three of us haven't had a chance to catch up in a while."

In the background, Jinx, Aiden, and Jake had begun cleanup.

Tansy gestured to the leftovers. "I need to take care of those, but after, I would love some girl time."

Which is how, half an hour later, they ended up in the living room, the fire crackling in the airtight stove. Petra rearranged the chairs to create a more intimate gathering for the three of them with a love seat and a single overstuffed recliner.

Aiden held a whispered conversation with Petra that ended with him nabbing both Jake and Jinx. "We're headed to my apartment. Jinx is going to let me beat her at three handed crib."

To which the teenager rolled her eyes. "Old-fashioned games are okay, but next time you guys have to play Wyrmspan."

Jake twisted toward Tansy and mouthed the word back at her, confusion on his face.

Amusement kicked into high gear. Tansy had played the boardgame with the girls a few times. She was totally joining that game to witness Jake calculating the odds of which was better—hatching eggs or deploying dragons.

But for now, she wrapped the fuzzy blanket around her shoulders a little tighter and stared into the flames. A little moment of peace after a whole lot of chaos.

Beside her, Petra patted her knee softly. "It'll be okay."

Tansy met her gaze, raising a brow.

Her friend smiled. "You let out an enormous sigh, and I get it. Right when I think I've got High Water lined up neatly, we get thrown another loop."

"Life would be boring if nothing ever changed," Sydney said pragmatically.

"I could take a little boring," Tansy offered, thinking of Jake's eye.

Her comment was greeted instantly by Sydney blowing a raspberry at her. "Bullshit, nonsense, and once more, *pffft.*" Sydney wiggled her toes toward the fire, her legs draped over the arm of the chair she was curled up in. "I wish the loops being thrown at us didn't involve abused kids, but at least we're here to offer them a chance."

Tansy caught herself taking another deep breath. Yeah. That was pretty much what she had hoped for when she signed on at High Water.

Time for a change of topic. She met Sydney's gaze. "We need to interrogate Petra. That or teach her how calendars work. As in time marches forward, there's no time like the present, yada, yada."

"She still not decided on a wedding date?" Sydney hummed intently.

"I'm starting to get worried. Maybe this is a sign that the wedding is not going to happen."

Unexpectedly, instead of laughing at their teasing, Petra made a face.

Beside her, Tansy jerked upright. "Wait. I was joking. I know damn well there's nothing wrong in Petra-Aiden-landia. You two are so disgustingly in love, it's obnoxious kissy-faces and woo-woo germs everywhere, all the time."

"We don't have a problem," Petra said slowly. Her gaze danced between Sydney and Tansy. "It's kind of the whole High Water thing."

Tansy considered what they'd just been talking about and rapidly came to a few conclusions. "You're worried that if you plan something, we might have ranch hands suddenly arrive, or a need to keep things secret..." Tansy paused.

Petra made another face. "Or Aiden might end up with a black eye that's hard to explain."

Well, shit. Something Tansy hadn't even thought of, but obviously possible, all things considered.

"That does make planning awkward," Sydney agreed. "Especially with the size of your family."

Petra sagged in her corner of the loveseat, misery on her face. "Holding the wedding at Red Boot ranch would make perfect sense since my brother's place is a wedding venue. That would deal with some of the issues like accommodation for my family and the rest of it. My parents know what we're doing here, and Zach and Julia. But..."

"But that means an extra four siblings and their spouses and their kids, and doesn't deal with the possible interruption of people arriving." Tansy's mind jumped from idea to idea, trying to come up with a solution.

Sydney cleared her throat. "First thing to ask is, do you *want* the big family wedding, or is it simply expected?"

Petra opened her mouth...then closed it. She frowned. "Well, shit."

She couldn't help it. Tansy snickered. "Hoisted on your own petard?"

The glare she got was quick and evil. "What does that even mean?" Petra demanded.

"Not exactly sure," Tansy confessed. "Other than I don't think you want a big wedding."

"But you do want to get married." Sydney said it as more of a statement than a question. "What we need to brainstorm is how to do that in a way that works for you and Aiden. Period. Because that's who this is important for. You two. Family expectations are good to think about—"

"And then ignore," Tansy suggested.

Petra snorted. "Please. You've met my parents."

"It's more your brother I was considering," Tansy said. "I can see him now, stuffing his pockets with tissues because he knows he'll bawl his eyes out during your wedding. No one wants to see that, so we should come up with that brilliant alternative Sydney assumes we're capable of."

"Do you need to check with Aiden before we put on our planning caps?" Sydney asked.

"One minute." Petra pulled out her phone and tapped a quick message. A second later, she grinned. "He says, and I quote, *Abso-fucking-lutely. Tell me when and where and I'll be there.*"

The three friends exchanged grins.

Sydney hopped up and came back with a notebook from somewhere. "I'll be the Jake stand in. Toss out your worries, Petra. We're about to do some problem-solving so you can get hitched."

The chill inside Tansy's gut had vanished, washed away by the rock-solid friendship enveloping her. An injured young man still lay in a room down the hall. Others with dangerous needs might show up at High Water unexpectedly. Maybe every time things changed, Tansy would have to do a mental and emotional reset.

But with the warmth of the fire and the warmth of friendship enveloping her, and maybe, just maybe something special brewing between her and Jake—Tansy was ready.

THOSE FIRST HOURS after Logan's arrival passed, sliding into days. He'd avoided serious consequences from his head injury, but he still slept an astonishing amount.

Tuesday, Jake walked into the spare room and found Logan sitting in bed with an expression on his face that said the kid was calculating how to cut and run, in spite of all the reassurances they'd given him.

"Good to see you're awake," Jake offered, taking a single step into the room. "Need help getting to the bathroom?"

"Think I can make it on my own. Is it okay if I get up?" The kid made a face. "Do I have clothes to wear?"

Jake gestured to the top of the dresser. "Loaners for now. They might be a little big, but they'll do until we can take you shopping."

Logan started shaking his head then obviously thought better of it, reducing his motions and rubbing a hand over the back of his neck. "I won't be staying long."

"Repeating this conversation all the time is getting fucking annoying." Jake folded his arms over his chest and glared. Maybe a little tough love would convince the kid. "You are not going anywhere until you're at one hundred percent. Then you can make up your own goddamn mind, but until then, stop making this more difficult than it should be."

Logan's eyes widened. Then his lips twitched and he dipped his head to hide his expression, which was more amused than frightened.

Yeah. Jake needed to work on his scary face a little more.

"Get dressed if you feel up to it. Jinx is already off to school, but everybody else is having a lazy morning. They're helping with wedding prep if you can believe it."

Logan didn't say anything, but curiosity had slipped in.

Jake left him alone and went to rejoin the others gathered at the kitchen table, coffee mugs in front of them, breakfast plates pushed to the side. Three of the ranch hands had already left to do chores or chill on their own. Only Brett remained, sitting beside Kevin as they shared a low, intense conversation.

From where she stood at the counter, Tansy twisted and lifted the coffee pot in question.

He nodded then spoke for everybody to hear. "Logan's looking much better. He plans to join us."

"Thank God," Petra said with complete sincerity before turning thoughtful. "I wonder how good his handwriting is."

"I don't know why you're fussing about that so much. You can use literally any font that has ever been invented and a printer, and yet you want someone to physically address envelopes." Aiden ducked as Petra aimed a mock punch at his arm. "I'm not saying that I won't be first in line to volunteer, but you have to admit, the computer girl wanting to do everything by hand is slightly odd."

"It's for our wedding," she pointed out smugly. "It's supposed to be—"

"Odd?" Tansy repeated.

Petra snickered. "I was going to say heartwarming and homey."

Tansy put a cup of coffee in front of Jake. He leaned toward her as she settled in the chair beside him. "I don't know. Odd worked for me."

A snort of laughter escaped Tansy. "I have all the food organized for Thursday."

Declan raised a hand. "I've arranged for the mailing boxes,

so the wedding cakes will go out with priority post Friday morning."

Petra took a deep breath, twisting in her seat to catch hold of Aidan's hand. "We're really doing this?"

The adoration on his face was front and center as he pressed his forehead to hers. "We're really doing this."

They stared at each other so intensely it was almost too much to take in. Jake dragged his gaze away and spotted Tansy, smiling from ear to ear as she watched with approval.

The girls had started the wedding *right now* train, but Aiden had been more than willing to jump on board. Which meant both Jake and Declan had as well, because anything that made their brother this happy was not to be ignored.

The biggest issue behind Aiden and Petra getting hitched had turned out to be the need to keep secrets, which was complicated by Petra's big family. After a whole lot of brainstorming that had involved dangerously strong margaritas, the girls had come up with what Jake thought was a brilliant solution.

If they couldn't have some of the family there, they wouldn't have any of them. Aiden and Petra would exchange their vows privately, location currently a supersecret. They planned to video the entire thing then send out a link so that family could enjoy afterward.

At some point down the road, they would have a family celebration with the Sorenson side, probably during their next Christmas in Hawaii getaway. The Skye family and all the Heart Falls friends would celebrate during a party this coming summer.

The only part of not gathering together that had caused Petra regret—the inability to have family photos— had been solved by Tansy's brainwave. It was a little unusual, and made everybody laugh when they heard it.

As unique and spontaneous as Tansy herself, Jake thought.

"What did everybody think about the *wedding photos in a box* you asked for?" Kevin asked as he and Brett rose to gather the breakfast dishes and pop them into the dishwasher.

"My oldest siblings sent me back eyeroll emoji," Petra informed them. "The niblings are all thrilled. Brother-in-law number three wanted to ensure he had the exact right box dimensions and aperture settings I'd need."

"So, pretty much situation normal?" Tansy offered.

"Pretty much. My dad did inform me that if I had thought of it sooner, he would've made sure to order all of us identical Amazon packages so that we would have the same cardboard box to work with."

A knock sounded on the door, followed immediately by Sydney letting herself in. "Morning, High Water. Is there still coffee in the pot?"

Tansy got ready to leap to her feet, but Jake laid a hand on her shoulder. "I've got it. Morning, Sydney. Our guest should be joining us in a minute if you want to see him."

"Oh, I suppose. I actually came here to interrogate Kevin." Sydney hung her coat and made her way across the room, stopping beside where Kevin and Brett were prepping to hand wash and dry the pots from breakfast. "What's this I hear about you making a play for my nurse?"

Kevin looked as if butter wouldn't melt in his mouth. "Edison is an interesting young man who shares a lot of common interests with me."

Jake passed Sydney her coffee then eyed their psychologist. "Is this who you had the date with a while ago?"

"A while ago, and a few days ago, and a day ago," Sydney teased. "I had to come and tell you that I've been getting a constant earful of the wonderfulness of Kevin."

The faintest flush hit Kevin's cheeks. "Always nice to be appreciated."

"It is." Sydney leaned toward him, hands pressed to the countertop. "Don't you go breaking his heart."

"Sydney, stay out of Kevin's dating life," Petra scolded.

"It's not his dating life I'm worried about. It's if they break up and then Edison finds it impossible to stay in a small town with constant reminders of what could have been, and suddenly I have to train another nurse to be able to handle the way I like things to work."

"Ahhh. That makes more sense," Declan offered, deliberately not looking at Sydney. "Heaven forbid anything interrupt your work."

Sydney made a face at him even as she paced toward the table.

She turned to Jake, pulling something out of her pocket. "By the way, this is yours. It got sent to your name, General Delivery, Heart Falls, which I had no idea was still a thing. I was at the post office and Marcy asked if I could give it to you."

"And there's a small town for you," Kevin murmured. "Anywhere else that would be considered tampering with the post."

"Here it's called *Mrs. Marcy's Too Lazy To Get Off Her Ass And Do Her Job*." Tansy coughed into her fist. "Excuse me. Did I say that in my outside voice?"

Jake took the envelope, eyeing it with curiosity. "I have no idea who would send me mail that doesn't already know our address—"

Shit. One glance at the handwriting and he knew immediately. It was from Melissa.

He shoved it in his pocket, ignoring the questioning gaze Tansy gave him.

A second later, distraction arrived from the bedroom

portion of the house. Heads turned as Logan stepped into the open doorway.

"Good to see you out and about." Sydney stood and marched forward. She was a good six inches shorter than the young man but seemed to tower over him as she looked him up and down. Nodding once, she gestured to the table. "If you're hungry, I'm sure we can find something for you."

"More than soup?" The kid sounded hopeful.

"Whatever the doctor okays, I'll make it for you," Tansy offered. She leaned in and placed her hand on Jake's thigh, speaking quietly. "We'll all be busy today, but save me a spot on the loveseat by the fire tonight? I promise to be in a cuddling mood."

Christ. He needed to set up their next date, stat. Yet, everyone's attention right now was on the wedding happening in two days' time.

So he took what he could and whispered right back. "I'll put it at the top of my to-do list."

12

The hammer glanced off the finishing nail and smacked into Jake's thumb. He cursed enthusiastically, shaking his hand as he stomped away from the trim hanging at a slant off his bedroom closet.

That's what he got for not having his mind on the task.

It wasn't the fact that Aiden and Petra were right now somewhere off getting hitched on the sly that had his thoughts tumbling like straw in the wind.

Well, not totally that. Damn Melissa—

He hauled the letter out of his pocket again for the fiftieth time, wondering why he continued to torment himself.

Hey, you,

It's been a while, but I had this feeling we needed to touch base. I think this is your new hometown—hope it's everything you've ever dreamed of. You deserve to find a sweet place that appreciates you.

You've always been a small-town guy at heart. I know there were things that we didn't see eye to eye on, but I always loved how you wanted to be a part of something intimate and close-knit. Somewhere you could connect with your people. I admired that about you, even while I complained about it.

Stupid, right? That I could see what made you special, yet I didn't tell you often enough how wonderful it was.

Anyway, I'll be traveling later this year and would love to stop by, even if it's only for a coffee. Let me know what works for you.

Lots of love,
Melissa

Nope. Even after re-reading it this many times, it still made no sense. The entire letter read as if she'd done a complete mental rearrangement of their past. Not once during the bits of correspondence they'd exchanged over the past years had she ever asked to meet, and she'd certainly never tossed off the word love.

Enough was enough. If he was serious about committing to the thing between him and Tansy, then it was past time to properly shut some doors.

His thumb throbbing, Jake grabbed writing supplies and an envelope.

Small towns have a charm to them, I agree.

I gave it some thought. Meeting up isn't a good idea. You and I chose to go in different directions, and that's how it should stay.

I wish you well, but don't write to me anymore.

Jake

Short. Not sweet, but not mean. Before he could start second guessing himself, Jake sealed the envelope, addressed it, and deliberately left the return address blank.

Any future *General Delivery* mail could go straight into the garbage.

Speaking of garbage...

He rooted in the closet until he found the wad of previous mail from Melissa. It was time for a clean break, once and for all. Shoving the newest letter under the elastic, he turned toward the door and got a full body slam from Tansy.

"Finally. You ever answer your texts?" Tansy stole the bundle from his hand and threw it toward the bed. "Never mind. Hurry up, Petra and Aiden need help."

"What?" Jake raced for the door and his boots. "Accident?"

"No, don't panic. Sorry, I said that wrong. They're healthy and breathing, but there's a glitch with the wedding stuff, so Petra sent me an SOS. I need you there to—" She caught his shirtfront and pulled, hard, jerking him toward the door. "Dammit, screw the details. Let's *go*. I'll explain as we drive."

Steps outside the door, Jake stole her keys from her fingers, pointing at his truck. "You're in no state to drive, especially not in that death rattle of an SUV. Tell me where I'm going, then start explaining what the hell could turn a simple wedding into a call for help?"

"Rough Cut pub. Go to the back alley."

He waited until she'd put on her seatbelt to put the truck in Drive.

She waited until he'd pulled out on to the highway to start talking.

"We're slim on details, but for sentimental reasons, Petra asked the owner of Rough Cut if they could use the dance floor for their wedding. Ryan agreed since the place is closed today until six. My dad is the officiant, and they set up the camera and were ready to roll when some sort of security system went off that Ryan didn't warn them about. They're locked in, and they can't get a hold of him or his main staff and need me to help."

"You know how to turn off the pub's security system?" Which made zero sense until he remembered she used to live a few doors down above Buns and Roses.

"Sort of? Turn here."

Jake turned then pumped the brakes to stop on time. He twisted to face Tansy. "Why do you need me?"

She shoved her door open then offered a nervous smile as she slid her feet to the snowy ground. "Heavy lifting? Or I might need you as a character witness."

She was gone.

Jake cursed under his breath as he chased after her, clicking the doors locked behind him with the key fob as he rushed around the edge of the truck.

The way she stood blocking the door made it hard to see what she was doing. Tansy suddenly stepped to the right, twisted the door handle, then bumped toward the wall with her hip. She pulled, and the door swung outward, and suddenly the faint beat of music he'd heard swelled to near deafening levels.

In front of them was the long corridor that held the bathrooms and a storage room access. The space was filled with bright lights that flashed along the walls, glancing off Tansy as she sprinted ahead of him toward the main room.

"Wait," he shouted, not a jot hopeful she'd heard.

It was like being tossed inside an arcade game where he and Tansy were two of the characters racing for the prizes. Music blared, lights whirled. He swore glitter floated in the air.

Jake had been inside Rough Cut dozens of times, but that

final step onto the dance floor had never looked like this. His gaze whizzed from spot to spot, taking in what could be still-life tableaux in the seconds when blinding white spotlights paused for long enough to let his eyes focus.

To one side of the dance floor, a tripod lay tipped over on the floor.

A few feet from there, Tansy's dad, Malachi, sat in a chair. He had his eyes squeezed closed and his hands pressed over his ears. Petra stood next to him, her hands over his, as if trying to help dampen the sound.

The next flash revealed Aiden by the front door, banging on the hinges with his boot heel. Which struck Jake as equal parts useless and hysterically funny since—well, a boot as hammer was part of it, but also no matter how hard Aiden hit his target, Jake didn't hear a single thump.

The entire time an epic soundtrack blared in their ears. Like a science fiction movie gone wild, it had the epic booms of evil overlords mixed with the occasional *whizz-zip-boop* of a ride at the fair.

Chaos.

Tansy laid a hand on her father's shoulder. Malachi lifted his chin and met her gaze steadily for a two count before nodding.

Instantly, Tansy motioned Jake forward.

He joined her at the office door. "What are you doing?" he shouted.

"Getting to the security controls. Grab Aiden."

Jake shoved aside his curiosity and made tracks for his brother.

He avoided getting beamed by an upswing, grabbing Aiden's arm to twist him around. "Love what you've done with the wedding venue," he teased at the top of his lungs.

Aiden grinned. "I'm going to be too deaf to hear her say *I do*. Thanks for coming."

"No problem. Tansy said—" Jake glanced over to where Tansy knelt in front of the office door. She was eye level with the lock, hands twisting quickly. "Not really sure what's going on, but come on."

Standing behind Tansy, it was suddenly all too clear. She had lock-picking tools in her hands, fingers flexing rapidly as she adjusted them.

Shock struck hard enough to kick some of the other sensory overload to the side as Jake soaked in this new information.

He'd worked in law enforcement. He knew what the tools of the trade looked like, and seeing the criminal paraphernalia in her hands didn't make sense with everything he'd ever thought about her.

She'd said Aiden and Petra were locked in, but Tansy had opened the back door without much fuss. Even now, she raised a hand in victory, pushing the door forward and gesturing them into the room.

There wasn't time to do much more than gape as Petra pushed Malachi into the office and the five of them huddled together, the door mostly closed to block out some of the noise.

"I'll try to access the controls." Petra settled in the chair in front of the computer and booted it up. She typed rapidly, a disheartened snort escaping her a few seconds later. "This won't take long."

Tansy peered over her shoulder. "No password required?"

"Easy password," Petra returned, typing madly.

The hush of silence as the system clicked and the lights and music cut off was nearly as shocking as the painful volume that had assaulted them seconds before.

For another moment, everyone stood motionless.

Malachi shook his head as if clearing it of cobwebs. "Well,

that was quite the adventure. Thanks for coming to our rescue, ladies."

Petra swung her chair around. "You're welcome, but trust me, I will be giving Ryan a few pointed suggestions to increase his online security."

"I'm sure he'll be glad to take them," Aiden assured her as he ushered everyone back into the main dance floor.

Since he didn't quite know what to say, Jake held his tongue. He just watched Tansy without looking as if he was watching her.

Aiden and Petra picked up the camera, but Malachi went straight to his daughter and gave her a big hug.

Tansy buried her face in his chest as if soaking in comfort.

When he stepped back, Malachi gave Tansy another one of those inexplicable nods. "With great mischief comes great responsibility." Her father pressed a kiss to her forehead. "My cochlea thank you."

"No going deaf for you," Tansy agreed. "And I cannot believe how many ways you can mess up that movie quote."

"It's a talent," her father said before lowering his voice. "You *are* loved."

Tansy took a big breath then nodded rapidly. "I know, Papa."

Malachi turned his attention to Aiden and Petra. "Our unexpected chaos seems complete, so if you're ready to get married, we can go ahead."

Aiden took Petra's hand, and they both nodded.

It only took a moment to get everything into place. The camera was repositioned with Aiden and Petra spotlighted in the centre of the dance floor.

Jake untangled his brain long enough to ask, "You guys want us to head out?"

Aiden shook his head. "I know we planned the whole

family not being here thing, but I think you guys sticking around is right."

Which was how Jake and Tansy ended up tucked into the shadows at the side of the room as his brother and Petra exchanged vows.

Tansy stood ramrod straight beside him. For a minute Jake couldn't breathe until he realized she stood like that because *he* had his shoulders back, the tumbling thoughts in his brain making him every bit the unapproachable uptight jackass she probably thought he was.

He'd learned something new and unexpected about her today. She'd trusted him, and while he wasn't sure how the information fit into the Tansy he'd grown connected to, he still wanted to be there beside her.

He still wanted *her*.

As Malachi stepped into position between Petra and Aiden, Jake slid his arm around Tansy's back and tucked her to his side.

For a second she remained stiff, then she sighed and softened against him. She slid her arm under his jacket and rested her head against his chest until she was tucked into position, nice and close.

Malachi kept talking in the background, but Jake was more focused on his own revelation. It wasn't what he'd expected, but when had anything with Tansy been predictable? It was worthwhile taking the time to find out more.

He had High Water to thank for that, he supposed. A place for new starts and new ways of thinking, even for him.

THE WEDDING SHOULD HAVE TAKEN MUCH LONGER, but

maybe that was because Tansy was comparing it to all the church weddings she'd attended.

Or maybe it was wishful thinking on her part because the longer the wedding took, the longer she had before she had to explain to Jake what he had just witnessed.

But the vows were happening, short and sweet.

Petra lifted her chin. "The first time I saw you I knew I wanted you in my life. The second time reaffirmed that same thing. Attraction, yes, but the bigger tug I felt toward you was deep inside. That tug gets deeper every day, and I'm so excited to be able to spend the rest of our lives getting to know each other better."

Aiden grinned. He glanced at the camera for a moment then back at Petra. "You know why I wanted to get married here?"

Petra raised a brow. "Good acoustics?"

Malachi guffawed, instantly schooling his features. "Sorry."

Both Aiden and Petra snickered before Petra offered more seriously, "Good memories?"

"The best. Because the first time I saw you I knew I wanted you in my life."

A small laugh escaped Petra at the repetition of her words.

Aiden continued. "And the second time I saw you I was so damn glad to be back here in Heart Falls at a point in my life that it was time to settle down, because you are it for me. Always and forever."

Then they stood there grinning at each other.

Malachi started the formal part of pronouncing them husband and wife, but Tansy was more aware of Jake, who had rearranged them so that he was leaning on the wall and she was leaning against him, cradled in his arms. Surrounded by him, protected.

Jake pressed a kiss to the top of her head as Malachi made

the final proclamation. Tansy held back a cheer so it wouldn't end up on the audio.

As soon as the camera had been turned off, though, Jake let off a loud whoop of congratulations, hurrying Tansy forward so they could share hugs with Aiden and Petra.

Her father paused once again, his gaze lingering for a moment where Jake stood talking to his brother. "So."

Tansy pushed Malachi's arm gently. "Don't go getting your hopes up too soon. But yeah. I like him, Papa."

"You trust him," her father added. "That's a good thing, sweetie. But yes, I'll hold my horses until otherwise told."

Which was a load of nonsense. "You're already planning some event so you can invite him over and interrogate him on the sly, aren't you?"

Her father peeked at her over the top of his glasses. "Wherever do you think you learned your best tricks?"

The party headed back to High Water, Aiden and Petra taking the video camera with them.

"Tansy and I will be home shortly. There's something I need to pick up," Jake told them before taking Tansy's hand and guiding her toward the back door.

"We'll see you there," Aiden returned.

As Tansy and Jake stepped through the back door into the wintry temperatures, he glanced at the door briefly. "Will it lock itself again?" he asked.

No matter how hard she listened, she didn't hear any judgment in his tone. "Yeah. I didn't unlock it. Just did a temporary override."

"Good to know. Come on. You look as if you need a hot drink."

Curiously, he led her around the corner and straight into Buns and Roses. It was like walking into a hug—a safe place as sweet scents and warm air enveloped them in a welcoming embrace.

Marina waved from behind the counter. Tansy waved back as Jake led her to the prime seating spot in the corner in front of the fake fireplace.

"Hot chocolate or anything else?" he asked.

"A small latte and a chocolate chip cookie, please." If nothing else, the sugar rush should help her maybe find the words she needed to explain— To explain her life?

Oh boy, this was going to be fun. *Not.*

Yet when he got back with the treats, Jake didn't give her time to get any more nervous. He put the food down on the little table in front of them then slipped his fingers into hers and stared into the fire instead of meeting her gaze. "I've been having quite the conversation in my head for the last hour. Which is a good thing because it let me get out a whole bunch of the stupid questions that instantly popped to mind. Once I moved past those and started to get to some of the more complicated issues, I realized you may not have explained much before we got into that situation, but you did say one thing really clearly."

"Prepare to be deafened?" Tansy cursed herself for trying to avoid the serious moment with humor, but as a defense mechanism, it was instinctive.

He tipped his gaze to meet hers. "You wanted me with you. That says you trusted me with a secret part of your past. That's pretty humbling."

Tansy took a shaky breath. "So, you still like me?"

Jake outright laughed. "Trust me back. You can't shake me off by showing me a part of you that's always been there that I wasn't aware of yet."

She nodded, the motion jerking free unevenly. "I don't like to talk about my childhood. It's not even really about the things that I learned to do that aren't normal, like picking locks. It's about the emotions that go along with them. It hurts less to not look back."

He dipped his chin slowly. "I get that. You don't need to tell me the details, but I hope that you keep letting me know more about *you*. Sometimes those things from our past that are hard— Hell, forget *sometimes*. The things in our past that are hard are important parts of what makes us who we are."

He picked up her latte and put it in her hand.

Tansy took a small sip then leaned back, still curled within his protective circle. "You get gold stars today for handling spontaneity so well."

His blue eyes flashed with amusement. "Gold stars are nice, but I'd like kisses more."

Great idea. "I can manage that."

"Perfect. Also, can you handle a date on Saturday night?"

Interesting. Tansy let her gaze drift over his chest and shoulders. "Am I finally getting the prearranged date with all the trimmings?"

He leaned closer, expression intensely heated. "You're getting the prearranged date. You need to let me know if we're a go for *any* activity we want to enjoy."

Oh, hell yes.

She met his stare with what she hoped was full-on approval. "I would be delighted to be your date. For any and *all* activities that might entice us."

It was a little surreal to be sitting in Buns and Roses—a place where she had so much history—with a man who intrigued her to an incredible degree and was definitely part of the present she had never imagined.

Perhaps even part of her future.

Back at the ranch house, more congratulations were shared

with the newlyweds, but pretty much otherwise the day went on in the most ordinary of ways.

Jinx got home from school and promptly had to watch the video of the wedding. "Awww. You guys are so cute," she said when it was done. She wiggled to the front of the couch and twisted toward Logan, who sat in the easy chair beside her. "Wasn't that adorable?"

Logan shrugged. "Not much up on weddings, I guess."

Jinx rolled her eyes. "Well, I am. And that was perfection."

She exited the living room with a huff and a flounce in her step.

Tansy exchanged glances with Petra, amused as all get out. "It's okay, Logan. You barely know the players. You're not expected to be gaga over their wedding."

"I mean, you guys look happy," Logan offered to Petra cautiously. "That's a good thing."

"It's a very good thing," Petra agreed before bringing Logan a pot of potatoes. "You can sit there and peel these, please."

She rejoined Tansy at the counter.

Tansy stole another hug. "I agree with both sentiments. That was an adorable wedding, and you guys look happy together. Congratulations."

"Thanks." Petra examined her face. "I'm guessing here, but it looks as if Jake handled your participation well."

"Pretty much," Tansy agreed. "He doesn't know everything, but he said some really perfect things that make me want to keep moving forward."

Happiness somehow got brighter on Petra's face. "I'm glad."

"Me too," Tansy said honestly. She paused. "Good job with the hacking. What was the password, by the way?"

"His daughter's name and birthday." Petra sighed heavily. "Which everyone in Heart Falls knows is Christmas Day."

"Ouch. Yeah."

A not-so-fancy but still delicious wedding supper was followed smoothly by a couple of pretty normal days. Suddenly, it was Saturday, and before she knew it, Tansy was getting ready for her date.

She eyed herself in the mirror on the back of her bedroom door, twisting from side to side. "You don't think it's too much?" she asked Sydney, who had shown up to check on Logan and been conned into staying to spend the evening with Jinx and Petra watching some classic horror movie.

Sydney got to her feet and did a slow walk around.

Tansy wore leggings under a long-sleeved, body-hugging, thigh-high dress. Both the leggings and the dress were a deep azure blue that made Tansy feel as if she was a movie star headed onto the red carpet. She'd left her hair down, the blonde waves falling to mid-back.

Black leather boots with a modest heel finished the outfit, and the idea of Jake undressing her set all sorts of delightful shivers down her spine.

Sydney rummaged on the counter for a moment then passed Tansy a new lipstick. "That dress colour is dynamite on you, but you need one final thing. This will keep him staring at your mouth until he's going wild," she suggested.

"We pretty much already established that he and I are about to be a happening thing, at least in the sex department." Tansy grinned. "I don't know if there's anything clearer than a green light, but we've flashed it."

"No sharing flashing stories," Sydney warned. "Not my kink."

Putting on lipstick while snickering was disturbingly difficult. "Are you getting some of what *is* your kink these days?" Tansy asked. "If you need a confessional." Or advice on who to hit on since Sydney didn't seem to be involved with anyone on a regular basis.

"I'm doing what works for me, and I'm happy."

Huh. Not the answer Tansy expected.

Sydney raised a brow at Tansy's face. "Seriously? You thought I was staying at home every night studying medical texts?"

"To be honest, I thought maybe you were getting some during your out-of-town trips," Tansy shared, dropping to the mattress beside her friend. "You found someone who is nice to you, girlfriend?"

"Yes, Mom."

Tansy poked Sydney in the side. "Be serious. Petra and I care, even if you're a Sphinx at times, so you just have to put up with our loving nosiness. Are you really okay?"

"I'm very happy with my situation," Sydney offered slowly. "It works for me. Yes, I'm being careful. No, I'm not looking for more. I'll let you and Petra be the starry-eyed romantics of our happy trio."

The idea shook Tansy for a minute. "Petra is the romantic. I'm the pragmatic."

The burst of laughter from Sydney was instant and annoying. When she calmed down, she patted Tansy's shoulder comfortingly. "No, sweetie. You can tell yourself that all you want, but you definitely have romance in your core. I'd guess, if anything, you lean toward pragmatic romanticism."

"Big words for I'm nervous about tonight?" Tansy asked quietly, finally admitting the truth. "I really like him, Syd. Things have been going well between us but this is right about when something usually rises up and kicks me in the teeth."

While he'd been so sweet and not at all intrusive over watching her pick open a lock the other day, Jake had to still be wondering and worrying. It was in his nature.

Sydney squeezed her fingers. "No teeth kicking. You're surrounded by people who care about you. Your family, me and Petra. Jinx, and many others. And now Jake, plus the other X-chromosomes in the house."

"So no need to worry?"

Her friend smiled. "You already did the worrying. Now it's time to let that romantic heart of yours enjoy the night. Trust me, he won't mess this up."

Suspicion rose. Tansy examined Sydney closer. "What did you do?"

"Me?" Sydney pressed a hand to her chest in mock innocence. "Your girlfriends would *never* think of interfering in your love life."

Tansy smacked Sydney on the arm with her purse. "I hope the power goes out at the key moment of the movie and you never find out how it ends."

"What a beautifully evil curse, but totally useless. Horror movies—everyone dies. Rom-coms, they fall madly in love. It's fated and true." Sydney shrugged as she rose to her feet and guided Tansy to the door. "No use fighting it."

13

When he caught himself adjusting the utensils on the table for the twelfth time, Jake knew he needed to get his ass in gear.

It was a heady feeling, ignoring his instincts and following the advice of people he had come to trust. Jake took one final look around his small apartment, ninety-nine percent sure he'd remembered everything. He pulled the door closed behind him, then got his truck started so the interior would be toasty warm when he picked up his date.

The thirty-second drive from his apartment under the art studio over to the main house wasn't long enough for his nerves to drop out of overdrive.

He stopped on the front porch, hesitating before simply walking in like he usually would.

A mocking laugh escaped. He was literally living in the house. There was no reason why he needed to stop and knock.

Which meant he was chuckling softly as he swung the door open and got his first glimpse of Tansy.

He'd caught her in mid-motion, twisting away from the

kitchen where Petra and Sydney leaned against the kitchen counter. The brief glimpse of her friends was all that registered before the only image dazzling his gaze was Tansy. Her body enveloped in the softest-looking blue cloud, hair tousled around her shoulders, just waiting for him to run his fingers through it. Her eyes—

She lifted her chin slightly as if in a challenge, and mischief flashed. With something else. A softness, just the trace of an emotion that said what he needed to do right now was to be very clear about exactly how beautiful she was.

"*Christ.*"

Tansy's lips quirked upward.

Damn it to hell. That wasn't what he wanted to say, but he couldn't seem to find actual words and make them come out. All he could do was stare, mouth working up and down in his best fish imitation.

Thankfully, Tansy seemed more pleased than worried by his faulty communication skills.

"You have struck him speechless," Petra pointed out helpfully. "I knew Aiden would be pissed not to be here to see this."

"We can fix that," Sydney offered. She pulled out her phone and held it up as if she was about to take a video.

Jake thrust his hand toward them, his gaze still firmly fixed on Tansy. "Hello, beautiful."

A full smile bloomed on her face. "Hello, handsome. Are you ready to take me away from here before they start the next round of torment?"

Jake stepped forward and offered his arm. "I'd say something about rescuing the damsel in distress, but I think you're rescuing me just as much."

Tansy slid into position at his side, and they headed for the door at a quick pace. "Don't wait up for us," Tansy called over her shoulder as she nabbed a coat off the side hooks and all but dragged Jake out the door.

"Don't do anything I wouldn't do," Sydney called.

"That sentence is such a waste of air," Petra complained. "Some time you'll have to make an actual list of what you wouldn't do so we can explain this to you in detail."

Jake pulled the door closed on the friendly teasing and put his attention back on Tansy. "Now that we're alone, can we try that again? Hi, Tansy. You look beautiful."

"Thank you. I'm looking forward to spending the night with you." Tansy followed willingly as he guided her to the truck and popped her into the driver side door. She slid to the middle seat and stayed there.

Spending the night. Thank goodness and thank God. He didn't want to assume, but he really hoped that meant he got to wake up with her in his arms.

As usual, she waited until they were on the highway before starting the inquisition. "You didn't turn toward Heart Falls. I assume we're headed out to Diamond Valley?"

"Nope."

Tansy leaned to the side and peered into his face. "Curious. Well, since this is the master-planned date of excellent dates, I trust you. Although, I have to say Sydney spilled the beans that my friends might have tried to give you dating advice over the past couple of days."

Dangerously true. "It's a good thing I think they like me. I can't imagine what they would have suggested if they were trying to warn me off."

Tansy groaned. "Like what?"

"Sydney insisted you are secretly afraid of the dark. Under no circumstances should I ever let you be anywhere without the lights on as bright as possible."

"I don't mind doing things with the lights on. Sometimes," Tansy teased.

Anticipation just might kill him. Then again, Jake planned to enjoy every step of the night including these little moments of torment. "Petra gave good and bad advice. She had a whole collection of candles, and she wanted me to pick out one so I could offer it as a gift."

"I like candles," Tansy informed him. "Not as much as Petra, but I do like them."

"Nearly every candle she offered had some reference to dicks."

A snicker escaped her. "Of course, they did. I know she's got a candle from your brother that's labeled *Big Dick Energy*."

"And that's a thing I didn't need to know."

Tansy beamed at him. "What other bad advice did you get?

"Kelli told me to make sure that I dressed right. That you really appreciated a man who was comfortable in bold-coloured clothing."

She leaned away far enough to look him over. "I take it you decided that advice was for the birds. I mean, while you look very dapper in your black jeans and black and gray shirt, neither are very bright or bold."

"I just smiled and nodded when she gave me her whole line of suggestions. I think she needed something to entertain her."

"Yeah. She's due any day. How did she look?"

"If I say like a bubble about to pop, am I edging into too-rude-for-words territory?"

"As long as you say it to me and not her, you're okay," Tansy assured him. She twisted to peer out the window because he'd pulled to a stop at their destination. She glanced back, a frown creasing between her brows. "We're at the lookout for Heart Falls waterfall."

"Appetizers al la fresca," he informed her as he pulled her

out his side of the truck and reached into the truck bed for the picnic basket he'd prepared ahead of time. He tossed a blanket over his shoulder and took her hand and guided her along the trail toward the bench seat less than a five minute walk away.

He'd been out earlier in the day and cleared both the walking path and the bench seat, so all he had to do was throw the blanket on the seat as a cushion and guide Tansy onto it.

"Hold this for a sec." He passed her the basket and reached behind the bench for the folding table he'd stashed there.

Moments later he had the table in front of them arranged with a tablecloth, two small mugs, and a lit candle.

Tansy leaned forward then snickered appreciatively. "*Come On, Baby, Light My Fire.*"

"It truly was the least offensive of them," Jake told her earnestly.

"I like it." Tansy tucked herself under his arm and focused on the view before them.

The water pouring over the edge of the cliffs into the pool below was at less than fifty percent but still spectacular. Ice dams and icicles clung to the edges, and in the middle where the downpour hit the lake surface, a circle had formed in the ice.

"It's pretty here," he said quietly, not wanting to interrupt her thoughts.

"I love the view," Tansy agreed. She pointed, tracing her finger in the air. "The heart shape of the lake gives the falls and the town their name. Sasha's grandparents donated this section of land to the town a year before my family moved here. I've always loved coming here."

Jake curled his arm around her shoulders and considered all the directions he could take the conversation at that moment. Ask about her family moving to town, ask about the Stones, who were no longer in the picture.

Ask if she was ready to have the daylights kissed out of her?

But the advice he'd been given that truly made sense was to be himself and focus on them, here and now.

He squeezed her shoulders briefly then reached for the basket. "Ready to start our dining experience?"

"Absolutely. What culinary delight have you created for me?"

"You have to help cook this course," he warned.

She held off from rolling her eyes. Barely. "Imagine that."

"Only because this takes multiple hands. We're having s'mores." He pulled out marshmallows, chocolate, and cookies.

"For an appetizer?"

"I hear life is uncertain. Eat dessert first."

Sweet approval shone in her eyes. "My thoughts exactly. Are we roasting over the candle?"

He pulled out the mini torch he'd ordered and held it in the air. "Not that I don't like apple-cinnamon-scented wax, but this might make things go faster."

She pulled out a couple of marshmallows, broke off some chocolate, then stabbed the first marshmallow. She lifted the fork for him. "Ready. Light me up, baby."

He clicked the trigger, careful to aim it to the side.

Nothing happened.

He clicked again.

Tansy snickered.

"One comment from you about all talk and no fire—" he warned.

"What about all wood and no flame?"

The torch lit, flickered feebly, then went out with a *hissssss*.

Inside, amusement rose hard and fast. Jake tried to keep from laughing, but when he glanced at Tansy to find her staring into the distance, lips compressed tightly as if she were desperately trying to hold it together, he caved.

He threw back his head and laughed until the sound echoed off the hillside. Her bright happiness joined his, and suddenly she was in his lap, hugging him tight as she cupped his face and grinned down.

"We'll save the s'mores for later. I need to give you something else right now instead."

She leaned in and kissed him, and the not-so-perfect beginning to their date turned into an awesome beginning at lightning speed.

Jake wrapped his arms around her, sliding his hands under her coat. Stroking and smoothing his palms over the silky smooth fabric of her dress.

Sexy, warm woman nestled in his lap, her tongue teasing with his—it was amazing. Not perfect, but it was a fine first step on the way there.

NECKING on the bench overlooking Heart Falls was a slice of hometown heaven.

Of course, when Jake adjusted position and kicked over the table, followed by the picnic basket tipping over and spilling all its contents, Tansy stopped kissing and started snickering.

"Don't squirm any harder," he warned.

"The bench won't tip," she assured him.

Jake picked her up as he stood, guiding her feet to the ground carefully. "I'm more worried you might end up kneeing me somewhere that will stop the evening before it's begun."

The warning was enough to make her legs go limp, but not enough to stop the amusement.

She helped him pack, and they headed back to the truck. "I still enjoyed my appetizer course," she informed him.

"Me too." He stole another kiss as she crawled into the cab, and another before he started the engine. They got distracted for a while. He hadn't put the truck into Drive, and she was tempted to crawl over him right then and there.

Jake broke their embrace, pressing their foreheads together. "Not that I want to stop, but we need to."

"You have an agenda?" Tansy asked.

"I have a timer going off in fifteen minutes," he admitted.

"Planning sometimes sucks," she pointed out.

They pulled apart, then had to wipe down the inside of the windows to clear away the steam. She was still hooting with amusement when he pulled back on to the main highway.

When he took the turn that led them straight back into High Water lands, Tansy frowned. "You forget something?" she asked.

Jake parked in front of his private apartment, tossing a shy glance her way. "I cooked for you tonight."

It felt as if a finger traced up her spine. Not scary, but very, very intimate. "That sounds lovely. Let's go rescue your timer."

She'd been in Petra and Aiden's suite any number of times. Jake's was slightly smaller. One bedroom sat off an open kitchen slash living space, with a decent-sized bathroom to finish the apartment. The finishing touches were mostly complete, but Jake hadn't done much decorating yet.

But the scent as he guided her in the door offered the most home-like feeling ever.

"Meatloaf?" she wondered aloud.

Jake hurried to the stove and checked the timer. He turned off the heat before slowly twisting. The slightest flush coloured his face. "My mom's recipe."

Oh my. Tansy stilled.

The guys talked a lot about their stepdad, Jeff. He'd made a huge impression on them, and had been the motivation for starting High Water in the first place. Tansy had heard the phrase *pay it forward* so many times it had also become part of her mantra.

But their mom?

Tansy took off her boots and hung her coat then made her way to beside Jake. He pulled a head of lettuce out of the fridge and was working on a salad. "Can I help with anything?"

"I've got the meal under control." He tilted his head to the side. "If you want, you can open the wine. Or if you'd like something else to drink, check in the fridge. I put a few options in there so you could choose."

"Of course, you did," Tansy teased softly. "Wine is wonderful."

She went to work on the cork as he assembled the salad with far more skill than expected. Not that she'd thought he couldn't cook, but—

No, she really had thought that. Tansy left the bottle open to breathe and leaned a hip on the counter and watched him. "Tell me to take a hike if I'm being too nosy, but I'm surprised to see how competent you are."

A low chuckle escaped him. "You are hell on a man's ego."

"Sorry. I meant right now, in the kitchen, considering how often you used to ask me to cook for you. Not because I don't think you're capable, but past history says something different than what the amazing scent in this room says."

He finished tossing the salad and put the bowl on the already set two-man table strategically placed to separate the kitchen from the living room. He didn't answer as he pulled the meatloaf out and placed it on a hot pad to rest for a few minutes.

Tansy approved, of course.

A moment later, Jake pulled out a chair for her. She sat, breathing deeply as he stroked his hands over her shoulders in a gentle caress.

By the time he sat in the chair kitty-corner to her, she had a plate full of food and a glass of red wine in front of her. "It looks delicious."

It truly did. The salad had all sorts of extra vegetables including crisp red peppers and the teeniest perfect curls of carrot. The meatloaf had crumbling caramelized corners and a savory juice pooling next to a mound of whipped potatoes.

Jake lifted his glass. "To women who know how to cook."

Tansy clinked her glass with his. "You're sweet."

They both dug in. Tansy nearly moaned as the meatloaf hit her tongue. The buttery richness of the mashed potatoes mixed perfectly with it, and she shook her head as she stared over at Jake. "I need your recipe."

He raised a brow. "A high compliment indeed."

"The highest." Tansy hesitated then decided to hell with it. She wanted to know more. She wanted more of this sensation of finding out exactly what it was that made Jake tick. "You said it's your mom's?"

Jake laid his fork on the table and leaned back slightly, wine glass in hand. He stared into the deep burgundy depths and answered slowly. "My mom was a great cook. Simple stuff, usually, because that's what we could afford. And that's what she had time for, especially after our dad was no longer in the picture. Single moms don't do a lot of fancy cooking."

"I imagine they don't. Not moms with three boys who could demolish everything she put in front of them and then some."

Jake laughed, placing his glass on the table. "There was always bread and butter to help fill us up, but Mom liked making different things for us to try. Even if it was just a new type of salsa to go on top of whatever meat we had that day. Declan didn't care what he ate as long as it was enough until the next meal. Aidan happily shoveled anything down, but cooking was something I did with my mom."

Tansy laid her hand on his thigh. "That must have made it even harder when you lost her."

He nodded. He hesitated for a moment then swallowed hard, speaking slowly as if making a confession. "When she died, I went on a hunger strike for a while. Not because I was protesting anything, but because everything they put in front of me reminded me of her. I just couldn't swallow."

God. Tansy squeezed lightly. "That makes total sense."

Jake met her gaze, linking their fingers. "I hated cooking after that. Would do just about anything I could to avoid it."

"Including hiring me when it was your turn to feed the family?"

"That was part of the reason," he admitted. He lifted his free hand and brushed his knuckles over her cheek. "The other reason was because there's something about you I just couldn't seem to stay away from."

Bubbles in her belly, lightning in her blood. The food still smelled wonderful but there was something that Tansy craved more. "Can we dance? If I'm not interrupting your perfect plans too much."

Jake rose to his feet, bringing her with him. "I'm working on my spontaneity, remember?"

He got music started, and as a slow ballad crooned in the background, he pulled her into his arms, dancing in the three by three space between his dining room table in the back of the couch. A slow rocking dance with them pressed tight to each other.

Tansy rested her cheek on his shoulder and savoured the closeness.

"There's a moment when life changes," she said. Screwing up her courage, willing herself to let him see a bit more of her truth as well. "Sometimes it's from the good to the bad, like losing your mom. Sometimes it's from the bad to the good. It's as if you can remember every single detail of that one moment in time, like a snapshot that's completely three dimensional. That's what it felt like when I met the Fields family. When Mom and Dad picked me up and brought me home and there was Rose, and Ivy, and Fern. Suddenly it didn't matter how bad my world had been before, this was everything good. I had a hard time believing it was real."

Jake brushed his hand up and down the middle of her back, dancing her slowly as the music pulsed in the background. "You've said before that they're pretty perfect as a family."

"They were a miracle. Still are," Tansy admitted. "Sometimes I can't believe that I'm worthy of being loved as much as I am."

They danced in silence for a minute, Jake's strong arms around her, his fingers tight with hers. Then he eased back and lifted her chin toward him. "Your dad called and asked me over. After the wedding."

Tansy didn't resist rolling her eyes, not even for a second. "Of course, he did."

"You're not mad?"

"Pretty perfect family, remember?" She met his eyes. "Except for the invasive as hell and being butt-inskies part."

"He said he needed help fixing the porch swing." Jake snorted. "I think he undid a single loop of chain. We sure fixed it easily."

Tansy linked her fingers behind Jake's neck. "So? What did my papa really want?"

"Not to share your secrets, but to give some fatherly advice." Jake took a deep breath. "I told you that day that I didn't need to know your past, and I meant it, but I think part of me still expected that I'd eventually find out. So, here's your dad, and out of the blue he's telling me this story about a wild night in college where he ended up knee deep in a mud bog. After we got done laughing, he said no matter how embarrassing, sharing a tale like that makes him remember how grateful he is for friends who haul him out of trouble, and how after, he was determined to be smarter."

Too funny. "I'll have you know that tales of the Wild Mud Bog Night has never been shared with me, so I will be poking him."

"It was classic," Jake agreed. "But also a great example of his final point. Memories that make a person smaller or less instead of empowered, those are not worth sharing."

Her father and her family knew her to the core because it was true. The past caused her nightmares. She worked to this day to believe she was worth being loved.

"Simply put, some stories help us move forward, but others drag us back." Jake shook his head. "I would never want you to share anything that makes you smaller or hurts you. Your past is done. It might have influenced who you are today, but you're the one who bravely stepped into the future. You made changes and made a life. *This* life."

Her throat had gone tight. "I promise I'm not breaking into buildings all over Heart Falls."

"I know that. Neither am I—" She startled for a moment, and he winked. "I got trained with lockpicks in my work as well. Having the skills isn't what gives us our job description."

"I never saw that one coming," Tansy admitted with amusement,

He stared at her mouth. "I like who you are, Tansy Fields. I like all sorts of things about you."

They'd stop moving. She had no idea what song was playing in the background because all she could focus on was his mouth. "This would be a good moment for you to kiss me. Plus whatever else you have on your perfect date agenda."

His lips quirked up at the corners. "No checklists, remember?"

But he did kiss her. Lips pressed to hers, a gentle pressure that built rapidly as he curled his arms around her and squeezed their bodies closer. When he nipped at her lower lip, Tansy gasped. He took advantage, sweeping his tongue in and teasing until they were both gasping for air.

Tansy slipped her fingers between them, working on the buttons of his shirt. Jake bunched up the fabric of her dress, bringing it higher until he could slide a hand under the fabric and skim upward to meet the bare skin of her back.

Hands roaming, mouths lingering. A slow steady seduction where Tansy definitely did not know what would happen next. He kissed along her jawline, lingering in the spot under her ear that made goosebumps rise.

He caught her fingers to his lips, nipping at the tips before sucking one into his mouth briefly.

Tansy moaned, and suddenly her dress was being lifted over her head. He licked the line along the edge of her bra, darting to the side and biting her nipple through the sheer fabric.

Then his fingers were in the waistband of her leggings, and moments later, Tansy stood in nothing but her bra and panties in the middle of their impromptu dance floor.

She approved, but there was one small problem. She caught his hands before he could remove anymore of her clothes. "Your turn."

She would have made it a slow, teasing event. Undoing one button at a time, pushing off his shirt and letting her mouth wander over all the naked skin she revealed.

Instead, Jake pulled his shirt up and over his head, flinging it to the side before undoing his jeans and dropping them on the spot. The hard length of his erection pressed the front of his boxer briefs.

Neon red boxer briefs.

A snort escaped. "Those are…"

"You like them?" Amusement tinged his words. "In case Kelli was right and you're gaga over bright colours."

"Very sexy." Tansy drew a slow line down his shaft with her finger, .

His entire body shook with the shiver that rolled over him. "You're fucking killing me," he groaned.

Anticipation was a wonderful thing, but they'd already had weeks of it. Tansy caught Jake by the hand and stormed toward the bedroom.

14

"Condom?"

"Side table." He picked her up and twirled, landing her on the mattress beside him. "In a hurry, sweetheart?"

She slapped her hand on his shoulder and pushed him back. A second later she straddled his thighs, trapping him in place—*ha*—leering down at him and enjoying every second of this wild, delightful dance. "You have no idea."

He reached down and fisted his cock, jerking it through the fabric of his briefs. "Trust me. I have some fucking idea."

Which meant they were both laughing when she grabbed the edge of his briefs and stripped them off him. He stopped laughing when she dropped and covered him with her mouth. She barely got in one delicious suck before he tumbled her off, peeled away her underwear and panties and slid between her thighs. Pinning her in place, his weight over her was heavy and perfect.

He stared into her eyes, gaze intent. "Some things we don't rush."

He rocked back, caught her legs, and lifted them skyward. A second later his mouth was over her sex as he licked every hot spot she had with incredible accuracy. As if he'd found the primer on *How To Make Tansy Into A Quivering Bowl Of Jelly In Thirty Seconds Or Less*.

Tansy closed her eyes and thrilled in the sensation of being wanted so desperately. Of being given to so freely. But as pleasure rose and the edge of the precipice neared, she used the fingers tangled in his hair to jerk him off her sex far enough to reconnect their eyes. "Put on the condom."

He grinned. "Yes ma'am."

She wanted to help. She wanted to do the next thing.

Somehow with the two of them laughing at their fumbling fingers, the condom was on and he was back between her legs. Lining up and sliding inside so slowly. So perfectly.

"Oh God. That's good," Tansy breathed.

Joined. Connected. Jake leaned on one elbow and brought his free hand to cup the side of her face. Rocking his hips slowly, keeping the pulse of pleasure inside her core hovering at an *about to explode* point. But his eyes—intense, hot. He examined her for another moment then leaned in and kissed her, tongues tangling as he picked up the pace and drove harder. Deeper.

Tansy lifted her legs and wrapped them around him, digging her heels into his butt and offering as good as he gave. Slamming together with what should have been too much pressure but again—perfection.

"Fuck." Jakes face screwed up, his rhythm faltering.

Tansy slid a hand between them to slick her fingers over her clit for the final touched she needed. His hand joined her a second later, harder and more direct as he took over and demanded her body's response.

A noise between a moan and a groan escaped her that was one hundred percent *hell yes*.

Pleasure exploded then fell around her like sexy confetti. Jake thrust in one last time and stilled, the groan from his lips the perfect musical accompaniment to her noisy climax.

They lay there, tangled together and panting into each other's faces until Jake chuckled. He pulled back far enough to kiss her gently before running his fingers over her cheek and jaw. "You know how to cook in the bedroom as well."

"When you've got a gift," Tansy teased.

She kept her hands around his face so she could pull him down for another long, slow, intimate kiss.

When he finally pulled away, there was amusement written all over him. "I need to deal with the condom. Then I really should feed you."

"You really should," Tansy agreed. "I hear that's what happens on well-organized dates."

His eyes sparkled. "We'll have to call this date the perfect blend of planning and spontaneity."

Tansy pretended to consider. "Maybe we should decide that in the morning over breakfast."

Jake grinned.

IT WASN'T AS if sex changed everything, Tansy thought. Yet somehow, it totally did.

From the minute they crawled out of bed the next morning and headed into their day, an additional thread of connection wove between them.

It wasn't only the smirk that Jake wore. Okay, she saw the same expression on her own face every time she looked in the mirror.

It was *more*.

Five days after the perfect date, Tansy packed a bag full of goodies and joined Rose and Fern as they headed to the hospital for a visit.

Stepping into the scent of antiseptic, with nondescript, white-walled corridors around them, Tansy slowed. This was not where she wished they'd be doing this.

Fern slipped her arm around Tansy and guided her forward, tipping her head into Tansy's shoulder briefly. "It's okay. Kelli's fine, and the baby's fine. They're just being cautious."

"I know that," Tansy said. "But of all the people to have complications during labour and delivery, I never expected it would be Kelli. She's bombproof."

On her other side, Rose took the goodie bag from Tansy then linked their fingers together. "We all know that's not true. There's no telling what might happen, especially when it comes to giving birth. But Fern is right. Focus on the good stuff. Everyone is doing great, and we're about to get to snuggle a brand-new baby."

Kelli wasn't alone in the room. Luke sat in the recliner beside the bed. His shirt was open, and he had a tiny bundle wrapped in a blue blanket against his bare chest. His big hand held the baby locked in place, but his eyes were closed and his breath flowed in a smooth rhythm that said he was sound asleep.

Tansy and her sisters slipped into the room quietly, pausing until Kelli motioned them forward.

"It's okay if you wake Luke. He's been out for a while, and if he stays in that position for much longer he's going to walk like a troll." Kelli reached a grabby hand toward Tansy's bag. "Tell me you brought cookies."

"Cookies, cupcakes, and apple turnovers," Tansy assured her. "How are you doing?"

Kelli patted the side of the bed for Tansy to join her then offered a smile to both Fern and Rose. "I have stitches in places where no woman ever wants stitches, but I have a healthy baby, and the doctor assures me everything is still intact. I will be out riding...*horses*...again, eventually."

Rose slipped in to give Kelli a hug. "That's good to know, but first you concentrate on healing."

"I will. Why don't you steal Kyle from Luke?"

Rose and Fern eased away, congratulating the groggy Luke as he woke and somewhat unwillingly passed over his son.

Tansy caught Kelli's fingers in hers, speaking quietly with her friend. "You with an emergency C-section was not the news I was looking forward to."

"Me, neither." Kelli made a face. "I love the fact that we made a baby. I am not enamored of the whole birth experience."

"I don't blame you," Tansy agreed.

Kelli leaned in so her words stayed private. "I know you're here to love on my son, but first, I never got apprised about the date. Tell me."

Warmth built in Tansy's chest. "It went so well. Yes, the sex didn't suck, but it was definitely about more than just sex. Jake's pretty amazing."

Her friend smiled. "I could have told you that from the expression on your face. But you take care of you, yes? You're worth it, girlfriend. Remember that."

"I'm working on it," Tansy promised.

The really fun thing was, as the days continued and she slipped into the busy routine of cooking and prepping for events in the art studio, Tansy found it easier to believe.

But the part that didn't change was they still had everything else to deal with. Jake still slept in his room across the hall from her. They had plenty of things to occupy their time without each other, between the cooking Tansy had to do for High Water, plus a slew of events in the art studio over the next couple of weeks.

Jake was kept busy making sure Logan got on his feet. The kid—and he really was still a kid, barely turned twenty—hadn't shared anything more about his past but had slowly accepted that he was welcome on the ranch.

March passed, part of April. The original hands moved on. While there was no reason for Jake to stay in the house anymore, he kept sleeping there, and no one said a word.

Being an established couple, accepted by her friends and his brothers—it felt right. Felt real.

It was such an odd sensation not to have her past hanging over them.

Jake kept being patience personified, and with every day that passed, she got that much closer to believing that this was really happening. That she didn't have to lay herself bare and yet he'd still care about her.

Maybe even love her...

A kazoo blasted in her ear and brought her back to the here and now. Tansy blinked then smiled at her nephew. "Hey, Carter."

"Happy birthday, Auntie Tansy. You're supposed to come and cut the cake with Auntie Rose."

"Perfect. You're my escort, then? Give me your arm."

Ten-year-old Carter made a face. "Okay, but you're too tall for me."

"It's good practice for when you get bigger and end up taller than all the girls in your life. You'll have some perspective." Tansy slipped her fingers over his elbow, adjusted them slightly, then nodded her approval. "Lead on."

The kid was a gem. He lifted his chin and got into it, back poker straight as if he were a gentleman. They slow marched all the way through the house from where she'd been daydreaming quietly on the front porch swing to the back garden where the rest of the family was gathered.

Jake glanced over from where he stood with Walker and Chance, his grin widening as he spotted her. Jake pivoted on a heel and made an interception course.

"May I take over?" Jake asked Carter politely.

"Nope."

Tansy bit her lips to keep from snickering as her nephew laid a possessive hand over her fingers and locked her in place. Carter lifted his chin, stubbornness written on every inch of him.

Jake straightened. "No?"

Carter shook his head. "Mom said if I found Auntie Tansy, I got an extra piece of cake. I'm not messing with that. I'm delivering her."

Amusement shot sky high. It was a great reason to be fought over. "In that case, I agree. No changing of the guard at this point." Tansy winked at Jake. "There is cake on the line."

Jake raised his hands in the air in surrender, smiling as he backed away.

In a tradition they'd started years ago when Tansy had first joined the family, she and Rose linked hands and cut into the simple pan cake for their shared thirty-third birthday celebration.

Everyone sang the birthday song, then Walker played his guitar and sang a few more of their favourites. Rose ignored her fiancée and tugged Tansy with her to the tire swing, curling up together as if they were once again thirteen years old.

Rose's eyes shone as she took in the gathered family,

lingering on Chance before moving over Jake. "He fits in pretty damn good," she offered.

Tansy leaned into Rose's side, left arm curled around her sister's waist. "He's a good man, Rose. I'm really enjoying having a steady boyfriend for the first time ever."

"That's good. But don't be afraid to take the next step when it's time," Rose said softly.

"Does this mean you'll take your own advice and pick a date for your wedding?" Tansy teased.

Rose's expression went thoughtful. "Yup."

Well damn. "Really?" Tansy demanded.

Her sister grinned back. "Midsummer. See how easy that was?"

Easy, huh? Tansy stared across the garden at Jake, coming to the conclusion that as much as she wanted more, it was too soon, all things considered.

For now, she'd just keep enjoying their here and now. Keep practicing looking into the future and not at the past.

JAKE STRODE through the living room toward the front door when he realized for once no one else was around in the High Water ranch house. Just him and Tansy, who was busily cooking, with pots on the stove and ingredients all over the counter.

It was too good an opportunity to miss.

He pivoted on the spot, stopping directly behind her, hands on the counter on either side of her hips. He pressed against her back and nuzzled his lips to her neck. "Hello, beautiful. What're you up to?"

"Making enchiladas. I thought you were out with the hands all day dealing with the arrival of the new flock?"

"Headed there soon enough," he said nipping at her earlobe. "Only, I'm hungry."

"There are leftovers in the— *Oh my God*, Jake." Tansy's head fell back on his shoulder because he'd slid his hands under her shirt and upward until he cupped her breasts. Working her nipples through the soft fabric of her sports bra, he kept up the assault on the sweet spot on her neck he knew drove her crazy.

Two and a half months. That's how long they'd officially been doing this, and Jake couldn't imagine it getting any better.

Well, except one thing at the immediate moment. He undid her button and zipper, jerked her pants down far enough he could slide his fingers between her folds, and went to work on her clit.

"Damn it, Jake. Anyone could walk in." A protest, except she wasn't moving away from him, she was rocking her hips in double time, twisting her head as if asking for his mouth to get back to where she loved it most.

"The way I'm standing, all they'll see is me kissing you." He put a foot between her feet and forced them farther apart so he could slide his fingers into her wet heat and work his thumb over her clit.

"You're far more of a brat now these days than before," she said between gasps. "Spontaneity looks good on you. Oh yes, that. *That.*"

"I had a good teacher." He took her lips, kissing her deeply until it was time to swallow the gasp of her orgasm. Her sex convulsed around his fingers and he slowed, bringing her down as gently as he could until suddenly the fire alarm went off and they finally clued in that smoke was billowing from the pan on the stove.

Jake scrambled for the pan as Tansy dealt with her pants.

By the time supper rolled around and they were gathered at the table, the scent of smoke was mostly gone.

"If anyone says anything, I'm throwing you under the bus," Tansy informed him on the sly as he helped carry plates of Mexican rice, the second batch of enchiladas, and the rest of the meal.

"Worth it."

The only one who seemed to suspect was Aiden. His brother eyed his dinner plate, glanced at Tansy, grinned at Jake, then wisely held his tongue.

The table was nearly full to capacity. Him and his brothers, plus Petra, Tansy, Jinx, and Kevin made seven. The current round of ranch hands, which included their first women guests, May and Helen, added six more.

The delicately featured blonde May sported a black eye, courtesy of her soon-to-be ex-husband, but she'd held her head high and said she needed a spot to breathe for a few days before heading back to deal with the rest of the divorce. Helen was an older woman in her early sixties who hadn't said much, but quietly stepped forward to help every chance she got. The two of them shared the final room in the house.

Three other men had arrived the previous week—Scott, Jon and Erik. Logan had moved into the men's quarters, and with Kevin in the fifth room, High Water was full inside and out.

Scott planned to leave in a couple days, Jon the week after, so the ebb and flow of the ranch had begun to fall into place.

Halfway through the meal the conversation turned to plans for the next day.

"We're all invited to Red Boot ranch tomorrow," Petra announced. She made it an open-ended offer. "It's Tansy's day off from cooking, so if you want to stay home, you'll have to fend for yourself. But if you feel comfortable joining us, it's a safe spot. My sister-in-law's baby is due this week, but the doctor has informed her that she'll definitely go late. She wants distracting, so my brother Zach has invited us all out for the afternoon and a barbeque. It's a quiet place with even better views than we have. Their foreman, Cody, says you're all welcome to try your hand at roping or to take a trail ride."

Jinx turned to May. "Red Boot is great. They have more horses than we do and a couple of really pretty colts that were born right after Christmas."

The young woman nodded slowly. "I'd like to go for a trail ride if someone comes with me."

"Aiden and I will go," Petra offered. "Jinx?"

"Sure. Can Dixie come?" Jinx's shadow sat at her feet as usual.

Declan snorted. "I don't think we could pry her off you with a crowbar. She's a well-trained animal. Zach won't mind."

Which meant after lunch the next day the entire bunch ended up at Red Boot ranch. Cody took one look at the ranch hands and immediately set up a barrel racing course. Most of the group went to the barns, but Tansy headed straight to Julia's side.

Jake walked slower, keeping pace with Logan. The kid refused to use a cane, but he was strong enough again to make the long trip from the parking lot to where Julia and Zach had a comfortable seating area around a firepit.

"You don't have to wait for me," Logan grumbled.

Jake lifted his face to the sun and continued at his slow but steady rate. "It's my afternoon off, kid. Stop trying to make me work harder than I have to."

A snicker of amusement rose quietly from his side. "You've got some good friends," Logan offered.

"Some of the best. I never expected it, but I really hoped for it." Jake waved a greeting at Zach, who had just put a glass of water beside his very pregnant wife. "You want to relax for a while?"

Logan pointed to the chairs ahead of them and nodded.

"Someday I'll get back up on a horse, but for now, my bones still ache."

It was a small group around the fire pit. Tansy pulled out a deck of cards and started playing crib with Julia. Logan put his feet up and closed his eyes, face upward as he soaked in the sunshine. Helen pulled out a sketchbook and began to draw.

At the railing, Zach was watching the crowd of men gathered in the arena. A smaller group were already on horseback, Dixie dancing at their heels as they headed out for their trail ride.

"We need days like this," Jake offered as he stopped beside Zach.

"Definitely. Although I would enjoy it better if my wife wasn't a million years pregnant."

Which is when Jake noticed Zach had strategically placed himself so he could see the arena and keep an eye on Julia. "Any reason to worry?"

Zach made a face. "Doctor says no, but I keep thinking back to Kelli, who ended up with an emergency C-section. I hate not knowing when and what's about to happen."

"I hear you." Although Jake had to admit he'd never had this situation to worry about.

Plus, he had gotten a little bit better at not freaking out over changed plans. It seemed his goal of learning to be more spontaneous was being beaten into him one day at a time, with Tansy's willing encouragement.

"Screw it. I can't even pretend I'm not hovering." Zach strode back to the chair at Julia's side. He dropped beside her so he could rub her back gently.

His friend occupied, Jake settled in the chair on the other side of Logan. He closed his eyes to soak in the sun, and shockingly, must have fallen asleep, because the next thing he knew he was waking to the sound of a low conversation to his left.

"You are getting stronger," Tansy said.

"I guess," Logan muttered. "Physically, maybe. It's not enough."

Jake stayed motionless, debating if he should move to show he was listening. But before he could decide, Tansy responded. "What do you mean?"

Logan sighed heavily. "I've had a lot of bad luck. One thing after another, it feels like. I've pretty much been on my own forever. I don't think my life's worth much."

The words hit like a punch to the gut. That was it. Jake slid his eyes open, and rolled, finding a seat.

Logan glanced at him but turned back to Tansy, who was nodding slowly. Julia and Zach were far enough away that it was just the three of them in this small quiet space, and Jake vowed to keep his mouth shut.

Because while he'd had moments like that—feeling as if the world had given him nothing but hardships—he'd always had his brothers. He'd had Jeff.

"I used to feel that way," Tansy admitted, her voice quieter now. She met Jake's eyes straight on, paused as if considering. She lifted her chin and focused back on Logan. "Before I was adopted, I didn't think I was worth much either."

Interest caught, Logan sat up a little straighter even as Jake wrapped his brain around the clear message Tansy had sent.

She wanted him to hear this. Wanted him near.

"I was adopted when I was twelve," Tansy continued. "The earliest memory I have as a child is being in a bad situation with people who should have cared for me but didn't. Even when I got pulled out of that trouble at age nine, I ended up shuffled from foster home to foster home. I never stayed anywhere long enough to feel as if I belonged. By the time I came to Heart

Falls, I wasn't sure I could trust anyone. I didn't think I'd ever find a real family."

Something like hope flared in Logan's eyes as he listened. "But you did?"

Tansy nodded. "The Fields took me in, and suddenly I had not only a home, but people who stubbornly loved me until I believed it was real. That changed everything."

She paused, and Jake wanted to wrap his arms around her and hug her tight. Brave, giving woman. Sharing bits about her past to help Logan—it meant something powerful.

"Point is," she continued, focusing back on Logan, "You might have had a ton of bad luck, but you've got a chance to start over here, with us. You have a home now for as long as you need it. It'll take time, but things can get better. You need to decide if you're willing to do the work."

Logan considered her words, his expression guarded but a little softer. "Yeah." He levered himself to vertical. "I'm gonna walk a little. Thanks for telling me your stuff."

As Logan headed to the railing, Jake felt Tansy's eyes on him. He slid onto the chair next to her, catching her hand in his.

"You were brave," he said softly.

Tansy shrugged, trying to play it off. "He needed to hear it."

"I needed to hear it." Jake rubbed his thumb gently over her knuckles. "We're all looking forward, though, right?"

"Working on it. Sometimes it feels as if I'm not fast enough, and I'm sorry," she said with quiet regret.

"Don't be. I think you're incredible. And sexy," he tossed out, just to lighten the moment. "Like *make me want to ravish you against the barn* sexy."

With a laugh, she climbed into his lap and kissed him

senseless. Things might have gotten out of control if not for the pillow that whacked into his head a few moments later.

"No sexy tomfoolery from you two," Julia growled. "I don't need to see it."

Tansy twisted in Jake's lap, holding tightly to his shoulders as she made a face at her friend. "You said you wanted to be distracted."

A second pillow followed the first. "Playing cards, you heathen."

"Fine. I'll save it for later." Tansy waggled her brows at him. "If that's okay with you.

"Excellent by me," Jake assured her.

The next hours were filled with good company and great food. The only one who seemed even the slightest bit put out was Zach. When Jake poked him about it, the other man sighed. "I was hoping the excitement of the day would send her into labour," he admitted.

After a wonderful evening, they headed home. Only a few lights shone in the windows, glowing warm yellow in the darkness.

The ranch hands and Logan waved goodnight, heading to their dorms. The ladies slipped from Aiden and Petra's truck, Declan bringing up the rear with Jinx and Dixie.

Jake shared Zach's tidbit with Tansy as they left his truck and walked slowly toward the High Water ranch house.

"Julia would have loved to go into labour. She's worried she'll have the only forty-five week pregnancy on record."

"Zach does like setting records."

Her laughter echoing in his ears, Jake swooped Tansy into his arms. He stopped in place and leaned down to kiss her. A hit of the heat that constantly flared between them struck, but mostly this time it was about what they'd just shared with family and friends. The new closeness that kept building.

A moment later, she hummed happily. "Nice homecoming."

He caught her fingers in his and strolled them toward the door. "It was a good day. Ready for a good night?"

"Always." She raised a brow. "Full week ahead, though, so I can't stay out all night."

"Too bad. I'll have to make sure I work a little faster—"

"Jake? Is that you?"

He jerked to a stop, hauling Tansy with him.

It couldn't be.

Yet five feet ahead of them, rising from the bench to stand in the porch light, was Melissa. She waved, the dark bags under her eyes completely out of place from the beautifully manicured face she usually presented to the world.

He was ready to demand what the hell she thought she was doing showing up uninvited when a little boy stepped out from behind her. More than a toddler, but not old enough to be *his* kid. A sad little white face with eyes full of fear.

A quiver in her voice, Melissa rested a hand on top of the kid's head as he stood beside her. "I need your help, Jake. I don't know where else to go."

15

———

May and Helen had eyes full of questions, but their mouths stayed firmly shut. Considering they'd recently arrived, they knew the rule was to keep their noses out of others' business unless invited, and they vanished back to their room after quiet *good nights*.

Jinx stared at the little boy for the longest time before giving Petra and Tansy hugs. "Do I need to give up my room?" she asked quietly.

"No," Petra assured her. "That's *your* room, and Dixie's. Lock your door, and let us figure it out, okay?"

Jinx nodded then snapped her fingers. Dixie came alert, gliding silently at her heels as the teen slipped away.

Before Jake could demand what was going on, Tansy spoke. "Are you hungry? When did you two last eat?"

Melissa considered, but it was the little guy's expression that clearly answered the question. Jake gestured to the main table. "Sit. Food first, then you can explain."

Tansy bustled off to make up two plates. Declan, Aiden,

and Petra settled in the living room, alert and wary as if ready to be Jake's backup.

He really didn't know which direction to turn. Just kept looking at the kid at the table and hoping something would eventually make sense.

"His name is Jeffrey," Melissa offered quietly.

God. Jake's throat tightened. "Hey, kiddo. We'll get you something to eat right away."

He turned to grab a glass of milk because that was safer than trying to speak. Of course, she'd named her boy Jeffrey. The name *he'd* talked about wanting to use to honour his stepdad.

If Tansy hadn't bumped into his side, he might have stood staring into the fridge for long enough for someone else to notice. "Deep breath. You got this," Tansy whispered. "I take it you know this woman?"

Dear God. She didn't know.

He poured the milk with shaky hands into the glass on the counter before putting the jug down and meeting Tansy's gaze. "That's my ex-wife, Melissa."

Tansy's eyes widened briefly, but other than that fleeting tell, her expression didn't budge. "Okay."

No. Nothing about this was remotely okay.

The entire house felt still and silent, even as full as it was. Tansy slid food in front of Melissa and her son, putting the plates down without a word before returning to the kitchen and keeping herself busy.

Thank goodness part of his brain was still working, because he registered Tansy keeping ample distance between the two of them. Which was a hell no in his books. He might not know what was going on with Melissa, but he absolutely knew hiding the relationship between himself and Tansy would do more to upset than help with any awkward situation.

He'd gouge out his own eyeballs before he deliberately hurt Tansy.

He slipped to the kitchen counter, standing close enough their bodies touched. "I didn't know she was coming."

"I figured." She stopped her busy work in the sink and met his gaze, forcing a smile to her lips. "Don't worry about me. You do what you need to do."

Which was enough of a go-ahead to slip his knuckles under her chin and lift her face far enough to press a sweet kiss to her lips. It was miles away from the heat they'd shared outside but exactly what was needed. Then he pressed their foreheads together. "I might need Declan to call the shots on this one."

"He's got your back," Tansy agreed. She slid her hands around his waist, a deliberate connection and comfort all in one. "We all do, Jake. With every bit of us."

Which made it easier to turn back to the table. Melissa's gaze was steady on him and Tansy, calculation in her eyes. It wasn't her Jake was worried about, though, but the little tyke next to her who hadn't stopped eating except to take deep gulps of the milk before returning to shoveling food down his gullet.

"Declan? You want to join us?" Jake met his brother's nod of approval as they pulled out chairs opposite where Melissa sat. "Finish your meal."

Melissa pushed her plate away. "Don't really have much of an appetite."

Declan eyed Jeffrey. "Hey, kiddo. You want to watch a show while we talk with your mom?"

"You can take your plate," Tansy said, standing to the side of him and curling her finger to motion him forward. "You want some more macaroni and cheese?"

The kid nodded, leaving the table willingly. Tansy had him settled in the living room at the coffee table, some Disney program clicked on with Aiden and Petra supervising.

"What's going on?" Jake asked quietly.

His ex-wife took a deep breath and let it out, her shoulders sagging. "I had to leave. The guy I was living with started to make demands that I couldn't deal with. Not with Jeffrey. I packed a few things and headed west. I didn't have anywhere in mind, then I thought of you."

Christ. "This guy you just left. Is he Jeffrey's father?"

She shook her head. "That man is not in the picture. He never really was, and it's better that way," she admitted. "He didn't want kids."

So no angry ex would be following her to get back his child. Good and horrifying at the same time.

Melissa went on, quiet but steady now. "After he left, I was doing okay by myself. Had a good job hairdressing with a great daycare for Jeffrey. When I met Nathan, it seemed like a good situation. He didn't mind that I had a kid, and he seemed gentle and understanding."

Her voice broke on the last word.

Examining her face, Jake would've sworn she was telling the truth. Or at least the truth that she believed, which wasn't necessarily the same thing. That had kind of always been the problem with Melissa.

"Where were you living?" Declan asked.

"Winnipeg." She pulled a tissue out of her pocket and dabbed at her eyes.

"Why didn't you go to your parents?" Jake knew his wife hadn't always seen eye to eye with them, but it seemed under the circumstances that would've made more sense.

Melissa gave a bitter laugh. "I haven't seen them in five years. Not since Jeffrey was born. They told me I made my mess, so I could live with it."

With every word, Jake's hands felt more and more tied. Again, if it'd only been her, he could have offered her temporary relief. Hell, he would've given her some money and told her to get her shit together somewhere else.

But there was a kid involved.

Jake turned to his brother. "Deck, can I talk to you for a minute?"

Out on the porch, the lingering cold of the tail end of winter surrounded them. It seemed suitable, Jake supposed. There was nothing warm and happy about this entire situation.

"Hell of a thing," Declan muttered.

"I don't want her here," Jake said, "but the kid—"

"I know." Declan laid a hand on Jake's shoulder. "This complicates things. I know we're set up as a rescue, but there's a level of trust involved for all the people who come here."

Crap. "Melissa's not done well at earning our trust."

Declan shook his head. He considered for a moment and made a startling suggestion. "We'll have to be smart to keep her from figuring out what we're doing."

"You want her to stay?" Jake sounded shocked, even to himself.

"Not sure we can turn her away. But we can reduce the interactions between her and the rest of the ranch hands."

"Going to be tough to do with her living in the house with the ladies once I go back to my space under the art studio."

Declan raised a brow. "I think instead of you leaving the house, we should put her in your apartment."

For a moment, Jake hesitated, then the wisdom of the suggestion hit. "That makes sense. Because she's got Jeffrey, that'll give them more private space without adding a kid to the other ranch hands' world."

"We'll help her out with groceries and that sort of thing, but she can cook for herself most of the time. And it will probably be less frightening for the kid than being shoved into a huge adult-dominated world."

Jake sighed. "I still don't like it, but I don't know how much of that is who we're dealing with rather than the whole messed up situation."

"The whole thing sucks," Declan agreed. "But if she's here for a couple of weeks, we can manage."

An uneasy feeling lingered in his stomach as they slipped into the house to inform Melissa of their decision. She took the news with a fresh bout of quiet tears. "Thank you. I'm really, really grateful."

Jake headed to his apartment to grab the few things he might still need. The rest he pushed to the side of the closet, and when Declan brought Melissa and Jeffrey in, he was ready to get out of there as quickly as possible.

Ready to get back to the house and take Tansy into his arms to reassure himself all the dread and negativity that *his* memories were throwing at him were a thing of the past.

As soon as Melissa and her son had left the house with Declan, Tansy wilted like week-old lettuce.

Petra curled an arm around her, guiding her to the living room where Aiden waited. "That was not on the agenda."

"It's total bullshit," Aiden agreed. He made a face. "I'm torn between not being able to believe that she showed up here and being one hundred percent convinced this is Melissa and status quo."

"And yet, this is what High Water is about," Tansy said slowly. "As long as Jake knows he's got our support, he can willingly put up with some bullshit for the sake of a kid."

Aiden and Petra both hesitated. "That's a completely mature response," Aiden offered. "I don't know that I'm quite there yet."

"Trust me, when Jake said she was his ex, I had an intense urge to do violence. But *I've* been a kid like that," Tansy admitted. She met her friends' eyes. "I would do a whole lot of bleeding to make a single kid's world better."

"I hope it doesn't come to that," Petra said, but she petted Tansy's shoulder as she got to her feet. "We'll wait to hear the rest of the details from Jake and Declan."

But after the guys came back from settling Melissa and Jeffrey in the apartment and the details they'd thought of were shared, there wasn't much more to do than go to sleep and hope that the next day ran smoothly.

Jake followed Tansy into her bedroom. "I'm running on adrenaline and nerves," he admitted. "I just want to hold you."

"Works well for my agenda," Tansy said, pulling him to the loveseat in the corner of the room. "Because I absolutely want to be held."

They ended up lying on each other, sprawled on the loveseat with Tansy half on top of Jake. Her head rested on his chest, and the steady beat under her ear was soothing and comfortable and exactly what she needed to be able to ask some tough questions.

"Are you really okay with her being here?" she asked.

His chest rose under her and then fell slowly as he sighed in frustration. "I have no choice."

"We always have choices," Tansy said quietly. "Some options take more time, or money, or energy. That's what my dad always says."

Jake pressed a kiss to her temple. "I'm kicking my ass and simultaneously grateful for having been an idiot. Remember those letters that were haunting me? The ones stuffed in my journal that you said I should get rid of because they were—how did you phrase it?—being mean to me?"

She thought back before nodding slowly. "Yeah, I remember."

"They were from Melissa. You were right to say I needed to let them go. And I had, because I wanted to make a total break from her to really concentrate on being with *you*."

The sweetness of the comment washed over a layer of her concerns. "I'm glad to hear that. But how does that make you an idiot?"

"It meant Melissa knew where to find me, although I never did give her my address. I wonder how she knew where to go?" Confusion laced his voice. "I suppose that doesn't matter now."

"If she didn't know where to find you, Jeffrey wouldn't be here," Tansy said. "That's the part that you're sort of grateful for, yes?"

"Yeah."

They both lay quietly for a moment. Jake stroking her hair, Tansy's hand pressed to his chest, fingers playing softly.

Her mind raced a million miles an hour. There were so many layers and so many ways that this could go wrong, but it came back to them not having many choices. They had to do something for Jeffrey's sake.

With that clear, Tansy pushed aside the rest of her worries. She pressed up to hover over Jake and meet his gaze. "Let me practice my best rookie planning moves."

Jake raised a brow.

"I know, bear with me. I'm a novice, but maybe it will help all of us get through the situation. Number one, we focus on Jeffrey. I will make things he likes to eat, and you can take him to see the animals, and in the meantime, we let Melissa do the adult things she needs to do to figure out the next step. But Jeffrey gets to be a kid."

Jake wiggled back until he leaned against the armrest. The hopelessness on his expression brightened. "Okay. I like that."

"Nice to get positive feedback from the master of the art," Tansy teased. "Number two, while Melissa is doing her adult things, she does not get to be alone with any of the ranch hands. Which does mean some juggling, but if she's only here for a couple of weeks, we can handle it."

"Number three, Melissa doesn't get to be alone with any of us either," Jake suggested. He grimaced. "I hope she'll be on her best behaviour, but in case she's not, I don't want her to spew her particularly toxic observations on anyone. You, Jinx—"

"Add yourself to that list." Tansy pressed a hand to his cheek. "Finally, number four, we get Declan and Kevin to deal with her adult decision-making checklist. Not you."

"Brilliant. Although Declan and Kevin haven't done anything to deserve it," Jake teased.

"Enough planning. My brain is exhausted, and I really want to kiss you," Tansy informed him as she rolled fully onto his chest.

"You did well for a rookie planner. I'm proud of you," Jake assured her before somehow finding his feet and lifting her with him.

Tansy smothered a squeal, but a burst of laughter escaped as he tossed her on the bed. A moment later, he was on top of her, hands on either side of her torso, a wicked smile in place as he stared at her lips.

"Are you going to reward me?" she asked.

"No. I'm going to reward myself."

Which, in the end, was the same thing.

Tansy crawled out of bed the next morning slightly achy in all the right spots and slipped into the kitchen with more enthusiasm than she had imagined possible. Not having to cook for Jake's ex three times a day was definitely a point on the plus side.

In fact, she didn't see anything of Melissa for three days.

Hopefulness rose that the woman was actually taking advantage of the gift she'd been given and trying to be as little trouble as possible.

In the meantime, Jeffrey showed up at the house on a regular basis in the company of one of the Skye brothers. By the third time he arrived, he and Tansy had fallen into a sweet rhythm. She couldn't always stop what she was doing, but she had plenty of experience getting others, old and young, to help in the kitchen.

Helen wandered into the kitchen early on Friday morning. She glanced around before heading to the counter where Tansy was piling muffins on a tray. "Can I help?"

"Be my guest." Tansy stepped away and switched to cracking eggs into a bowl.

Quiet settled for a couple of minutes then Helen cleared her throat. "I don't want to make trouble for anyone, but something happened, and I think I need to tell you."

Tansy paused and turned all her attention on the older woman. "You okay?"

"Yes, but my wallet is missing two twenties." Helen said it softly then met Tansy's gaze straight on. "I'm certain of it. But if May took the cash, I don't want to make a fuss. She needs it more than me. I thought you should know, though."

"I'm sorry, Helen. If you want to put anything away, we do have a safe."

"It's fine, really," Helen insisted. "I'll be gone next week to my daughter's. I'll keep things close until then." She eyed Tansy hard. "And don't you dare offer to give me money out of your own wallet, you hear?"

Tansy offered her a hug instead. "I'll talk to the guys. How about we arrange for a drawer with a private lock for every one of our guests in the future?"

"Good idea. Now, we should get back to work or breakfast will be late."

There was always something new to learn around High Water, Tansy decided as she scrubbed dishes after breakfast and got working on the food needed for the next day's retreat.

The spring was slow for bookings for the retreat house side of things, but Tansy didn't mind. Not with the added stress of having Melissa around. But tomorrow they would have the local Girl Scout and Brownie pack in for activities from nine to five, and she wanted to get as much ready ahead of time as possible so her Saturday wasn't so rushed.

Around nine thirty, the door opened and Jake's firm voice echoed in a happy greeting. "Hello to the house."

Jeffrey came rushing in. "Tansy," he called excitedly.

"Hold up, cowpoke. Shoes off at the door," Jake reminded him.

Jeffrey dropped to the floor, ripped his shoes off his feet, and all but threw them toward the wall. Dumping his coat on top, he rushed to join Tansy. "We making cookies today?"

"Cookies and, even better, veggie trays." Tansy announced it as if she'd just promised him endless candy.

The little guy looked at her with suspicion before shrugging and heading to the stepstool that had migrated into the kitchen. He dragged it to the counter and climbed on top, thumping his hands on the countertop.

"Melissa has a couple of interviews in Calgary," Jake informed her. "I already lined up to help Declan this morning, but Aiden and I can take care of the Jeffster this afternoon in case Melissa isn't back until late."

Tansy offered a wooden spoon to Jeffrey which he excitedly banged on the outside of the enormous cookie dough bowl. "Not a problem. I'm headed to my sister's tonight at four o'clock, though. I promised to take care of my nieces and nephew while Ivy and Walker go to some school event. I'll have the meal for High Water ready in crockpots for everyone to serve themselves—chili, buns, salad."

"Want some company babysitting?" Jake asked.

She waggled her brows at him. "You're a sucker for punishment. Of course you can come. You'll make Carter's evening."

"I have an ulterior motive," he assured her solemnly. "For supper, you're making grilled cheese sandwiches and tomato soup, yes?"

Tansy laughed. "It's the number one request when I go over to babysit." She glanced down at Jeffrey. "You know what, why don't we bring him along? It'd be good for him to have playtime with other kids."

Jake considered for a moment. "As long as you don't think Ivy and Walker would mind. Melissa will be okay with it."

Tansy worked hard to keep a smile on her face. It had only been three days, and she was already hyperaware that the amount of attention Melissa gave her son was nowhere near what Tansy considered sufficient.

It was fine to say they were caring for him to let the woman get things accomplished. But Melissa didn't seem to want him around at all.

Tansy focused back on what she was in control of, which right now was offering Jake a heartfelt answer. "Then it's a date."

A happy whistle sounded as Jake stole his way across the floor to give her a kiss. When he bent and tussled Jeffrey's hair affectionately, a hint of warning struck in Tansy's gut.

It was good things were going smoothly, but there was a line she couldn't cross. Falling in love with Jake? Well, she was most of the way there, to be honest.

Falling in love with an adorable little boy who could never be hers?

That would be a terrible idea.

16

---

*B*efore four, Jake slipped out of the barn with Jeffrey on his shoulders.

"I like the kitties, but the puppy was all *woof*, and the kitties run away." Jeffrey banged enthusiastically on Jake's hat. "Run away, run away."

"Easy on the hat, cowpoke," Jake warned. "Yes, kittens are good at running and hiding. But now we're done with kittens and you need to get cleaned up. You've got kitten fluff and hay all over you, and we're headed to Tansy's sister's house. You wash up and put on clean clothes, okay?"

"'Kay." Jeffrey wiggled. "Fly me."

It was too easy to oblige. Jake flipped the little tyke off his shoulders and proceeded to twirl Jeffrey in circles all the way to the apartment. The kid squealed and laughed the entire trip.

Melissa stood waiting on the porch, a small smile dancing on her lips as they arrived. "Someone is having a good time."

Jeffrey nodded, squirming to be put down. He vanished into the apartment.

"I hope it's okay, but I told Jeffrey I was taking him over to play with Tansy's nieces and nephew tonight." Awkwardness hit hard and fast. "I should have asked first."

"Don't apologize," Melissa insisted. "I just got home, and you probably had to make plans much earlier. I wasn't answering my phone while I was busy."

"We did." He looked her over. "How was your day?"

"A lot of driving, but I think it was worthwhile." She glanced over her shoulder. "Come in for a minute."

"Oh, I should—"

She was already marching away from him, the door left wide open.

Jake gingerly stepped into the space that was legally his, closing the door with reluctance. "I need to get changed. If you can bring Jeffrey to the house once he's got clean stuff on, that would be great."

"Oh, I'm sure he'll be ready in a minute. Then he can walk over with you." Her eyes brightened, and she reached into her purse. "This gives us a minute alone. There's something we need to discuss. And I need to apologize."

That would be a first. "Apologize for what?"

"For not suggesting this right away. It might have made things go smoother between us." She laid a piece of paper on the table and pushed it toward him. "I only want what's best for my son."

Jake leaned forward and scanned the official looking document quickly, not quite sure what he was seeing.

The piece of paper was an application for adjusting a birth certificate. Name: Jeffrey Drea. Birthdate: September sixth.

In the place to name the father it said *Jacob Anthony Skye.*

For a second, Jake couldn't breathe. His gaze snapped up to Melissa's. "What the hell?"

"In Alberta, there's a thing called voluntary

acknowledgment of paternity, and it doesn't require a DNA test. So it would be simple enough to say that you're his—"

"It's a lie."

"But it's a lie that doesn't hurt anything. It would mean that Jeffrey has two people in this world who love him and care about him."

How she said it with a straight face, Jake could not fathom. "Melissa, you're making it sound as if I'm his father. And while I do care about him—I'm caring for him while he's here to help you out. I'm not his dad."

Melissa dropped her chin for a moment then her lashes fluttered upward. "You could be. You and I could be together again, and that would make—"

"Holy crap, Mel. What fairy-tale world are you living in?" Somehow Jake kept his volume from rising too far. Jeffrey did not need to hear him shouting at his mom. He eyed her hard. "Are you high?"

"I found the letters."

Jake froze.

She twisted and went to the side counter. Sure enough, she lifted the entire bundle of letters and cards and cradled them in her arms as if they were precious. The bundle that he was certain he'd destroyed.

Hadn't he?

"They were under the bed. I dropped an earring, and when I went looking for it, I found the bundle just under the edge of the frame."

Jake's brain scrambled for the how and why. He'd stashed the bundle in the closet and then he'd gotten rid of—

Shit. The day of Aiden's wedding. Tansy had rushed in and tossed the bundle away and Jake hadn't thought of it even once since. It must have landed out of sight and out of mind.

Melissa made a small noise, somewhere between a sigh and

a sob, and he jerked his attention to her face. "I know we didn't work out, but we were young. I know now that I was selfish. I didn't come here specifically thinking that we'd get back together, but once I saw you again and then found these letters..." Moisture filled her eyes. "You wouldn't have kept them if I didn't mean something to you. It made me think of Jeffrey's future and everything I can't give him without your help."

Speechless. Jake was struck utterly speechless. He just stared, not really sure what was happening.

"You don't care about me at all?" It came out all wobbly and innocent.

"Dammit, Mel." Jake changed his tone, speaking softer, regret tinging his words. She did have a reason for her hair-brained idea, even if it was completely out of line. "I'm with Tansy. She's a caring, giving woman who challenges me in all the right ways. I'm not— I'm sorry. I'm not looking to get back together with you."

Melissa nodded slowly. "Okay. I'm sorry, too. I never imaged that you'd have someone in your life, and of course, I don't want to get in the middle of that."

Jake extended his hand. "I'll take those."

She hesitated then passed the bundle over. She smiled hesitantly. "Okay. Mental reset. I still need some time to figure out my future, but now I know the truth. You will not be a part of it."

Being together had never been an option as far as he was concerned, but that didn't need to be resaid. "As long as we're clear."

"Absolutely." Melissa's gaze darted to the side. "Jeffrey, baby. Come here and let your mom see you."

The kid stopped a pace away from her, back straight but smiling. "I'm going to play with Tansy's niblings."

"What fun. You make sure you're on your best behavior, yes? Don't disappoint your mother." Melissa nodded firmly then turned toward the kitchen. "I haven't eaten since breakfast."

Jeffrey was already at the door, shoving his feet into shoes as fast as he could, ignoring the fact he had his left shoe on his right foot. He grabbed Jake's hand and hauled him outside without another glance at his mom.

Jake shook his head then scooped up the little tyke. Time to ignore the crazy that had just happened and focus on what was more important. "It's better to put the shoes on before you start running. Silly buckaroo."

"Silly Jeffy," the kiddo corrected. Then he shrieked with delight as Jake held him upside down and carried him, still swinging, toward the main ranch house. "Silly Jakey."

"You're full of beans," Jake offered with a grin.

His mama might have a few tools loose in the shed, but the kid? One hundred percent joy. Jake flipped him right-side up and settled him back onto his shoulders.

Jeffrey grabbed on tight and laughed with childish abandon.

SOMETHING SEEMED so familiar about Jeffrey, but Tansy couldn't put her finger on what it was. Something she hadn't really noticed when it was just the two of them in the house, but mixing him up with her niblings, especially Harper, who was the same age, the sensation grew stronger.

He'd slipped into the middle of Carter, Chloe, and Harper like a greased pig, with complete childish enthusiasm and all the energy of a five-year-old.

At ten, Carter was on the cusp of insisting he was far too

old to join in the games that Chloe and Harper wanted to play. But the instant Jeffrey arrived, evening out the boys-versus-girls ratio, everything changed.

With Jake there as well, Tansy's amusement level was through the roof. They weren't only building a racetrack for Hot Wheels that went around ninety percent of the playroom. They were building a *Space Mover Deluxe* with a loop in the middle and a Lego bridge for all of Harper's favourite toys to gather and cheer each time a car went flying down the track.

Controlled chaos at its finest with Jeffrey wide-eyed and quieter than the others and very, very observant.

Tansy alternated between joining in and building as directed by Harper and Jeffrey, and hitting the kitchen to make a crumble to go with the rest of supper she was assembling.

She slipped out to the washroom, but the kids' bathroom in the hall was occupied. So she followed the usual family protocol and slid into Ivy and Walker's room. Her sister insisted it was never a problem, but Tansy still kept her head down and didn't take too much time admiring the beautiful quilt on the bed or the family pictures in black-and-white on the wall.

After washing up and silently opening the door, Tansy took one step into the room to discover Jeffrey motionless at the foot of the bed.

"Did you get lost?" she asked.

He nodded, eyes going wide.

She held out a hand. "This is my big sister's room. It's very pretty, but we should stay in the other parts of the house."

"Okay."

That was the first, but not the last time that Tansy turned around to discover Jeffrey not where she expected him to be.

The kid moved like a ghost.

"My mommy works at the school," Harper informed Jeffrey

as they sat next to each other at the dining room table. "And my daddy rides horses."

"He used to ride bulls," Carter added enthusiastically, "but he said he likes his head attached to his spine, and bull riding can make your bones shake apart, so he doesn't do that anymore."

Jeffrey's eyes were the size of dinner plates. "His head could come off?"

"It's an expression." Chloe lifted her nose like the little expert she was. "It never really came off." She frowned then turned to Tansy. "Right?"

Oh, the temptation to tell a whopper right then. Auntie Tansy could get her brother-in-law tangled in so much mischief, but she restrained herself. "You're right, it's only an expression. Like when we're having fun, and we say we're having a blast."

Carter snickered. He put his hands together as if he were holding a ball then threw them into the air as he shouted, "Kaboom."

After supper, and after dishes were done and the playroom had been deconstructed, Chloe had a request. "Can we play hide and go seek?"

"Absolutely," Jake said, instantly dropping to the floor and covering his face with his hands. "I'm counting to twenty," he warned.

Four children and Tansy darted from the room.

Of course Jake found her first, standing against the wall near the front entrance. He pushed aside the coat she'd used to cover her face and upper body, one brow raised high. "It usually helps if you cover both the top and the bottom."

Tansy looked down to discover the second jacket that had been hanging from the bottom hook lay on the floor by her feet.

Which of course, left her entire lower body in full view. "Some little sneak took my cover off," she complained.

A giggle sounded from behind the couch.

Jake winked. "Good thing there's no one hidden nearby who might've tried to commit sabotage on their auntie."

Another giggle, and this time Tansy pressed her hand over her mouth to keep from joining in.

Being found first was perfect. Getting to follow along behind Jake allowed Tansy to watch the precious moments when he discovered each of her nieces. Harper was the little mischief maker hiding behind the couch. Chloe had somehow snuck around behind Jake's back as he counted and covered herself in a blanket. She looked like nothing more than a messy lump on the edge of the loveseat.

Funniest though was the expression on Carter's face as Jake slowly peeled back the curtain in his room. His little boy face was screwed up tight, with his eyes closed as if truly believing that ostrich story of if you can't see them, no one can see you.

Finally the only one missing was Jeffrey. He wasn't in the kitchen, the living room, or either of the two children's rooms.

There was a moment's excitement when Jake tried the bathroom door and discovered it was locked. He motioned Tansy forward. "I assume you can do something about this?"

She reached above the doorframe and pulled down a wooden skewer from where Ivy kept it in case of emergencies. "Next time give me something challenging," she whispered.

A moment later, he'd slipped the end of the stick into the emergency unlock button in the center of the doorknob, and the lock clicked easily.

Jake eased the door open. "Ready or not, you will be caught."

No one. Not in the bathtub, not behind the door. Jake even

opened the cupboards under the sink, but while there was room for a child to hide, the space was empty.

He turned back to her, frowning. "These kids are amazing. They're even using misdirection. I could've sworn the door was locked for a reason."

Five more minutes of looking, and Tansy decided to call it. The other kids were still looking, but it was time. "Come out, come out, wherever you are, Jeffrey. You won the game."

To all of their shock, ten seconds later Jeffrey popped out of the bathroom, a huge grin in place as he rushed forward to wrap his arms around Tansy's leg.

She tousled his hair but kept the rest of her questions to herself. "Good job. Okay, it's time for pyjamas and stories."

Jake gave her a look, but he took Jeffrey into Carter's room with the bag with pyjamas that they'd brought along.

Tansy went and examined the bathroom. She knew they hadn't missed seeing him, so there had to be another explanation. But she didn't really want to ask him because—

The laundry chute. Set to the side, behind the door, was the sliding opening that led to the basement. Tansy used her phone's flashlight and took a peek, but she already knew the answer. The width was more than big enough for a child to fit.

There were open spaces between the bare two by fours lining the inside of the passage, and she was pretty sure they would make a dandy ladder.

That uncomfortable feeling in her belly didn't go away, not through story time or the goodbye hugs and kisses once Ivy and Walker got home.

Jeffrey fell asleep in the car seat as they drove back out to High Water.

"You're quiet," Jake said, his strong fingers linked with hers.

"Just thinking," she offered quietly. She didn't want to say anything until she was sure. She wouldn't allow uncertain parts of her past to dump suspicions on an innocent child.

Jake squeezed her hand. "I'll take Jeffrey back to the apartment. Hopefully Melissa is there. And then there's a couple of things I should do in the barn."

"I'll probably head to bed early," Tansy told him, offering him a smile. "You were awesome tonight, as usual."

"You're far worse at hide and go seek than expected," he teased.

He had no idea how much effort it took to be bad at something she'd been trained to be better than good at.

Three days later, Tansy volunteered to drive May to the bus stop for her journey at nine a.m. The young woman had spoken with lawyers and the police, and with Jake and Declan's suggestions, she had a full list of things to take care of with her family and friends' help.

"I'm glad I had a chance to stay somewhere quiet while I got myself straightened out," May said. She paused as if considering her next words. "I really am grateful, and so I don't want to say this, but I feel as if I should. I think maybe you should keep a close eye on Helen."

"Oh? Is there something wrong?"

"Not anything dangerous," May said quickly. "And I do hate to mention it, but I could've sworn I had a pair of earrings with me that I can't find now. They weren't really valuable, but they were from a trip I took that made me happy. I don't think it's Jinx—that girl is amazingly sweet."

"I am sorry," Tansy offered immediately, dazed by the somewhat surreal conversation. "Sometimes it's worse to have something that's got sentimental value go missing. I'll make sure we take an extra good look around when we clean up. And I'll take the warning to heart."

May waved a hand. "You know what? In the big scheme of

things, it's small beans. If she wanted them, I hope they help her down the road. But I thought you should know."

"Of course." Tansy sat in silence for a moment, unlocked doors and confusing thoughts tangling together. "If by chance you find them when you get home, please let me know. I'm glad you said something."

"Thank you." They slipped outside and May took her suitcase and stepped into Tansy's arms to hug her tightly. "You're making a difference. That's not always easy," she said firmly.

"You're making a difference in your own life," Tansy returned. "I wish you every happiness going forward."

May lifted her chin, nodded once, then got on the bus.

Tansy's uneasiness lingered far longer than the trip back to High Water. What were the chances two of their guests had stolen from each other?

ZenBaby made a strange noise for a moment, and Tansy tightened her grip on the wheel. She tapped the brakes lightly, but they seemed to engage. Still, not a good sign. Fine. She'd make an appointment for the poor thing at the shop ASAP.

She was just about at the ranch when her phone went off.

Tansy hit answer and sent it to hands-free mode. "Julia?"

"What are you up to this morning?" her friend asked.

"It's Monday, so I was planning on going for a walk and maybe bugging my parents at the bookstore for a while. You need company?"

"Yup. There's someone I want you to meet. Come over now."

Julia hung up without a word of explanation.

Suspicions high, Tansy instantly contacted Petra. "Have you heard from Julia this morning?"

"Yes. I've been summoned." The rush of voices in the background quieted slightly. "I was about to head over."

"I'm turning into High Water right now. Jump in and we'll go over together."

Less than five minutes later, Petra was buckled up and Tansy laid rubber as she headed straight out to Red Boot ranch. "Julia's either out of her mind with boredom or she had the baby."

"We were over last night, and she never said a word," Petra protested. "And we didn't leave until after midnight."

"A lot can happen in a few hours."

Truer words had never been spoken. The sheer number of vehicles outside the small cabin Petra and Zach lived in was a dead giveaway that Tansy and Petra weren't the only ones who had been called.

A slightly slimmer Julia answering the door with an armful of pink and blue blankets was the final answer. "Hey, you came."

"Julia Sorenson, you take the cake." Petra swooped in and hugged her tight. "Congrats. You look wonderful."

"I feel wonderful, and I can see my toes again. It was a hard labour, but quick, thank God. I've already had a nap. This is Anneka, and one of you needs to take her because I need to pee."

Which is how Tansy ended up with a newborn baby in her arms and laughter dancing on the air.

Thank goodness there were enough sound-minded adults around that one of them—Zach's mother?—guided Tansy to a chair and got her settled. Which meant she got to examine tiny fingers and a wrinkled-up nose and tiny puckered lips without worrying about dropping her precious cargo.

Sydney settled on the arm beside her with Petra to her right.

"Pretty baby," Sydney offered quietly.

"She's beautiful." Anneka wiggled, and Tansy tightened the bundling around her. "Did you do the delivery?"

"I did, little as I was needed." Sydney offered a grin. "I think Zach's been studying because when they called me at three a.m., he gave a complete report of dilation and contraction timing, and it wasn't Julia's doing because she was too busy swearing to answer the questions I asked."

"My big brother always was an overachiever," Petra offered dryly. "He caught the baby, didn't he?"

"Absolutely. Best catcher positioning I've seen in a long time." Sydney was still grinning. "Didn't even twitch out of place when Julia started describing in graphic detail what she would do if he came near her in the next while even thinking about sex."

Tansy snorted.

Petra made a vomiting noise. "Enough. It's funny and all, but he is my brother, and ick on the sex talk."

"You want to hold her?" Tansy asked, lifting Anneka toward her auntie.

"In a bit. You enjoy for now." Petra glanced over her shoulder at the filled room. "Once you give her up, you won't get her back for a while. Not with this horde."

It was a full room. With Julia's three sisters and their spouses, Zach and Petra's parents, and the three of them, there wasn't space to turn around.

Which was fine. Tansy shoved down everything else she'd been worrying about and focused on the very good thing in the here and now.

A tiny new life coming into a world of love.

17

They had barely sat down to supper when a knock sounded on the door followed immediately by it swinging open.

"Hey. Is it okay if I come in?" Melissa stuck her head around the corner, Jeffrey in her arms. He squirmed to be let down, but she held him locked in place.

Declan rose and went to the door. "Did you need something?"

"I finally got back from that meeting I had down south, and Jeffrey's crying for supper. I don't have the energy. Is it okay if he joins you? Don't worry about me, only if there's something for him, please?"

Tansy was already moving, reaching for extra plates. "Of course you can join us. There's enough for you both."

Heart Falls was down to a single ranch guest. The ladies were both gone, and only Logan remained in the men's quarters. Tansy, however, was still cooking for an army.

There might be enough food, but it was the third time this

week Melissa had invited herself into the house, and Jake didn't appreciate it.

Three weeks. What he'd hoped might be a short-term visit was now passing three weeks, and Melissa was still around. Which meant Jeffrey was still there, and maybe that had something to do with the dangerous teeter-totter going on in Jake's gut.

"Thank you so much." Melissa put Jeffrey down and gestured him toward the table.

He instantly climbed into the chair next to Tansy that he'd been using when he spent the morning with her.

Melissa settled herself in the chair across from Jake.

The conversation lull was epic. Where moments before they'd been laughing and enjoying Jinx's story about a school project she and Sasha were working on, it seemed no one really wanted to talk anymore.

Jeffrey crawled up on his knees, staring over the edge of the table at Dixie. "'inx's doggy is nice."

There was nothing Jinx enjoyed more than talking about her pet. "Dixie is a nice doggy, but she's also a guard dog. You have to not chase her or pull her tail, remember?"

"No pulling," Jeffrey said firmly. He turned and patted Tansy on the arm. "Can I please have noodles?"

"Oodles of noodles?" Tansy teased. She leaned down so she was eye to eye with him. "Yes. And you can have a rainbow. See?" She tumbled the brightly coloured vegetables onto his plate.

As conversation at that end of the table continued regarding the meal, Melissa accepted the breadbasket from Jake, broke off half a bun, and sat back in her chair. She sighed heavily.

Ignoring her would be so much easier. "Having any luck?" he finally asked politely.

Melissa shrugged. "I'm doing my best." She sat upright, leaning across the table a little bit and lowering her voice. "You're working so hard. This is a wonderful place you and your brothers have set up."

Jake nodded, filling his plate as bowls passed but trying his best to pay attention to the conversation now continuing up the table.

"I was thinking," Melissa continued, drawing his gaze back to her. "Maybe I should look for something a little closer for work."

That was confusing as all get out. "Closer to what?"

She laughed. "Never mind. I'm so tired I'm obviously not making any sense. Jeffrey's really enjoying himself. He said you took him for a horseback ride. Thank you for that."

Jake had enjoyed it as much as Jeffrey had. "You're welcome. He did a good job. Wasn't scared at all."

"No, he's not scared of much." She said it so matter-of-factly that it sounded odd. As if she'd done her best to scare him and hadn't been successful, although where that idea came from, Jake didn't know.

He wished it had stayed away.

That seem to be how things continued over the next couple of days. Everyone at High Water took turns caring for Jeffrey while Melissa took off during the days, supposedly working on plans for her future. Then half the time she showed up and expected Tansy to feed her.

In the middle of the afternoon on Tansy's day off, when she'd headed out with Rose and Fern for some springtime activity at Red Boot ranch, Jake offered to keep an eye on Jeffrey.

They'd spent the morning taking care of the animals in the shelter, and the instant they came into the house, Jeffrey crawled onto the couch and fell asleep.

Jake pulled out his journal, but his heart wasn't in it. There was a real sense of something out of kilter. No matter how much he tried to balance his to-do lists, no matter how he tried to be spontaneous, nothing seemed to fix it.

The door opened, and Jake glanced up. He expected one of the girls, but it was Melissa.

She smiled as if pleased to discover him. "Just the man I hoped to see."

She pulled out a chair, and Jake was suddenly reminded of Tansy's warning that they should never be alone with Melissa. Unless he wanted to run screaming from the room, there seemed no way to stop it. "I've been meaning to ask. Do you have a date for heading out on your own? You need to start thinking about that."

Melissa shook her head. "I'm trying, Jake. And I can't tell you how grateful I am that you've been there for me. You've been a lifesaver, just like I knew you would." She laid a hand on his arm.

He pushed back from the table, freeing himself and folding his arms over his chest. "Glad we've been able to help, but there is a limit."

"I suppose." Melissa stared at him for a minute then over at where Jeffrey was sleeping on the couch. "If you don't mind, I'm going to leave him here. He seems so comfy, I'd hate to wake him."

Then she was gone, out the door, leaving confusion in her wake.

It felt as if the whole house was under some kind of a spell. Even as the spring weather warmed and the snow melted away, there was none of the happy optimism that usually accompanied the changing of the seasons. Jake felt tired to the soles of his feet.

Tansy seemed distracted as well. The impulsive, vibrant

woman he couldn't keep his eyes off had a dull fog over her bright veneer.

Enough already. When the final day of May arrived and they were all dragging their collective feet, Jake had enough.

Time for another moment of spontaneity.

He swooped into the house at four thirty, eyed the food on the counter, and calculated his chances of succeeding. "If I bring in a pinch-hitter, can I convince you to play hooky with me?"

Tansy turned from the counter, drying her hands on a towel. "Since the only people who expect me to feed them are somehow related to you or in your employ, I will abandon everything right now, pinch-hitter or no."

Jake turned back toward the door. "Come in. She said yes."

An instant later, Sydney was through the door and tossing her things over the arm of the couch. "Hey, chica. Unless you're doing something very *ooh, la la,* I'm here to take over."

Tansy snickered. "Perfect. I hope you brought your knife— there's a ham to carve."

"Delightful. It always makes Aiden slightly green when I sharpen my blades." Sydney winked at Jake.

"Doesn't do much for the rest of us guys either," he admitted before turning to Tansy. "Don't dress up. Jeans, runners, warm enough coat for outside."

"Give me five minutes," Tansy offered.

Which meant seven minutes later they were on the road.

Tansy leaned back in the middle seat and closed her eyes. "God, you don't know how much I need this."

"Even without a clue to what we're doing?" Jake teased.

"I'm not in the house," Tansy returned. She snorted. "Maybe it's spring fever. I know that cabin fever is a real thing in the middle of winter, but is there something that makes your brain go into tangles in the spring?"

"I doubt it's the time of year," Jake offered quietly. "I think it's Melissa. Having her and Jeffrey around... It's messing with all of us."

They sat in silence for a minute before Tansy nodded. "Yeah. It's not getting any easier, that's for sure."

While he agreed, that's not what tonight was about. "Time for a distraction. You're not cooking, and we're not in the house. And if *anyone* tries to do anything stupid tonight, Sydney's there to take care of them. Enough said?"

An evil snicker escaped her. "Enough said. But also, *woohoo*, Sydney. I really hope she's in the middle of wielding her knives at some appropriate moment. If necessary."

"Enough said," Jake reminded her.

Tansy tilted her head toward him. "It's not warm enough for a picnic. We've already gone to the Heart Falls lookout."

"Because heaven forbid we ever have a date to the same place twice."

She wrinkled her nose. "Yeah, I suppose that's a silly rule, all things considered. Small towns being small."

"I've missed spending time with you alone," Jake said softly.

"I'm across the hall," Tansy pointed out. She grinned. "You seemed to remember that a couple of nights this week."

Because the temptation to be together physically was too strong to resist. But they tended to mostly be quiet—well, as quiet as they could be while fooling around. Then they'd cuddle for a while before he'd go back to his own room.

It was starting to not be enough. Maybe it had never been enough.

He pulled to a stop in the back alley behind Buns and Roses.

Tansy peered at the door, confusion on her face. "Okay."

"Not what you expect," he promised. "Not Rough Cut, either."

Instead of guiding her in the back door of her café, or in the back door of Rose's flower shop next door, he used the key he'd been loaned to access the third business on the block.

The temperature inside was slightly cooler, with dark shades over the windows but clear security lighting along the edges of the room.

"We're at my future brother-in-law's art gallery." Tansy walked forward, seeming to listen hard. "Closed for the night?"

"We have a private viewing," Jake informed her. He offered his arm. "Right this way, m'lady."

She laughed as he guided her past the art draped with protective cloths then up the stairs into the top floor. One room was an interactive techno-art area where Fern reigned supreme. Another was a room that Chance used while teaching lessons.

But it was the third space that Jake guided Tansy to. It held a single table with two chairs artistically spotlighted—of course. He'd have to give an extra thanks to Chance for the mood lighting.

A small table to the side held covered plates. Tansy spotted them and instantly laughed out loud. "You got Marina to cook for you."

"I have a long history of getting Buns and Roses café to provide me with food when I'm not able to cook." He held out a chair.

Tansy settled into place, pulling his chair closer to hers. "I seem to remember some of that long history."

"Time to make some current history," he told her firmly.

It was a moment out of a dream. The stress that had enveloped him fell away as he and Tansy took turns lifting the covers on the plates, laughing to find some of the treats that

Marina had put out to accompany the hearty beef stew and cheesy scones.

They ate and drank and talked without having to worry about someone else being in the room. Without having to worry about being overheard or any of the other things that constantly sat at the edge of Jake's attention.

When they'd sated their stomach's appetites, Jake took Tansy's hand and led her away from the table.

"You're making me very curious," she told him.

He pushed open the door to the classroom, striding to the far wall covered with a large bulletin board and a whiteboard. "I discovered something intriguing this past winter." He grabbed the hidden handle and pulled, and suddenly a Murphy bed swung down from the wall into position.

He turned to discover Tansy grinning at him.

"I assume Chance has a bed in his studio for visiting artists." Tansy stepped up to Jake and wrapped her arms around him, lifting her lips until he closed the distance between them. Kissing soft and deep and meaningful.

That same sense of peace that had hovered around them the entire meal remained as they pressed together, their hands and bodies caressing and bumping. He jerked his shirt over his head and tossed it to the side. A second later he had his hands under Tansy's sweater, crinkling it up until it slid off, and he meshed their torsos together while he wrangled with her bra hooks.

"If you need me to get down to skin faster, let me know," Tansy offered. She eased her head to the side as he nibbled his way down her neck and across her cleavage.

A moan escaped her when he dragged the shoulder straps free, easing the bra over the tips of her nipples in a slow-motion caress meant to tease.

"Faster is overrated," Jake insisted. He meant it, too.

He found her nipple and sucked lightly until she squirmed against him. He pressed his palms to the small of her back to keep her in place as he nibbled a little more, easing down her rib cage even as he worked the button and zipper of her jeans.

He could have sworn he was going slowly, but suddenly she was absolutely naked, stepping away from him with mischief in her eyes.

"Some time you'll have to do the thing where you keep all your clothes on and I'm naked, but right now? I'm fully on board with the lights-on-eyes-open idea." She waggled her brows.

"So you're saying strip?"

"Naked as a blue jay," she agreed.

He wasn't sure what birds had to do with it, but shucking his jeans and the rest of it only took a split second. He caught her outstretched hand and guided her to the bed. "I've missed this."

She laughed as he tumbled her back onto the mattress. "Canoodling in strange places?"

He adjusted until they were side by side, lazily running his hands along the length of her torso. "Being naked with you. Being able to talk, and make noise, and be together. No worries about other people. Just us."

Her eyes danced, something infinitely happy in their depths. "I like you Jake Skye."

"I like you too, Tansy Fields." He stared at her for a moment, the words itching to come out. There was more here than just *like*.

Love hovered on his lips.

Instead, though, he eased down her body, tasting and teasing until she quivered, tugging on his hair and gasping as he slid his fingers gently in and out of her core. As he took her up and over the pinnacle, his name escaping from her lips—

That's what he wanted to hear. Not just sometimes, but every time.

He wrangled on a condom then stretched out beside her. Hand on her thigh, he draped her top leg over him as he lined them up and gently slipped his cock between her folds.

She moaned happily. "Oh, God, yes."

A palm fisted around him, and Jake grinned. "This is going to be over before we begin," he warned.

Tansy swore softly then kissed him, sliding until she straddled him, knees on either side of his hips as she worked him hard and deep, the whole time kissing and petting him, fingernails scratching lightly until his rhythm broke and he came.

She collapsed on top of him, breathing hard. "It's all good," she panted happily. "It might be over, but that only means we get to start again."

Which was, Jake considered, very deliciously true.

18

It was the smallest of sounds, but Tansy woke instantly. Her heart leapt into her throat as she opened her eyes and stared into a pair of blue-grey eyes hovering at mattress height.

Jeffrey stood next to her bed.

Her door had been locked, the house had been locked, and yet he stood there in the pre-dawn light.

After her heart started again, she managed a smile. "Hey, you. Does your mama know you're here?"

He hesitated then shook his head. A second later, he shocked the hell out of Tansy and crawled onto the bed, cuddling against her like a kitten.

The death grip on her quilt said neither of them was going anywhere soon.

Dammit. Tansy wiggled up enough to be able to wrap her arms around the kid and hold him tight.

Like knows like she thought. Both of them had been so trained by abuse that they craved unconditional love with everything in them.

She no longer doubted her suspicions. Not after the phone call she'd had with her sister earlier that evening.

She kicked herself that it had taken so long to act, but in her favour, there had been distractions like babies arriving and daily to-do lists. Gah, she sounded like a *planner*.

But finally, before heading to bed, Tansy had called Ivy and been completely upfront about her concerns. If she could trust anyone, it was her big sister.

"I need you to check to see if you're missing anything from your bedroom. Look for small shiny items, like rings or jewelry."

Not even five minutes later, Ivy had returned to the line, her voice gone serious. "I'm missing the necklace Grandma Sonora gave me and the set of diamond drop earrings Walker got me for our fifth anniversary. And strangely, a set of ladybug earrings that the kids gave me last Mother's Day. I could see the girls maybe taking the necklace to play dress-up, but neither of them have their ears pierced yet for the earrings. And they could take the ladybugs anytime they want, but they were so proud to give me something they bought, I really don't think this is some childish mix up."

"It's not your kids," Tansy assured her instantly. "And it wasn't me—"

"Oh my God, of course not. But the only people who have been in the house recently have been family. We both know no thief would break in and only steal a few trinkets when there are other things of value readily available."

"Jeffrey came with us that night I babysat. I think he stole them."

Ivy went silent then sighed. "Dammit. Are you okay?"

The fact she instantly put all the clues together and went straight to worrying about Tansy was so Ivy. The love in her voice swept around Tansy like a wave and made it easy to focus on the important parts of this disastrous discovery. "I'm too worried about Jeffrey to be upset by memories of my past. Unfortunately, I don't think we'll have much luck pinning this on the real person behind the theft."

"Maybe we can scare Melissa enough to get her to stop." Ivy's tone went icy-sharp. School principal at her finest. "We have your back, both Walker and me. I won't say anything to anyone else in the family. Not unless you think it's wise."

"Let me sleep on it," Tansy requested. Ivy had blown kisses at her and offered her a hug through the phone along with the firm reminder of how much she was loved.

Tansy had come this far with the help of her family and friends.

Jeffrey? If she was right, he was still being molded and formed by cruelty, and she desperately needed to change his future sooner than later. No five-year-old should have to fight that battle alone.

She'd fallen asleep trying to figure out how to approach the topic with him, and here he was.

Tansy thought back to those days. To what someone would've had to say to get *her* to admit to her sins, and the longer she thought about it, the more she realized pretty much nothing would have made her confess.

But having options would've been nice.

She pressed a kiss to the top of Jeffrey's head. "Sometimes it feels as if there are scary things around every corner."

He stiffened enough she knew he was awake and listening.

God, give her the wisdom. "Sometimes, though, if you look hard enough, you can find safe places. Safe places to hide. Safe people who want the best for you, no questions asked. People who have smiles that go all the way down to their toes."

"Puppy smiles," Jeffrey offered in a near whisper.

Tansy hesitated. "Tell me."

Jeffrey patted her hand with his. "Jinx's puppy is scary because she's a guard doggy, but she gives *me* kisses."

Perfect. His little mind had found his way to reason through this. "Yes. You know you have to do the *right* thing around her, and if you do, Dixie will give you kisses and smile at you." Tansy squeezed Jeffrey. "Anywhere you go, you need to find the people who will give you puppy smiles. Okay?"

"Okay."

He was gone the next minute. Out of her room, closing her door so quickly and quietly it was as if he'd never been there.

Tansy shot to her feet, pulling on her robe as she chased after him, but by the time she made it into the living room, the front door was closed. Outside the window, the yard light spotlighted a little boy flying across the yard back to the apartment where Melissa slept on, oblivious to the fact her son was missing.

Tansy waited until he was back in the apartment, the door closed, then she moved decisively. There was no reason to hesitate any longer.

She slipped back to the sleeping quarters and opened the door to Jake's room.

"Jake?"

Of course, that's when she finally clued in that it was only five o'clock in the morning.

"What's wrong?" Jake's question came out of the dark far more alert than she expected for having woken him.

"No emergency," Tansy assured him. "But we need to talk."

He clicked on the light beside the bed, blinking at her groggily. "Okay?"

She dropped onto the mattress beside his hip. "When I was five, my mom and dad died, and there was an aunt and uncle who took me in. I hadn't known them before, and I was still really little. So suddenly, I didn't have the people who loved me, but I had people who *said* they did, and that's where it started. Life got really confusing."

She had to give him credit. Jake went from bleary-eyed to fully awake and alert in the time it took to hear that brief confession. "Tansy? You don't need to tell me this. I mean, unless you need to tell me this, but—"

"This isn't about sharing my past in a way that's bad for me. It's about telling you for a good reason. Trust me?" she asked quietly.

He caught her fingers in his. "Absolutely."

The truth in that word made it infinitely easier to go on. "Long story short, my aunt and uncle were part of a ring of thieves. They didn't have children of their own, thank God, and they didn't really want any. But after I arrived, one of them suddenly realized how perfectly distracting a child can be. And how if you train them right, a five-year-old is small enough to fit into tiny places that offer access to big payouts."

Jake swore softly. "They made you steal?"

Tansy shrugged. "Love was conditional. So was food. They didn't often physically abuse me, but the only time I got any sort of affection was when I was *being good*. Which usually meant I had found a way to lift some item of value and get it back to them."

He pulled her close, settling her against his body, innocently cradling her tightly as if giving comfort to the child she had been. "That's all sorts of fucked up."

"I know that now, but they were very good at what they did, and it turns out so was I. It took almost five years before anyone figured it out, which meant they landed in prison and I ended up in the foster system at nine years old."

The sharp ache in her chest hit again. *Unworthy. Dirty thief.*

Tansy pushed past it. She had to. "The foster system has some issues, but overall, they try their best. The biggest problem struck because I *was* a thief. The only way I knew how to get affection was to steal. Trust me, that's not a way to endear yourself to a new family, so I got transferred a lot before the Fields adopted me."

Jake held her for a moment, stroking his fingers through her hair. "I don't want to rush past your trauma, but why are you telling me this? What's your good reason?"

"I think Melissa is doing the same thing with Jeffrey. The stealing part."

He went very still. "Christ."

"I have no solid proof, but the signs are there. Plus, there's this sense I have—I know what he's thinking because I used to do the same thing." She pushed back and met Jake's eyes. "Looking around the room, spotting purses that are accessible. Trinkets that fit into a child's pocket."

Jake paused as he considered then nodded slowly. "I know what you're saying. I can see it." Anger had replaced his initial shock.

"He trusts us," Tansy said slowly. "Maybe we can do something?"

"He really trusts *you*," Jake offered softly. "So, what do you suggest?"

There was no good route forward. "I'm not about to set Jeffrey up so we can catch him in the act."

"God, of course not. That poor kid." Jake tucked his fingers under her chin. "We'll meet with my brothers and come up with a plan, but for now, I need to hold you."

Tansy swallowed around the knot in her throat. "I'm okay, really I am."

Jake shook his head and man-handled her until she was under the covers, little spoon to his big spoon. "I'm pretty sure this is what needs to happen, even if you're okay." His lips brushed her ear. "You were very brave right now, Tansy."

"And it's not even time to wake up," she joked. Instinct again, no matter how wrong.

"*Shhh.*" He nuzzled her. "We'll find a way, okay? We'll make a difference."

"We will," Tansy repeated, flipping over to bury her face against his chest. Because the nightmares didn't have a chance of hitting with his arms holding her close.

JAKE TEXTED his family and got them gathered around the table extra early in the hopes they'd be done with their conversation before Melissa showed up on the scene. Or before she sent Jeffrey out on his own.

He hadn't messaged Jinx, but she wandered out of her room early, Dixie on her heels as usual. Jinx blinked hard as she took in the full table at not even seven a.m. and instantly made her way to Petra's side. "Trouble?"

"Some, but we got it covered. Can you get yourself together fast enough to be a casual guard on the front porch for us? Until it's time to catch the bus at least."

"Of course." The teen raced back to her room and reappeared before Petra and Tansy had finished bagging her lunch and organizing a handheld breakfast.

Jake poured everyone coffee, but no one seemed interested in anything but what he and Tansy had to say.

After sharing their suspicions with Declan, Kevin, Aiden, and Petra, the faces around the family table were the solemnest Jake had ever seen at High Water.

Once again, Tansy laid out her past, meeting everyone's eyes steadily until the very end when she let out a shaky breath.

"I don't share this often. Talking about it often brings on nightmares and negative thoughts."

"No one here will share your story," Declan assured her in his deep, quiet way. "I'm sorry you had to face that as a kid."

"Thanks."

"I'm sorry as well, and if you ever do need to talk on a professional level, please ask." Kevin paused. "I've heard of this a few times," he admitted. "From individual crimes to the whole Oliver Twist gang." He met Tansy's gaze. "To get it out there, I feel as if your story has been used in a recent psych class—all names redacted, of course. But I think I read about you."

Tansy sighed heavily but waved her hand. "It's history, and as much as I hate it, if sharing my story in a textbook or class helps other kids be spotted before they're as messed up as me, it's worth it."

"As messed up as you *were*," Petra offered quietly, her fingers squeezing around Tansy's. "You are a strong, beautiful force of nature now."

"Agreed." Jake caught Tansy's other hand. He met her gaze until she lifted her chin.

"You're all a bunch of bossy McBossyPants." Tansy wiggled her hands free. "Now that we're done with my therapy session, what are we going to do about Jeffrey?"

"Can we call in the police and see if the missing jewelry is in Melissa's possession?" Aiden asked.

"Chances are Melissa's already sold them," Jake said.

"This long after the fact, definitely sold. But even the day of, she wouldn't usually keep it on her or in her room. Unless we catch Jeffrey in the act, which we won't, there'll be little evidence." Tansy stared into space, face wiggling as she considered.

"We can phone the local pawn shops," Petra suggested.

"Maybe get back your sister's things. Plus, proof that Melissa took them in to sell."

"Possible, but she's been all over the province these past weeks. It'd be like finding a needle in a haystack," Aiden pointed out.

Jake wanted to pick Tansy up and protect her, but she'd insisted she wanted to be here, finding a solution. He spoke softly. "We need to confront Melissa."

"With no evidence?" Declan frowned. "She'll just deny it."

"She will, but if she's worried she might get caught, she'll have to be more careful going forward, and that alone might make a difference." Aiden turned the question to Tansy. "Or am I completely out in left field?"

"I really don't know," Tansy admitted. "I was only a kid when my aunt and uncle got caught, and no one ever shared the details."

"It comes back to challenging Melissa with what we know and insisting she makes the right choices for Jeffrey." Jake braced himself. "I think I need to do it."

"By yourself?" Tansy shook her head.

Declan pulled a face then looked Jake straight in the eyes. "She'll clam up completely if we all go in there, guns blazing. She might react better to just Jake."

"I don't like it," Aiden tossed out. "She's never been—" He broke off then winced slightly as he spoke to Jake. "She's got your number, bro. The divorce might have been both of you not knowing how to get along. You might have been young. Whatever the reasons were, she still had you good and convinced it was your fault for a long time."

"She did," Jake admitted.

Aiden paused then shrugged. "I don't want her to strike those nerves again. She's going to lie, and she's going to hit low. She'll probably ask for money. We need to make sure you know what to say to every possible demand she throws at you."

Including the one Jake was dreading the most. "Most likely she'll simply hightail it out of here with Jeffrey. There's nothing we can do to stop her."

"No, you're right." Declan rested his hand on Jake's shoulder. "But that doesn't mean we'll stop trying to make a difference."

Petra held up a finger. "I can make sure we know where she is at all times." She coughed lightly. "Um, I might have already planted a couple tags in her stuff, but you never heard that if the police ask, okay?"

A burst of laughter rippled around the room, exactly what they needed at that moment. Jake nodded. "There's one plan in place already."

Something hit his hand where it rested on the table. He glanced over to see Tansy pushing his journal toward him, a pen held at the ready. "This is where your skills shine. Let's make some plans."

For the next half hour they brainstormed.

They'd covered just about every scenario possible when a knock sounded and the door swung open. Jinx poked her head in. "My bus will be here in five, and Logan's on his way across the yard. Is it okay to let him in?"

"He's fine to join us." Petra slid toward the door, and Jake went with her. "Thank you. Did you have time to grab everything you need for the day?"

"I'm good." Jinx glanced at Logan who was still walking slowly toward them. "Is it Melissa?"

"Yeah, but we're dealing with her." Jake offered his hand to Jinx. "It might not seem like you did a lot, but knowing you were out here to stop interruptions helped us concentrate. Thanks."

To his surprise, Jinx ignored his hand and tucked herself in tight for a hug. "You guys take good care of me. When there are little things I can do, I want to help."

Petra hugged the girl as well then pushed her toward the road. "There's the bus. Scoot. We'll talk tonight, okay?"

"Okay. Bye Petra. Bye Jake. Hey, Logan, you're moving better today."

Logan waved at her.

"Yup, definitely better. More like a turtle than an amoeba," Jinx tossed over her shoulder. Dixie barked excitedly, racing back and forth from her to the porch.

"Just you wait. I'm going to run circles around you someday," Logan called after her before shaking his head and pausing at the bottom of the steps. "Someday that is not today or tomorrow. Morning, guys. I hit the barn this morning, but no one was around. I did the chores, but did I miss a message?"

"Just a ranch organizational meeting," Petra offered.

Jake nodded. "Thanks for doing all our jobs. I bet we can find you breakfast."

"Sounds like a plan." Logan took his time up the steps then motioned back toward the living quarters. "The kid is awake. He helped in the barn for a while, but when you didn't show up, he went back to the apartment. His mom was messing around in her car when I went by. Looks as if she might be heading out soon."

Dammit. Which meant there was no time to hesitate. "Thanks." Jake met Petra's gaze. "Guess I'm off to have a chat with Melissa."

"Okay." Petra looked worried but she nodded. "No matter what, we've got your back."

Funny how every step toward the apartment felt as if Jake's legs were made of lead. There was none of the joy he'd had a few days ago, playing with Jeffrey and taking deep breaths of the spring air.

He paused just shy of the corner of the residence complex. The doors were open on Melissa's car, and she had boxes and bags piled on the walkway outside the apartment.

She hurried to the car and tucked away a couple more items then turned and made eye contact.

The change in her expression was nearly comical. She smiled brightly, all the intense focus gone as she carelessly closed the car door and paced toward him. "Morning. I was just about to come see you. Maybe we can get a coffee in the house—"

"We'll talk here," Jake suggested.

She raised a brow at his interruption. "Well, let's go inside then. I need to listen for Jeffrey. He fell asleep again right after breakfast."

Melissa twirled on a heel and slid into his suite.

Jake took a deep breath. Maybe this wouldn't end up a shit show—but he'd have to be Suzy Fucking Sunshine to believe that bull.

Just inside the door, Jake stopped. There wasn't a single sign of food or breakfast dishes around, and he ached for Jeffrey all over again. But the kid was asleep on the couch, so that much was positive.

Melissa twirled toward him, face expectant. "What's up?"

The one part they hadn't nailed down was how to start, so Jake just went for simple and cut to the chase. "I know what you've been doing."

Her brow arched skyward. "Really? And what would that be?"

"Using your son to steal things. Small stuff, like money and things that you can sell—"

Her laughter danced around the room, completely wrong when contrasted with the tension in his gut.

"It's not funny, Mel."

The laughter stopped instantly. "But it is. What on earth are you talking about?" She shook her head. "It's a good thing you're no longer on the force, because false accusations like that could get you in a lot of trouble."

Jake folded his arms over his chest. "How have you been paying for your expenses over the past two months?"

She smiled sweetly at him. "You and your brothers were kind enough to pay for food for me and Jeffrey. Plus, I had some money saved from before I had to escape that dreadful abusive situation."

She was simply going to deny everything, just the way Declan had said she would. So be it.

Jake knew the one guaranteed way to get her talking.

Make her mad.

"You know, when you showed up, I was shocked, but there was a part of me that was glad to see you." Jake looked her over for a minute. "I'll admit it. I kept those letters of yours because I did think about you often."

Her eyes brightened. "Are you seeing the light, Jake? Interested in being with someone who would be very good for you?"

Wasn't that enough to make him nauseous? Instead, he grinned. "You're resourceful, I'll give you that. But yeah, those letters you wrote had me hooked for a long time." He stepped closer, looking down at her. "Luckily, I've realized some feelings that linger are ones we should take advantage of. Others are like mold. Toxic and gross, but they cling to us until they poison the good things in our lives. You're the latter. Dangerous, toxic, and gross."

No trace of the soft, teasing woman remained in her eyes. "What the hell?"

Jake shrugged as if he was talking about the weather. "You see, once I got to know a real woman with a heart of gold and a spine of steel, your flouncy baby ways and noxious attitude finally flipped into focus. Add in the fact you'd abuse your own kid to make your life easier? I got over you real fast, and for good."

"Fuck you, Jake Skye." Melissa slapped him, fists landing on her hips afterward as she glared daggers at him. "You don't know anything about me. What I had to deal with after you divorced me. If you'd just given me a little more time—"

Jake shot up a hand to stop her. He had notes on this reaction. "Whatever happened in your life ten years ago wasn't my fault. Not after we signed the papers and walked away from each other. Don't blame me for your bad choices."

She actually stopped for a moment, head tilting to the side as she examined him. "Okay, so it seems it's over. Thanks so much for the charity. I'll need another week to deal with—"

"No." Another point they'd covered in their family plan. This one was harder to say. "Two days, max."

"This is because of that woman, isn't it?" The face Melissa made was downright ugly. "The one you're fucking now?"

Jake glanced over, but fortunately, Jeffrey was still asleep. "This is because you've been given a gift, and you're abusing it. I suggest you think about changing your ways. I might not have proof, but I do still have contacts in the force who would willingly keep an eye on you."

Melissa waved a hand as if brushing the idea away. "No, I think this is all about Tansy. You're still in love with me but trying to prove to her that you're not. She's a paragon of virtue, isn't she? Butter wouldn't melt in her mouth."

"Watch what you say right now," Jake warned. "We've all

given you time and space to fix your shit, but adding in the probable abuse, your welcome here is officially over."

Her chin lifted. "You're throwing me out?"

"Asking you to leave. There's a difference," Jake said calmly.

"What about Jeffrey?"

Jake steeled his heart. "I hope for his sake you figure out your life and priorities." He marched to the door and yanked it open, readying his escape. "Be out of here by tomorrow—"

"You want him?"

The earth fell away at least five feet. Jake turned to stare at the woman he'd once thought he loved and tried to comprehend that she had just offered to give up her son.

That had not been one of the variables they'd planned for.

"There's a catch," she added. "I mean, he's a good kid. Handy at times, although that's not a confession you can take to your buddies on the force. Truth is, I'm not really mother material."

"Get to your damn point, Melissa. What do you want? Money?"

"That would be nice, but the other thing I want is sweeter. You can have Jeffrey. I'll sign papers saying he's all yours." She narrowed her gaze. "But not if you're with Tansy."

He was flying by the seat of his pants, but even so, the answer was clear. "Bullshit. You can't make that kind of demand."

"Watch me," she all but snarled. "Jeffrey or Tansy, you pick."

19

The rest of the family had lingered in the house, waiting to hear what Melissa had to say. As soon as Jake returned, Logan was asked to take his breakfast out onto the porch.

The kid surveyed them all then nodded sagely. "I'll just keep an eye on things, okay?"

Jake squeezed his shoulder in thanks then helped carry Logan's meal to the small table tucked into the morning sunshine.

A few minutes later, Jake was back inside, dropping the bombshell.

"She wants you to *what?*" Tansy quivered she was so mad. "Are we sure the woman is mentally stable?"

"Obviously she's not," Declan muttered.

"No sane woman offers to give up her son." Kevin shook his head. "Only proving it will be nearly impossible."

"A while ago she wanted me to sign a form that would put me on his birth certificate," Jake informed them. "Would that help at all?"

Declan cursed. "'When did that happen?"

"Shortly after she got here. She also suggested that we'd make a great family, but I shut her down." Dammit. Had he screwed up? Jake paused his pacing to demand of no one, "Should I have signed it?"

"If you're on the birth certificate she can sue you for child support," Kevin offered quietly. "I think it's set at three years of back payments right now. You want her to have the legal right to what I'm spit-balling to be over thirty thousand dollars?"

Petra whistled softly. "She'd keep Jeffrey in a shot if she could nab that kind of money. And ongoing support, I'd bet."

"That's definitely not a solution." Tansy shook her head. "I don't know how she expects to monitor keeping us apart long term, but if pretending is all it takes, we'll go along with it. Maybe it'll only be for a short while, and once she's convinced—"

"I love you." Jake's words echoed in the suddenly silent room.

Tansy's eyes widened.

Hope and pain swirled, tumbling together in the center of his heart.

"I love you, and I don't want to have to pretend that's not true." He stared at her, an awful nothingness in his soul that shouldn't be there. Not at the moment he'd confessed to a life-changing truth. He kept going because he had to. "Because I don't believe Melissa for a minute. I don't believe anything she says. No matter how much it hurts, there is no way in hell I can give you up just so she can jerk us around with false hopes and broken promises."

A brittle gasp escaped Tansy. "We can't let her leave with him. It's every nightmare I've ever had."

"Our hands are tied." Jake's hands tightened into fists, and he closed his eyes and took a deep breath before letting it out slowly. "I'll have her followed. We'll do everything we can to find a way, but it can't be by having to endure her in our lives, in person or dictating our behaviour from afar."

Tires squealed in the background as Jake wrapped his arms around Tansy.

They all turned. The front door opened and Logan leaned in. "Hey, guys? Melissa just left. She didn't look happy."

"Dammit." Declan paced toward the door. "I'll go see if she left anything in the apartment."

Jake ignored the rest of the chaos and focused on Tansy. He lifted her chin and examined her tear-filled eyes. "I'm sorry. We couldn't just take him."

"I know we couldn't, but that doesn't make it any less heartbreaking," she whispered back. "For you as well as me, yes?"

"Yeah." The knot in Jake's throat was the size of grapefruit. "I mean it though. I can't give you up."

Tansy's face twisted as she fought back tears. "I love you too."

He pulled her against him, limbs tangled together as they stood there, hearts breaking. Fear for Jeffrey and what Melissa might decide to do was a nearly tangible thing, and hopelessness was a weight pressing on Jake's chest.

But this other part—falling in love with an amazing, kind, and beautiful woman—this was the seed of hope he needed to push toward the light.

He tugged Tansy with him out of the living room and into her bedroom, looking for privacy. Twirling her, he dropped into the loveseat with her in his lap. Arms tight around her torso, he rested his chin on the top of her head.

Tansy burrowed in and clung even harder. She rocked lightly, and his shirt grew wet with her tears.

"I'm so sorry, Tans. I'm so sorry."

She sucked for air, wiggling back to stare at him with eyes full of moisture. "Me, too." She pressed her palms to his cheeks. "It's lousy timing because inside it feels as if I just got tossed in a frozen lake, but you get some major spontaneity points for what you said out there."

He caught her fingers and pressed them to his chest. "I'm frozen right now, as well, but I'm serious about being in love with you. I should have said something sooner—" He laughed softly. "For once I can honestly say it wasn't because I had big plans of how I wanted to tell you. I was just being a dumbass cowboy, struggling to figure out what this need in my heart meant. It's definitely love."

"I know. Me too." She sniffed, lips quivering. "I'm really happy right now, even though it doesn't look like it."

"I get it." Jake took a deep breath. "Good thing humans are complicated creatures and we can be devastated and glad at the same time."

"We'll find a way to save him."

It wasn't a question, so Jake nodded. "Somehow. I know she took off, but I'll reach out to my contacts so they're on the alert. Petra will do her tracking magic, and we'll make sure we know exactly where Melissa is at all times." It wasn't one hundred percent certain, but he had his suspicions about another matter. "I don't think she'll try to take advantage of Jeffrey in the next while. She'll be scared someone is watching her."

"Good." Tansy wilted against him. "We need to get our brains to aim at the next thing. Or at least I do, otherwise, I'll start spiraling."

"Then we do the next thing." Jake stroked her back gently. "Need me to make a list of possible activities not remotely related to our current situation? And I hope that doesn't sound glib or make light of what just happened—"

"Of course not." She let out a sigh that echoed off the wall.

"I just admitted I need distraction, so I suppose this is as good a time as any to warn you I set up a surprise birthday party for you for tonight."

Christ. With everything that had happened that morning, he'd completely forgotten. "Oh. It's my birthday."

"Yeah." Tansy wiggled until she was sitting next to him, hands still tightly connected. "I didn't organize anything elaborate. It's not really a jump-out-of-the-cake surprise event, just a few people gathering in the barn and by the firepit. But all things considered, I figured you should know what's up."

"Thanks for that. Yeah, being prepared is better today, although I am working hard on my Boy Scout spontaneity badge." Jake brushed his lips over hers. "You okay rejoining the family and making plans?"

"Okay." She rested her forehead against his. "I love you."

"That sounds really nice," he offered softly.

Tansy snorted. "Excellent, but try again."

A smile arrived far easier than he'd imagined. "I love you, Tansy Fields."

"Good." Her lips twitched upward. "Let's go make plans."

MELISSA HAD LEFT A NOTE.

If I get harassed by the police, I'll deny everything and you'll never see us again. If you're good, I'll be in touch. Be ready to make a choice.

It wasn't much to go on, but they all kicked into action mode. Petra set up her tracking grid, and Jake contacted the couple of friends still in the force he promised could be relied on to be more than discreet.

Tansy pulled herself together and tried her best to figure out how to balance the sheer joy in her head and the painful, stabbing pain in her heart.

Pulling together food for the birthday celebration helped. There was comfort in the familiar, although far too many people hovered nearby, ready to offer her a hand or a random hug. Far too much support for her to spiral.

That night as the barn rang with music, and friends from the community danced around them, Tansy slipped into Jake's arms and hoped.

He held her, swaying together in an easy intimate embrace.

Tansy glanced around at the contented gathering. "One task done. Which means I can now make some major plans."

He raised a brow. "Going for your master's degree in planning?"

"Absolutely. I've had this great instructor during my exchange program." She stole her hand from where it had rested on his hip and lifted a finger with each comment. "First, Petra, Sydney, and I are fumigating your apartment tomorrow."

Utter confusion flashed before something she swore was disappointment rushed in. "Okay, I think? Does that mean I'm getting kicked out from where I'm sleeping now?"

"Yes. That's point two on the agenda." She lifted another finger. "Grab your stuff and join me in my room. The apartment is bigger, but I'd like to stay in the house because it makes things simpler for cooking without bothering others, and someone still needs to live there to supervise Jinx and any women ranch hands who show up."

His lips curled the slightest bit. "Are you asking me to move in with you?"

"Yup." She made the *p* pop with a great deal of satisfaction. "That's what I hear people in love do, and I'm not letting anyone muck that up for us."

"Good." Jake grinned and twirled her. "Then why cleanse the apartment? And what do you plan?"

"At some point, someone will stay in that space. The girls are coming over with candles, and we're getting the negative vibes out of there before the bad juju messes with the entire ranch."

"Candles have that sort of power?"

Tansy poked him in the chest. "Go with the flow. It's more about the ritual than anything else, but Petra promises it will help."

He twirled her then, holding her tight. "I'm on board."

That night Jake took less than fifteen minutes to move his stuff into her room, and a good solid hour to tease and tempt and kiss every part of her until there was no room for worrying or nightmares. No room for anything but pleasure and the promise of a future with him.

Even after the heavy breathing was done and bonelessness had set in, Jake made sure to cuddle her in tight. "You wake up and need me, I'm here, okay?"

"We both don't have to be awake if I have a nightmare," Tansy informed him, the heat of his chest to her back and the still racing endorphins making her eyelids droop.

"People in love are willing to give up a little sleep," he informed her. "Or so I hear."

Tansy linked her fingers through his where they rested on her belly. "Okay."

The nightmares didn't dare come close.

Post breakfast, Tansy hauled Jake out to his apartment. Sydney was already there, along with Declan. Petra arrived a minute later, dragging Aiden with her.

"Are we in a rush?" Aiden asked, amusement on his face.

"No, I just like pulling you places," Petra admitted.

Tansy snickered then gestured them in the door.

One glance was enough to confirm the apartment had already been cleaned. Petra had said it was good to go, but with her food prep demands, Tansy hadn't had time to get out to check.

"When did someone deal with the place?" Jake asked.

"I did it yesterday afternoon," Declan said quietly. "Figured it needed to be done sooner than later for a bunch of reasons."

"And that was without knowing about the uncursing. Good job, Deck," Sydney offered.

Aiden raised a brow. "Uncursing?"

"I know, strong words, but I believe people leave energies in a place, and we have better things to focus on than running into that person's shitty aura." Sydney frowned at Declan. "What?"

He shrugged. "You're a doctor. I didn't expect to hear you talk about auras and energies."

"I'm a well-rounded doctor," she said with attitude. "Deal with it."

"On that note, here are your candles." Petra stepped forward and handed each of them a paper bag. "Jake, it's your room, so you get the master candle, and we'll light ours off yours."

"This is not my typical morning, but I appreciate the sentiment." Jake took the tall candle she held out to him. "Thanks."

"Always."

He glanced down and read the note attached to the taper out loud. "*One Fuck Left (and It's on Fire).*" He glanced at Tansy. "This is one of *those* kinds of fumigations, is it?"

"Petra's in charge. I'm just along for the ride," Tansy said with a grin.

It might have been somewhat inappropriate, but having the people who meant the most to her and to Jake there made it hugely meaningful. Especially as everyone attempted to solemnly read their candle labels and slowly failed more and more hysterically.

Laughter was therapeutic, right?

Aiden's candle read *Sometimes You Have to Take It One 'Are You Fucking Kidding Me?' at a Time.*

Petra made direct eye contact with Jake then announced, *"Some People Just Need a High Five in the Face."*

When Sydney read, *I Will Gladly Tittiepunch a Ho for You,* Declan choked briefly. He waved them on. "Sorry. That was a little on the nose."

"Wasn't it?" Sydney offered in her best Disney princess voice.

Before reading hers, Tansy nodded slowly. "I like this, and it goes well with yours, Jake. *May the Bridges I Burn Light the Way.*"

"Nice." Jake nodded. "Very appropriate."

Declan was the last to go. He raised a brow as he lit his candle and intoned, "*I Cleanse this Room of Your Negativity.*"

Huh. Tansy glanced at Petra. "That was boring."

"Not the candle I bought." Petra glanced at Sydney then rolled her eyes. "Never mind. Last thing, carry your candle to your assigned part of the apartment."

Tansy carried hers into the bedroom, standing where she could still see Jake where he remained as the hub of the candle spoke. The teeny light of the candles bounced off the walls as every corner of the apartment got hit by very profane sentiments.

The event was somewhat childish if she'd had to describe what they were doing, but at the same time, warmth radiated through her. Friendship and family, all doing their best to find the good and move toward the light.

One fucking candle at a time.

It was almost anticlimactic when he finally got the text. For two weeks, Jake had silently stewed and tried not to obsess so that he could help the rest of the family, and especially Tansy, deal with their uncertainty.

When the notification showed up, Aiden was the only one near at hand. The two of them huddled together over the phone and hoped Melissa had come to her senses.

That faint hope was dashed pretty damn quickly.

> Melissa: Hello, darling. Miss me?

> Jake: What do you want? Get to the point.

> Melissa: Such a bad attitude. Don't you remember that saying about catching more flies with honey?

> Jake: If you don't have anything to say to me regarding Jeffrey, goodbye, Melissa.

> Melissa: Still a stick up your ass. Fine. I gave it a lot of thought, and you're right. There's nothing to say you'll keep away from that woman a second longer than you have to, so I'll accept a show of you humiliating yourself and her. Your precious new town holds an auction every year. Sign up for it.

For a moment, Jake truly had no idea what she was talking about. "An auction? What auction?" he demanded.

"For fuck's sake." Aiden shook his head. "The town fundraiser on Canada Day. We arrived after it happened last summer, but someone has to have told you about it."

He didn't have a clue. "What auction? Do I need to sell my truck?"

Another curse rang from his brother before Aiden caught

him by the shoulders and forced him to stop pacing. "It's a *bachelor* auction. You offer a date to the highest bidder. It's somehow all rated PG, but it's real."

"There are far worse things she could have asked for," Jake muttered.

Aiden raised his hand. "If you want to sign up, you'd have to not be dating Tansy. As in, you'll have to convince the *organizers* that you're not dating Tansy, or they won't let you in."

Jake's stomach dropped at the warning in his brother's eyes. "Who are the organizers?"

Aiden made a face. "Malachi Fields. And I heard Chance Gabrielle say he was involved this year."

Great. Fucking great. Tansy's dad and her future brother-in-law.

Jake met Aiden's gaze. "I know Tansy will be good with telling her father what's going on, so he at least wouldn't kill me. But we can't tell anyone else, like her mom or her sisters, because at some point we risk everyone finding out and Melissa running before we find a solution."

"Which means you're about to have at least ninety-five percent of Heart Falls pissed at you." Aiden nodded. "Yeah, that's pretty much what I see as well."

It still really wasn't a choice. "If there's even a chance this will work, I have to do it." He turned back to his phone.

Jake: Fine. I'll sign up. What then?

Melissa: If I see you get sold off to someone other than her, I'll consider dropping my problem on you permanently.

Of course she'd have figured to add that twisted demand.

Jake: How do I know you'll keep your word?

Melissa: Don't you trust me, sugar bear? Oh, I guess not. Too bad. That's the deal.

Jake: Take care of Jeffrey. That's all I ask.

Melissa: Your move. I'll be in touch—

Jake and Aiden stood in silence, staring at his phone. Impossible. What a goddamned mess.

Aiden scuffed a foot on the ground. "You know if you do this, chances are she'll say *fuck you* and just keep jerking you around for a long time to come."

"She might, but she also might decide she'll be happier not having to care for a child." Jake breathed out so long and slow his head spun. "I have to take the risk. For Jeffrey's sake. And for Tansy's."

20

Tansy had a decidedly uncomfortable two weeks heading into the Canada Day weekend.

The frustration started with the meetup with her dad. She and Jake joined him out by the firepit at High Water, hoping for less eyes around than if they showed up at the bookstore or her parents' house.

Her father listened to their entire story without interrupting then shook his head. "This could all end really badly," he warned.

"It could, but even a slight chance of success means we have to take it." Jake motioned to her. "I wouldn't do it if Tansy said this wasn't what she wanted as well, but we're both on board. We just hope that you'll understand and help as much as you can."

"Oh, I understand, and I approve. To be honest, this is exactly the type of thing I expect from my girls." His wry smile took them both in. "Courage is knowing something might hurt and doing it anyway."

"Stupidity is the same thing," Tansy punted back.

"True." Malachi patted her hand gently. "And this is why life is hard."

Jake snorted so violently he choked. "Sorry."

Malachi's expression softened. "I won't give it away, which means I apologize now for the dirty looks I might have to give you. And the dirty looks you will absolutely get from Sophie and the girls. And their grandmother."

"I get it," Jake said. "Just as long as in the end you know the truth and can vouch for me, I hope that will make the difference down the road."

Her dad examined Jake again. "Sounds as if you plan on being around for the long term."

Jake turned to Tansy as he answered and made her heart go pitter-patter at the expression in his eyes. "As I was informed by a very smart and wonderful woman, sticking around is what people in love do."

Love. It was there in his touch. In every glance in her direction.

That's what made it easier to focus on the good parts.

She had five full days of cooking for a weeklong booking that kept her brain more than busy. Jake was there at High Water ranch house every morning, noon, and night. Whenever he could, he passed through the house and offered a kiss or a wildflower or something that made her smile.

"You're spoiling me," she informed him when he brought out the massage oil and gave her a very satisfying rub down in the hour break she had between prepping breakfast and lunch for the crew in the art studio.

"Getting to have my hands all over you?" Jake leaned down to make eye contact where she was sprawled on the bed. "Not much of a sacrifice, Tans."

She eyed the tent in the front of his jeans. "You're into pain and suffering? Because there's no time to deal with that."

Jake rubbed a hand over himself, grinning as he watched her dress. "Nothing saying I won't go deal with it myself."

A shiver raced up her spine. The image of him in the shower, hand stroking his hard length, made her whimper. "That's mean."

"You can watch," he offered. "Or I can tell you about it later."

Revenge was served when she tormented him that night by doing a striptease and not letting him touch. He was swearing slow and steady by the time she crawled over him and settled onto his hard length with a happy sigh.

Yeah, the sex was great, and a good distraction because the other part of her brain never forgot that somewhere out there, Jeffrey still didn't know he had lots of people in his court.

That courage her dad had mentioned? She needed a boatload of it as she pushed through the doors of the community center on Canada Day and headed for the bachelor auction.

Not that she intended to bid on anyone, but they all thought it was important she was there in case Melissa somehow had tapped into the town rumor mill.

Tansy didn't intend to play any games this year, not the way she usually did. In spite of the messed up situation, a hint of amusement trickled in. Of course. For the first time, it wouldn't be only her father she could torment, and here she was, on her best behaviour.

All the familiar faces were there, with families gathered around the long tables. She'd come too late for the potluck meal —feeling sorry for herself had really cut a hunk of time out of her morning. Plus, she didn't need to do another round of explaining where Jake was without outright lying.

But now she was here, and ready to support her community the way she always did. Even though she wouldn't buy any bachelor, she'd still donate to the fund. Because that's what community-minded people did. And she was a positive, glowingly wonderful part of this community, and they were damn lucky to have her.

She'd just focus on those parts of her life instead of worrying what twisted bombs Melissa would drop on them next.

Rose waved at her.

Tansy marched over with her head held high and settled into the chair saved for her between Rose and Fern.

"Is Chance excited about today?" Tansy asked.

"Quivering," Rose informed her. "If he gets much more excited, no one will be able to understand a word he says. His brogue gets really thick when he's flustered."

Fern offered a tight smile. "Even if they don't understand him, you know the girls will still go gaga. Everyone loves an accent."

Their little sister seemed extraordinarily out of sorts. Tansy eyed her for a moment. "Are you okay?"

Fern raised a brow. "Are you?"

Low blow. Tansy made a face. "No, but I will be."

Her far too honest response seemed to deflate Fern's sails. She stared for a moment then dipped her chin once. "Yeah. I guess I will be too."

There it was again. She'd been so consumed by her own problems she'd missed the signs that something was definitely up with Fern. Before Tansy could interrogate her, though, their father's voice rang over the loudspeaker.

"We meet again, Heart Falls. And I for one couldn't be more delighted." Relaxed and immaculate as always, Malachi waved as he walked across the stage, microphone in hand.

"Wasn't that the most delicious lunch? Many thanks to the hands that prepared it. Including a loud round of applause for Marina Ray, and Buns and Roses, for continuing the tradition of providing pies for this event, even though it is no longer my daughter at the helm."

"Yeah, Tansy," someone shouted from the back of the room.

Malachi grinned. "Yeah, indeed. Which is a good introduction for the next thing I need to inform you of. Considering how many years I've been doing this, and all the excess excitement I've had to deal with—*cough*, Tansy, *cough*—I've decided it's time to begin training my replacement."

A huge roar of protest shook the auditorium.

Tansy exchanged amused glances with her sisters.

"You knew he would milk this for everything he was worth," Rose said.

"Which makes it so tempting to be naughty," Tansy returned, even though she really didn't have the heart for it this time.

Damn Melissa to hell. Jake was supposed to be here, sitting by Tansy's side in the audience. He was supposed to be her reason to not bid on the bachelors. He was supposed to be here because they *meant* something to each other, and they wanted to shout it to the rafters.

It was a small sacrifice if it meant Jeffrey got a second chance, but it gave Tansy another reason to be royally pissed at the woman.

Up on the stage, her father continued with great enthusiasm. "Now, now. I don't plan to vanish on you, but I figure it's a good idea to train someone before it's necessary. I couldn't be more delighted to be able to introduce to you someone you already know and love. My future son-in-law, Chance Gabrielle."

Chance walked forward from the back of the stage, his bespoke three-piece suit cut to his frame like perfection.

"Holy shit, sis. You got yourself a looker," Tansy said with approval.

"He's dreamy," Rose said with a sigh. "I'm a lucky woman."

Fern sighed as well. "I'm happy for you."

Tansy glanced over again, highly suspicious. Fern was not a sigher or a moaner. Fern was a do-er. "You and I are having a talk real soon," she said quietly.

Her little sister blinked. "Don't worry about me. I'll figure it out."

"Thank you for that welcome," Chance said from the stage. "I'm delighted to be here today to uphold the high honour of this position. Mr. Fields has done a marvelous job keeping you entertained and on the straight and narrow, and while I can't promise to do either of them nearly as well as he, I think we'll have ourselves a bloody fine time." Chance surveyed the audience until his gaze landed on Rose. "I have good memories of this event in my own right. I look forward to possibly shepherding more couples to their happily-ever-afters. And if not that, at least to a good date and some money raised for our community."

Malachi stepped back slightly, approval written all over him as Chance continued.

"This year the money goes to the women's shelter in Diamond Valley and to the care baskets for any new bairns in our community." Chance paused and smiled over the audience. "I know you're eager to meet this year's bachelors. We've got a lovely crop for you to enjoy. Shall we meet them now?"

A cheer rose.

Behind Chance, the curtain that normally would've swept open to reveal the bachelors seated nervously in a long row remained sealed shut. Someone was jerking on the cable, but nothing moved more than a quiver.

Malachi held up a hand. "Small technical difficulties. One minute."

Tansy's phone vibrated in her pocket, and she absently fished it out as her father slipped behind the curtain.

Chance smiled at the crowd. "Starting me off with a challenge, are you? No matter. We'll get you the bachelors in short enough order."

Malachi poked his head through the curtain. "It's stuck. I'll send them out one at a time."

In the pause, Tansy took a quick glance at her phone screen, and her smile froze on her lips.

> Melissa: I'm at the Heart Falls lookout. You want Jeffrey? Come get him. Just you, or no deal.

Holy crap. Tansy's legs moved before her brain registered what was going on. Only as she stood and prepared to leave, the curtain fluttered, and cheering began as one long jean clad leg after another slipped into view.

Jake stepped onto the stage. He handed a card to Chance then stood to the side, arms folded resolutely over his chest.

Completely caught unaware, Chance glanced between Jake's oh-so-familiar face and where Tansy stood next to Rose.

The clapping died down, and a bit of whispering rose on the air.

Rose caught Tansy by the hand. "Sit," she murmured. "We're here for you."

No, Tansy needed to leave, but right now? When all attention was firmly on her? Not a good idea. She reluctantly lowered herself back to the folding chair.

Chance raised his hand in the air to get everyone's

attention, although it wasn't as if he needed it. People were fixated on what was about to happen. "First bachelor for auction this afternoon is a relative newcomer to the community. But then again I've been told if you haven't lived here for twenty years, you're a relative newcomer. Please give a warm welcome to Jake Skye."

Applause rang out, and more than a few heads turned in Tansy's direction as she resolutely kept a smile on her face. She deliberately didn't meet Jake's gaze, but instead focused intently on Chance. Willing him to move quickly to get this over as soon as possible.

As if he'd heard her thoughts, Chance cleared his throat. "We should get started because we have a lot more gentlemen waiting trapped on the other side of that curtain. Don't know what might happen if we keep them in the dark for too long, so do I have any bids from the audience?"

At the side of the stage, one of the old-timers stood. Over seventy, with a long white beard that hung to his chest, Martin Fogell wore his ever-present overalls, albeit they *were* a clean pair today.

"I'll start it off." Martin ignored the good-natured laughter and shook his finger at the nearest table. "None of that. Not bidding for me, although I could use someone strong to help me clean an old outbuilding. No, I'm in charge of the pre-set offers. There's a set bid of fifty dollars offered for the first bachelor."

No.

No, *no, no.* Tansy's smile barely clung to her lips, and her stomach was somewhere in the vicinity of her feet. She'd completely forgotten about this particular bit of pre-planned mischief. She'd set this up ages ago, like last fall, well before she and Jake had gotten together.

Martin pulled out a sheet of paper and read carefully.

"Says here *Time to get things rolling,* and the fifty bucks is offered by Tansy Fields."

If she thought the rafters had shaken before, now she was nearly deafened by the shouts of surprise. Only for a moment, though, before utter silence fell.

Chance glanced around the room in shock at the strange response. "Well now, that's a fine first bid. Do I hear fifty-five? Fifty-five for this fine bachelor who says..." He lifted the information card in front of him. "He's highly skilled in planning and organization. So if you want to organize your shed, Martin, he's willing to help."

Usually that sort of a straight line would've provoked some innuendo. Instead, there was nothing but a hushed buzz. Only now there were smiles as well, and a shifting of shoulders as people glanced around the room, ping-ponging between Tansy and Jake.

Then the murmuring rose in volume.

"Not falling for it."

"She's only going to bid us up," someone else said.

"Nice try, Tansy. Won't work this time."

Every comment was accompanied by a wink or a wave or a smile from people who were loving the drama of the moment.

For fuck's sake.

All those years of having a marvelous time messing with bidders at the bachelor auction was coming back to bite her. All around the room it was clear that everybody thought this was a set up. No one believed she and Jake had actually called it off.

All of Heart Falls appeared to believe they were in it together, and that this was simply another ploy to raise money.

Tansy lifted her gaze to Jake's. She didn't know what was worse. The fact that she had somehow accidentally bid on the man she loved exactly when she needed *not* to bid, or that everyone around them thought she was trying to pull a fast one.

All she wanted was for this to be over and Jeffrey to be safe.

"Come now. Do I have any other bids?"

Tansy couldn't take it anymore. Social media would have this sale posted in seconds flat. Maybe if she got to the falls quick enough, she could explain the mix up to Melissa. Maybe it wasn't too late.

"I need to run. Take care of the bill for me, and I'll explain later." She forced a smile on her face, squeezed Rose's hand, then slipped from the hall without a word.

21

Watching Tansy leave the hall was the worst sort of torture, and suddenly, Jake couldn't deal with the lies anymore.

"Tansy—" he called, but the door slipped closed as he finished. "I love you."

If he thought the crowd had offered a roar earlier, now they were a raging storm. Heads turned and there were smiles and shouting and waving hands as everyone told their neighbour what had just happened at high volume.

The entire floor of the hall turned into bedlam.

Malachi Fields stepped next to Jake. "You hanging out here for any particular reason, son?"

"That's not—"

"Explain later." Malachi gestured for him to get a move on. "I know my daughter. When she's hightailing it like that, you'd better catch her sooner than later."

Thank God. Jake jumped off the stage and headed through the chairs for the exit door Tansy had escaped through.

Behind him, Malachi must have gotten to the microphone, because as Jake struggled forward, Malachi's booming laugh rang out, comforting and contagious at the same time. "That's a twist I never saw coming. Never thought your first day on the job would be this exciting, did you, Chance?"

Behind him, Chance responded. "No, sir. Seems as if we have one bachelor in a hurry to collect his date. Let's get him out of here as quick as we can, shall we?"

Thank God Chance had said something, because it seemed the crowd had all leaned into Jake's path instead of out of the way.

"Misunderstanding," Jake shouted, not caring how foolish it made him seem. "I love her."

"Then go get her."

One of the men in the crowd leapt to his feet and threw a fist into the air. "Don't mess this up, man."

"Tansy deserves the best," someone else called.

"I love her," Jake repeated, still fighting his way toward the door.

"Tell her, not us," some card in the far corner of the hall shouted.

"Tansy rocks," another voice cried, and the sentiment was greeted with applause and cheering.

If he wasn't trying to get away as fast as possible, Jake would have found it rather enchanting to know exactly how many people were Team Tansy.

He tried calling her phone the entire way to the ranch but kept being sent to her voice mail. "Dammit, Tans. Making it harder to find you than usual isn't nice."

Fine, he'd start with logic. Home first.

Dust flew as he braked in front of the main house. There was no sign of her SUV, but he still hurried out just in case.

A note fluttered on the front door of the High Water ranch house.

I don't feel safe here anymore. That Tansy is nothing but trouble, so before she does something to hurt me, I need to get away. I don't know where I'm headed yet, so I'll leave Jeffrey with you for now. Take care of our baby for me, darling, until I find a way to come back to you both.

XOX Melissa

Shit. Melissa had been at the house? Was that why Tansy had left?

He tried the door, but it was locked. He raced over to the apartment Melissa had used, but it too was shut up tight.

He stood in the yard and tried to call Tansy again as Petra and Aiden pulled up to the porch, poured out of their truck, and raced toward him.

"We got here as fast as we could. Is Tansy here?"

"No sign yet, but Melissa was." Jake handed his brother the note.

Aiden swore softly. "She's clearly out of her mind."

"Oh, she knows exactly what she's doing. She's setting up an alibi for down the road when she returns and claims to have been doing the best thing for her son." The chill from the frozen spot in the middle of Jake's chest seeped into his words. "Where's Jeffrey?"

"The barn?" Aiden turned to Petra. "Can you track Melissa? Or Tansy?"

"How about both? I'm on it." Petra had her phone out, fingers flying.

Jake and Aiden raced for the barn. "Declan wasn't at the

auction. He should be here," Aiden said breathlessly as they pushed through the door.

"Shit." Jake shot toward the crumpled form lying on the ground outside one of the horse stalls. He rolled his brother carefully, cursing harder as blood slicked his fingers.

But Declan's eyes fluttered open and he swore softly. "Fucking Melissa."

That answered that question. "Sorry, bro. We'll get you fixed up, but do you know where Jeffrey is?" Jake demanded.

His brother shuffled to a sitting position, one hand cradling the lump on his head as he pointed. "He was there. Standing at the end of the hall. I came out of the stall and he was there, but when I went toward him, Melissa must have brained me. The last thing I remember is his face."

"Jeffrey's?"

"Yeah." Declan pulled his hand from his head and examined the blood. "The kid was pissed, and I don't mean at me."

"Good. Maybe—"

"Jake, I got a bead on Tansy," Petra shouted from where she hung on the barn door. "And the she-witch. They're both at the Heart Falls lookout."

Christ. "Come on, Deck. We'll get you to the house—"

His brother waved him off. "I have my phone. I'll message Sydney to come rescue me. Go find Tansy. She needs you right now."

Jake squeezed Declan's shoulder then hightailed it for the truck, Petra and Aiden on his heels.

Minutes earlier...

Speeding at the maximum allowable before the RCMP would pull her over, Tansy put all her attention on keeping ZenBaby on the road. It had been a long winter and a busy spring, and her poor SUV needed a tune up in the worst way possible. She'd kept putting it off, and now she was regretting it with every fiber of her soul.

At least the dangerous trip kept her mind on the road and not on the crazy she was headed to meet. Leaving when she had might have been foolish, but she didn't see any other way around it.

Ten minutes later, when her phone started going off with a series of text messages from Jake and Petra, followed by insistent phone calls, she ignored all of it, both for safety's sake and so she didn't cave and tell them exactly how foolish she was being.

Besides, she was nearly there. Nothing anyone could do to stop her at this point.

The final turns up the forestry service road to the lookout were extra tricky, and the undercarriage seemed to shimmy harder than usual. Tansy fought with the wheel and finally convinced it to head in the right direction.

At the top of the hill, the road leveled out to a slight incline instead of the steep slope it had been to that point. Melissa's familiar black car was parked past the usual pullover spot, nose down toward arriving traffic.

Tansy manoeuvered to the left, off the road and facing uphill. Hand brake on, wheels locked. God, she hoped the beast didn't decide to give up the ghost right now.

As she slipped from ZenBaby and approached the other car, Melissa stepped into view. She snatched Jeffrey off the ground and balanced him on a hip, and the plan Tansy had to rush the other woman vanished. They were too close to the escarpment on the eastern road edge, and Tansy knew

Melissa would drop Jeffrey in an instant to save her own skin.

Melissa grabbed a tire iron out of the open trunk of her car. Great. That was a potential problem.

Still, it was time to focus on the part she was in control of. Tansy was close enough now to check Jeffrey. "Hey, kiddo."

"Don't talk to him," Melissa ordered. "Throw your phone over the edge."

Tansy sighed. "Really? That sucks. I just put a new case on it. Also, not very environmentally friendly."

The other woman's nostrils flared, but she held onto her anger by a thread. She waited until Tansy had done as ordered before speaking again. "Here's the deal. I'll leave Jeffrey with Jake if you get in the trunk of my car."

What the hell? It wasn't much of a threat—not in Tansy's books. Trunks could be gotten out of fairly easily. "You're not serious."

Melissa raised a brow. "Either you get in, or I throw him in and leave for good. Which will it be?"

Maybe trying to overpower Melissa was worth the risk, but fear Jeffrey would get hurt held Tansy back. Whatever else happened, the kiddo needed to have the chance for a better life. That couldn't start with him in the trunk, vanishing from Heart Falls.

Good thing she and the little tyke were both thieves and sneaks. They spoke the same language.

Tansy looked Jeffrey straight in the eye. "People who don't make Dixie smile get something else, don't they?"

Her attention elsewhere, Tansy couldn't move fast enough to dodge. Melissa had dropped the iron and slapped her hard with an open palm. "Stop spewing nonsense and get in the damn trunk."

Climbing into the enclosed space wasn't an ideal situation,

but then again, Tansy had some options not available to the average person. She knew better than most how to get out of a trunk, so while it was a bad idea, it was better than any of her other current options.

In fact, it was one way to guarantee Tansy could get the jump on Melissa.

Tansy made eye contact with Jeffrey again. The kiddo was tight-lipped, with eyes wide as saucers, but he was also hyper-focused.

"No puppy smiles," he whispered, and Tansy bared her teeth in her best Dixie impression.

"Shut up," Melissa ordered, shaking Jeffrey as she stepped closer to the car.

"Cool your jets, I'm going," Tansy offered, setting a foot into the back. She needed to move fast and smart and not leave her fingers in vulnerable positions. Just in case Melissa slammed the trunk shut before Tansy was all the way in.

She'd barely ducked her head when the lid crashed closed.

A second later, Melissa screamed. A thump sounded, followed by a scramble of rocks.

Cursing rang for a full minute before Melissa got herself together. "What the hell? The little asshole bit me."

Good for Jeffrey. Tansy hoped he escaped along the path to the lake. There were a ton of places for someone with his skills to hide along the way, and it was a warm enough day. He'd be safe until Jake came and found him.

"You taught him to have that shitty attitude. Fine, Jake can have him, but he can't have you as well."

"Someone needs to up her meds," Tansy sang out. She peered around for the emergency trunk latch releases. The car was new enough it had to have them. Somewhere close to her should be a glow-in-the-dark latch.

"*Bitch.*" Overhead, metal rang like a kettle drum as Melissa slammed something on the trunk. The tire iron? "You messed everything up."

"Tell me about it. Oh, wait, maybe don't. You're nothing but a liar, and a thief, and far too stupid to have any sort of long-term plan. Do you even know your right hand from your left? Crazy bitch."

Crude insults, and not very politically correct, but Jake had said a mad Melissa made unwise choices. Maybe she'd get close enough Tansy could open the trunk suddenly and smack her in the face.

Maybe she'd stand there beating on the metal until the cops arrived. Because by now Jake had to be looking for Tansy, which meant Petra as well, and there was no way her bestie didn't have some kind of tracker to follow.

"Fuck you," Melissa screamed, "I was *brilliant*. You ever wonder how I knew where to find him? I sent Jake a bunch of letters. I'd lost track of him and had no idea where he was anymore other than southern Alberta, and for some reason, his past employers wouldn't give me his forwarding address."

Because you're clearly not mentally stable? Which didn't matter at this point because as long as Melissa kept talking, she wasn't going after Jeffrey. Tansy spotted the glowing catch release for the trunk. One problem solved. "How does that mean you showed up on his doorstep?"

"He answered back." Melissa gloated. "I sent one letter a month until I got a response. That narrowed it down to two different towns, and as soon as I got here, people were more than happy to talk about the gorgeous Skye brothers and them taking over the animal rescue and running their retreat house. Ad nauseum."

Mentally unstable, but slightly smart. Tansy clapped slowly then went back to feeling for the other release that should be close, just as a backup. "Well done. You could get a job with the police force, except for the fact you're a thieving, cheating, psycho bitch."

The screaming that followed was drowned out by the deafening volume of Melissa beating the hell out of the trunk with the tire iron. With every blow, the metal over Tansy's head dented more until she figured it was possible the trunk latch would no longer open.

Tansy gritted her teeth against the racket, adjusted position, and found the second release pull. The one that when she decided to tug it, half the back seat would flip down and let her access the passenger space.

If Melissa took off now, getting access to attack her directly would be risky but still the safest possible solution. Surviving a car going off the road, especially if Tansy could time her escape to be in town when they were at lower speeds, was far better than whatever the hell else the woman had in mind.

The banging stopped and quiet fell, but Tansy's ears still rang as she listened for a clue of what Melissa was doing. Headed to the driver's door? Heading out to find Jeffrey?

If Mellissa walked away from the car, Tansy could be after her in seconds.

But what she heard was a low, menacing laugh. "You know what else? I went to your cheesy little café. Found out all about the Heart Falls lookout. How this is where sweethearts often meet. I figured you came here sometime with Jake, so this is where you get to stay. Maybe they'll put up stuffed animals in memoriam for you."

The car rocked suddenly then slowly began to roll.

"You should have left him alone," Melissa taunted. "He's mine."

Crap. The nose of the car had been pointed down the hill toward the sharp U-turn corner. The only things at the edge of the road were rosebushes and scraggy little trees. Beyond that, it was a cliff all the way down to the heart-shaped pool at the base of the falls.

The car picked up momentum, rocks under the tires loud as Tansy scrambled to free herself. She jerked the glow-in-the-dark release cord.

Nothing happened.

22

———

on't panic. Don't panic.

Easy to think, tough to follow through. The car bounced slowly over the rocky road, and even as Tansy switched gears and pulled the seat latch, she was picturing the cliff edge.

How far away was she?

She scrambled through the opening into the back seat and all but dove for the front. There were too many types of door latches and locks for her to know for sure she could get out of the backseat in seconds, but she could do this much.

Brakes were brakes in all vehicles.

She rolled over the top of the back rest and sprawled into the driver's seat, foot extended to stop her forward motion as quickly as possible.

A gasp of relief escaped as the pedal depressed and Tansy finally had a second to breathe and look out the window.

The hood of the car was maybe five feet from the edge, a whole lot of open air right beyond it. God. Tansy pressed her hand to her chest to try to stop the pounding—

"*Nooooo.*"

Tansy whipped her head around to discover Melissa running at high speed toward her. "Shit."

No time to get out safely. No keys in the ignition. Not a new enough car to be a push start, and no time to hot wire it. Tansy scrambled for the door panel and hit the power locks just as Melissa grabbed the latch.

"You *bitch*." Melissa smacked her fists on the window.

Tansy jerked up the parking brake then slid over the center toward the passenger door. "Look who's talking."

Unfortunately, Melissa wasn't giving up. She sprinted to the back, planted her hands on the smashed trunk and pushed.

Nothing. She rocked forward futilely a few times as Tansy held her breath, but the weight of the car combined with the shallow incline meant the brake held.

A deafening blare rang out. Melissa had set off the car alarm, which also security locked the doors, effectively sealing Tansy in.

Damn it. Tansy ducked under the dash and went rooting for the fuses she needed. Now the only way to get out was to short the system.

She peeked up every few seconds but didn't see or hear Melissa. Then again, all she could hear was the alarm at deafening levels as she went back to work on the panel.

Pulling the plug brought sweet silence to her ears, and Tansy breathed out in relief. She reached for the door and froze.

Barreling down the road toward her was her SUV. The red taillights flickered, but Melissa had obviously had the bright idea of grabbing the vehicle to, what? Bump the car over the cliff to finish the job? Make a quick get away?

Tansy wasn't sure.

What she did know was that ZenBaby's brakes were even

less reliable in reverse, and this trip wasn't going to end the way Melissa hoped.

For either of them.

~

JAKE ROUNDED the corner and froze, slamming on the brakes so hard that a scream escaped Petra in the backseat.

In front of him, Melissa's car was parked almost off the cliff. Above it, Tansy's SUV bounced backward erratically, crossing the final five feet separating it from the car. A second later, the SUV made contact.

The car went sailing over the cliff toward the lake, the SUV right after it.

"Holy shit." Panic flooded his system as he shot his truck forward another twenty feet until he was mostly off the road. Somehow he threw the thing in Park before scrambling out the door and heading for the cliff edge as fast as his feet could go. "*Tansy.*"

"Watch it." Aiden caught Jake by the arm, jerking him back when he would have raced right over the edge.

"What the hell just happened?" Jake demanded, trying to shake free from his brother. "*Tansy.*"

"You falling after her doesn't help anyone," Aiden shouted.

Denial shot to his lips, but Jake was more interested in moving than arguing. He jerked to the left and broke away, leaping to the side of the hill where there was at least something to grab onto as he leaned toward the—

Beyond the rocky edge, a small brown-haired boy popped into sight out of seemingly nowhere.

"Jeffrey?"

"The hell?" Aiden muttered from behind him.

Jake stayed focused on the kid, looking for a way to reach him. "Stay there, buddy. I'm coming to get you."

"No." Jeffrey lifted a hand, worry in his eyes. "I'll fall."

Shit. Jake froze. "What are you standing on?"

Jeffrey looked down. "A rock. It's wiggly."

Christ. "Okay, stay still. I'll find...something." Jake glanced up the hill, hoping for inspiration.

"I'm going down the path. I'll try to get below him," Aiden called, his voice fading as he ran.

"I'll check the truck. You have booster cables if nothing else. They'll make a decent rope," Petra offered before turning and sprinting out of sight.

Jake took a deep breath and returned his gaze to Jeffrey. "You okay?"

The little tyke dipped his chin solemnly once before shaking his head. "Scared."

"Me too, buddy. Stay very still, okay?" Jake used every morsel of strength to stay in place and stay calm when everything inside him was screaming to find Tansy. To go to her, to see if there was any chance—

"Jake?"

Oh God. That was her voice, out of the empty air. "*Tansy?*"

"No, Tansy. Don't move." Jeffrey stared in the opposite direction now. "Stay secret so no one will see you."

A long, dragged out groan sounded. Tansy sounded drunk or maybe semi-conscious. "'Kay. You too, then. *Shhh.*"

"*Shhh,*" Jeffrey repeated back. He met Jake's eyes. "She's in a bush. It's not a very big bush."

Fuck. "Can I reach it?"

Jeffrey glanced upward to the edge of the cliff above his head. "Nope."

The phone in Jake's pocket rang, and he nearly jumped out

of his skin. He somehow kept his footing and answered the thing on speaker. "Yeah?"

"I can see you guys, but there's no route from here." Aiden gasped out the words. He must have sprinted the entire way to be at the bottom already. He lowered his voice. "Ah, shit. Melissa didn't make it."

"She's there?"

"Driver's seat of Tansy's SUV. Sort of driver's seat—she got tossed. Christ, this is a mess." Aiden took a deep breath. "I've checked again. She's not breathing, and there's no heartbeat. She's gone."

Maybe Jake should have felt something other than numb at that news, but terror and fear for Tansy and Jeffrey outweighed everything. "Keep looking for a way to access the hill. Or at the least, stop them if they fall."

An impossible task, but Aiden was kind enough to not tell him that. "Be smart, bro. Think through every move."

"Jake, I got the cables." Petra inched her way toward him.

"Call for help," Jake told Aiden before shoving his phone away and motioning Petra forward. "You feel like a little climbing?"

"Sure." Petra stopped a foot away, watching as he pulled his belt free from his pants and offered it to her. "Excellent. Double knot the cable to it in the back, and you can anchor me so I can see what it looks like."

"Jeffrey says he's not on firm ground, and I heard Tansy."

Petra's eyes widened as she tightened the belt around her waist. "She's here?"

"Partway down. Not out of danger yet," Jake said softly. "You don't take risks, okay? Just...check it out first."

As much as he desperately needed Tansy and Jeffrey to be safe, if anything happened to Petra, Aiden wouldn't survive.

Petra squeezed Jake's arm. "I'll do everything I can."

Jake double-looped the end of the cable around his forearm and gripped the bendy plastic as tightly as possible. Bracing back slightly in case Petra slipped, he spoke to Jeffrey. "Hold on tight and watch. If anything starts to move, tell us to stop. Can you do that?"

"Yup." Jeffrey glanced over his shoulders. "Tansy?"

"I'm here, kiddo. Just hanging out."

God. Only Tansy could joke at a time like this.

"We're coming to get you, Tans. Don't move," Jake ordered.

"Not moving is a good idea. I think I'm stuck. And partly broken."

Petra had made it about five steps away from Jake, and she peered over the edge, a soft laugh escaping. It sounded a hell of a lot more forced than usual, but it still helped. "You're upside down, my friend. Stuck is good for a few more minutes."

"All the blood in my body is pooling in my brain," Tansy began before stopping. "Maybe hurry? I just felt something shift."

"Hurrying, I promise." Petra eased onto her belly, one leg over the edge as she wiggled toward Jeffrey. "Hey, bud. As soon as I reach you, grab on and climb, okay? Jake has me tight, so you go right ahead and climb like a monkey."

The booster cables were the longest on the market, but Jake was rapidly running out of his makeshift rope. "How much farther?" he asked Petra.

"Another arm's length." Petra cursed softly. "Jeffrey, look at me. I need you to hold out your hand."

"The rock is wiggling," Jeffrey whispered.

"I see it. But I'm nearly there. Hold on—"

Sudden weight hit the cord as Petra vanished, nearly jerking Jake off his feet. Jeffrey yipped sharply before the sound cut off.

"Petra," Jake roared.

"We're good. I got him. I got you, kiddo. It's okay." Petra spoke loudly to be heard over Jeffrey's crying. Jake ignored everything as he dug his heels into the dirt and pulled the cable up hand over hand.

Petra's head popped over the edge, and a second later, Jeffrey scrambled over her shoulders, headed straight for Jake. A second later he had a death grip on Jake's neck.

"Let me get Petra—" Jake began, but Petra cut him off, crawling on her hands and knees.

She coiled their makeshift rope in her arms and headed for the road above them. "We need to go from directly above. Come on. I got the line."

Jake scooped Jeffrey up. "Tansy. You okay?"

"Peachy." The word was soft and slurred.

"Stay awake, baby."

"'Kay. Jake? Love you."

This was not happening. "Love you too. Hold on tight. We'll get to you in a jiffy." Ignoring the urge to head over the edge right there, Jake shot up the hill after Petra.

Time had to be running out on their luck. How much longer could Tansy's precarious perch last?

23

———

The throbbing in her head wasn't going away. Then again, the pain meant she wasn't dead at the bottom of the hill, so it had to count for something positive, Tansy decided.

If she could have thrown herself out of the car a couple of seconds *before* ZenBaby made impact instead of after, things would have been different. "Note to self. Next time, move faster."

Please, God, let there be a next time for bad choices.

Her left leg throbbed in time with the pulse in her temple, but she'd already made the mistake of trying to adjust position once—nope. When she hit the ground and the ground had decided to hit back, something had definitely gone *snap* in her shin.

Now that the adrenaline rush was over, the numbness in her brain was helpful. It meant things didn't hurt quite as much as they should. But the whole *head lower than the rest of her body* position meant she was beginning to see spots in front of her eyes.

Then suddenly, she saw the face of an angel. If angels looked like Ryan Zhao, one of the Heart Falls fire hall volunteers.

"This is a new one for you, Tans." His hands moved rapidly, but his smile stayed firmly in place. Something clicked at her waistline, and he breathed a sigh of relief. "You're attached to a lifeline now. If the cliff goes, we'll swing a little, but you're safe."

"Excellent." The word came out slightly slurred. Tansy's tongue didn't seem to fit in her mouth anymore. "How's Jeffrey?"

"Better than you," Ryan assured her, reaching for the spinal board dangling to his right. "This part will get a little awkward. Feel free to scream if you need to."

"Can't." Tansy grit her teeth as Ryan slipped the board into position beside her. "Can't scare Jake."

Ryan chuckled. "Interesting he's the one you're worried about."

"He loves me," Tansy informed Ryan.

"So I hear. Brace yourself. Moving on three. Ready?"

Oh God, this was going to hurt. Tansy counted with Ryan and breathed out as he slid her onto the board. The scream behind her teeth stayed there from sheer willpower, a gritted growl escaping instead.

Sometime during the strapping in process, Tansy let the darkness wash over her.

The next thing she felt was coolness on her skin and the sound of gentle beeping in the background. A tentative inhale brought the scent of antiseptic and a marked ache in her ribs. "Gah."

"Tansy?"

Fingers tightened on her hand. Tansy blinked to discover

familiar blue eyes in a worried face hovering beside her. "It's you."

"Thank God you're awake." Jake cupped her face tenderly with one hand, clinging to her hand with the other. "Jeffrey's safe."

She'd been about to ask. "Good. That's good. No, that's wonderful."

"It is. You, on the other hand? You've got a broken tibia. It was a clean break and set well. Other than that, how do you feel?"

Tansy took a moment to do a real assessment. Aches and pains danced over her body, her palms were scraped, and her lower left leg was definitely in a cast. She glanced around the hospital room, gaze hesitating on the mystery man who stood in the open doorway. His outfit clearly said cop, and his feet were braced wide and hands clasped in front of him. While he wasn't staring, he was most definitely keeping an eye on her and Jake.

Then she couldn't see the man anymore because Jake cupped her face in both hands and kissed her tenderly.

Screw the aches and pains. She was alive. Tansy kissed him back, curling her arms around his neck the best she could while hooked to an IV. Jake hugged her back so tightly Tansy had to pull hard for air. Did she care?

Not. One. Bit.

The hug eased slightly as Jake took a big breath and let it out slowly.

Tansy took a big breath as well and let it out, only she pursed her lips and blew in his face.

His lips twitched, and some of the fear in his expression lightened. "Mischief."

"You know you love me."

"I do." His expression went serious. "You up for an important talk?"

"Yup." Because once it was over, she could ask for more painkillers. Plus, the guy watching them from the doorway—it was creepy, to be honest.

Jake leaned back, speaking softly but clear enough to be heard by the man in the door. "I called in a few favours. Jackson Murray is a friend, and he's taking point on the investigation. You remember what happened?"

"Yeah." Tansy hesitated, searching her memories. "Did I hear Aiden right? Melissa didn't make it?"

His expression went grim again. "Yeah. And I can't say much more because Jackson needs to ask you official questions, but the fact Melissa died while in your SUV is messed up."

Tansy shivered. That could have been her—

"*Shhhh.*" Jake's strong arms curled around her again. "You're alive. You're safe."

"Jeffrey is safe, too." Tansy nodded against Jake's chest. It still didn't feel possible, but she would cling to all the good she could. "Investigation? Am I a suspect in her death?"

"No. Not really. But he needs to talk to you." Jake tipped his head toward the door. "Okay if he comes in?"

She would have liked a ton more time to talk first, but that probably wasn't an option. "I guess."

Jake squeezed her hand as he rose. "Don't worry. Jackson is on our side. It'll be okay."

Jackson was a dark-haired white man with silver at his temples and a pair of wire-framed glasses he pushed up immediately after shaking Tansy's hand. "Sorry for having to do this right away, but the sooner we get the info in, the better."

"Okay." Tansy sat up straighter. "What do you need to know?"

"Petra found your phone, so we found the message Melissa

sent you." Jackson took out a notebook and pen. "Why did Melissa ask if you wanted Jeffrey?"

God, what was the right answer? How much of the truth had Jake told his friend? Tansy deliberately didn't look at Jake as she mentally raced through options of what to say.

In the end, she went with a simple truth. "I wanted Jeffrey to have a better life than Melissa was giving him. Both Jake and I wanted that, and Melissa knew it."

Jackson made a couple of notes. "What happened when you got to the lookout?"

Explaining about the trunk incident, and her shitty SUV brakes, and the mad scramble to get out of the car took more energy than expected, and in the end, Tansy felt like day old celery as she leaned on her pillows and sipped the water Jake handed her.

Jackson nodded slowly a few times as he finished his notes. He glanced between Tansy and Jake then dipped his chin. "I got enough. You get a copy of that paperwork we talked about in as soon as possible, Jake, and that'll cover all the bases."

"We appreciate it," Jake offered his hand as the man stood.

Jackson shook it firmly then smiled gently at Tansy. "You're a lucky woman. Second chance at life and all that."

"Never a dull day," Tansy quipped back.

The door closed, and Jake returned to her side. "Sorry I couldn't warn you ahead of time. You did great."

"Does he know all the bullshit Melissa put you through?" Tansy asked quietly.

"Sort of?" Jake offered. "Jackson is one of the guys I asked to track Melissa when she vanished. So he knew things weren't great—how she was treating Jeffrey."

Tansy's brain couldn't line up everything neatly, but she did remember one part. "What paperwork?"

Jake took another deep breath. "Remember when Melissa

wanted to add me to Jeffrey's birth certificate? During the apartment purge after she left, Declan found the paperwork she'd already signed in the garbage. He kept it. I've signed it, and Petra's loaded a copy into the database. I'm officially listed as Jeffrey's dad on paper, which means no one can take him away from us."

A sudden spark flared in Tansy's chest, and she gasped at the sensation. It was painful and perfect, and the next second, tears burst free like a dam had exploded, and there was nothing she could do to stop them.

"Oh God, *Tansy*. What's wrong?" Jake brushed his hands over her as if searching for a new wound. "Do I need to call the doctor?"

"No. I'm happy," Tansy gasped out between sobs. "So happy."

They'd held onto hope for so long that having an answer that meant Jeffrey was safe seemed unreal.

She let herself cry it out, leaning into Jake's arms. Letting the sadness of her own five-year-old self fall away and find a solid footing with High Water and all it stood for.

A solid footing with Jake by her side.

When she eased away, he didn't move. Just stayed close, offering his support. "Thanks for being here," she whispered.

"There's nowhere else I want to be," Jake offered quietly. "I'm not the only one, by the way. Your entire family stuck around for hours until I convinced them to head home."

She snorted. "How did you do that?"

"Bribery," he admitted. "We're expected at your parents for dinner as soon as you feel up for it. Then a visit with Ivy and Walker followed by Rose and Chance." His grin widened. "Plus, it appears your sister Fern has big news she wants to share with you in person."

"Really?" Tansy thought back to her sister's odd behavior at the auction. "Okay. So we're booked for the next week?"

"Definitely."

Tansy hesitated. Jake had said everything was okay, but fear lingered like an ache in her soul. "Where's Jeffrey?"

Jake tenderly brushed a final tear off her cheek with his thumb. "He's at High Water with the family. We didn't know how long you'd be out after the operation to set your leg." He made a face. "Plus, I didn't really want him around for the police investigation. Jackson is rock solid, but just in case—"

"No," Tansy said quickly. "I'm glad Jeffrey's not here. Although I'd love to see him. He was so brave, Jake. So scared, but so brave."

"He's a brave little boy. You'll have to wait until tomorrow to tell him that, though, because it's late. It's already after visiting hours, and they've got him settled down at the house." Jake indicated the clock on the wall. "You missed supper."

"Not hungry." She hesitated. "I'm sorry Melissa's dead. I never wanted that."

"None of us did," Jake said softly. He linked their hands together and stared at the connection for the longest time before lifting his gaze to hers. "Melissa made choices, Tansy. Same as you and me. Every step of the way, we had to decide how we'd act and react to the hand we'd been dealt in life. Somewhere along the line, she broke and took a wrong turn. That's on her. All we can do now is try to make a difference in the life she left behind."

"Jeffrey."

He nodded. "Jeffrey."

A knock on the door sounded an instant before a nurse paced in. "Time for your meds," the young man offered cheerily. "It's better to stay ahead of the pain so you get some rest tonight."

"Okay." Tansy watched as he administered the dose into the IV tube beside the bed then quietly left. She turned to Jake, "Tomorrow I go home, though."

"Absolutely," he agreed.

Home. Which was a place, but more than anything, it was a feeling. It was the people in her world who meant everything to her.

It was love.

How did she tell him that? How did she make it clear that this thing inside her, for him, and for Jeffrey, was big and huge and shiny, even in the sadness of loss, and the messed up cliff, and trunks with glowing pull handles and—

"Those are good drugs." Tansy blinked hard, the floaty sensation in her brain twisting in circles even as she chased an important idea. "Home is love. You and me. And Jeffie. And the guys. And gals—Sydney too. She says *guys* is unisex, so all of us."

Jake's lips twitched. "You're getting high."

"High on love," Tansy agreed. "We're almost a family."

Wait.

That wasn't what she wanted to say. She needed for him to know they *were* a family in all the ways that mattered.

Only Jake had risen to his feet to press a kiss to her forehead. "*Shhh.* Go to sleep. I'll be right here when you wake, bright and early."

"Marry." Tansy's tongue twisted to a stop before she could get it all out.

"Merry and bright, yes," Jake parried back. "My unstoppable Tansy."

Dammit. That was nice, but it wasn't what she meant. Fighting to get the words right through the furry blanket on her brain wasn't happening.

She'd have to ask him in the morning. Or as soon as she had her feet under her. Cast and all.

They were meant to be together.

24

A gentle touch landed on his shoulder, and Jake jerked upright.

"You won't be able to move after sleeping like that." Sydney shook her head. "Crawl onto the bed beside her."

Jake peered at his watch through bleary eyes. "Is Tansy okay? What are you doing here?"

"They're short staffed, so I took a shift." Sydney glanced at Tansy's chart then nodded firmly. "She's doing fine. They cut back on the painkiller on the second dose, so she should be wide awake by ten. She'll be cleared to head home then."

"How's my brother?"

Sydney snorted. "Stubborn."

Jake resisted the urge to roll his eyes. "Other than the usual. How's his head?"

"He refused to come into the hospital, so I stitched him up at High Water." Her eyes flashed with annoyance and a hint of something Jake would guess was satisfaction. "He whines a lot."

"Declan?" What exactly had Sydney done to his stoic oldest brother? "What did you stitch him with, a staple gun?"

"Tempting idea. I'll consider that for next time." She shrugged. "He's fine as well. The stitches will come out in a week. Other than a bump to the head, I think his pride was hurt more than anything."

"Melissa wasn't what we expected, on so many levels." Sadness mixed with his sense of happiness, and it seemed very wrong.

Something of what he felt must have shown on his face because Sydney raised a brow. "You had better not be feeling guilty for surviving. You, Tansy, Jeffrey."

"No guilt about that." He measured her and decided to go for it. "Can you keep an eye on Declan for the next few days? Just to make sure he doesn't do himself permanent damage?"

"He's a big boy," Sydney pointed out. "Probably not keen on a babysitter."

"No, he'd hate it." Jake nodded seriously.

She reacted as expected, a wide grin crossing her face. "I'll be sure to drop by often."

Amusement danced through him even as Jake rubbed his neck, easing closer to the bed. The idea of joining Tansy was tempting. She slept on her side, fingers meshed with his. "I don't want to wake her."

"An earthquake wouldn't wake her," Sydney assured him. "Also, if she does have any bad dreams, you'll be that much closer if you're already in bed with her. Go on," she insisted, pulling the IV cord out of the way and gesturing him onto the mattress. "Doctor's orders."

Tansy muttered something softly before nestling back into his body. She tucked his hand against her belly and let out a contented sigh.

Sydney wiggled her fingers in farewell then closed the door behind her.

Jake was asleep before the door clicked shut.

Waking up with Tansy alive and laughing softly, her torso wiggling against him, was a sweet heaven.

"Did I miss something funny?" Jake asked quietly.

"No." Tansy patted his hand. "Just thinking how nice it was to be here and then realizing this is a terrible place to be happy about. I'm happy to be alive but not thrilled to be in a hospital."

"Situation normal then, all fucked up?"

"Pretty much," she agreed.

It wasn't until they were home that Jake felt he could take a full, easy breath.

Tansy seemed the same. They paused on the porch, and she met his gaze straight on, leaning on her crutches. "I love you."

"Convenient, since I love you too."

Which meant she was laughing as they stepped into the house.

A second later, Jeffrey leapt on Tansy like a feral kitten, clinging tightly as tears poured out of him.

Tansy patted his back, a slightly watery look in her own eyes as she smiled at Jake. She teetered slightly, but somehow kept her balance, one crutch held as an anchor.

"He was fine a minute ago," Jinx insisted, joining them at the door. "We were playing a game, and he was okay."

"He's okay now, too," Tansy assured her. Jake wrapped his arms around Jeffrey and Tansy, and the three of them swayed gently in the front foyer.

"I'm glad you're safe, Tansy," Jinx offered.

"Thanks. It's good to be home."

"Thanks for all you did to help," Jake told Jinx. "It made a difference."

The girl's chin rose. "Good." She dipped her chin and made eye contact with Jeffrey. "Hey, buddy. Come give Auntie Jinx a hug so Tansy can get off her feet. You can cuddle with her once she's sitting down."

Jeffrey unlatched himself from Tansy before clutching tightly to Jinx. "Tansy?"

"Yes, Jeffster?" Tansy asked politely.

"I live here now." The words came out as a whisper, but most definitely a statement, not a question.

"You live here now," Tansy affirmed, smiling at him and bopping him on the nose with a finger. "That okay with you?"

His chin dipped up and down like a bobblehead on a bumpy road. "Yup."

Jake wrapped an arm around Tansy's shoulder and hugged her briefly. "Come on. Time to make some plans with the family."

She grinned at him. "Breaking out the notebook, are you?"

"You'll see."

He kept quiet, his heart in his throat as every member of the family came and greeted Tansy with a hug or a kiss or some kind of outpouring of love. Tansy fussed over Declan's head bandage. Petra squeezed Tansy so tightly he thought they'd be stuck together like a *best friends forever* statue.

Even Logan made his way over and offered Tansy his hand. "Glad you're only partly broken."

"You and I aren't winning any races these days, are we?" she teased.

"We'll get there," he said, determination in his tone.

She pulled him in for a hug. "Darn tooting we will."

By the time the gauntlet of greetings was run, Tansy looked tired. She settled at the table and offered him a grateful smile when he rearranged a chair for her to put up her foot. "Lifesaver."

"Tough mentor," he corrected. "There's work to be done."

Tansy frowned briefly as everyone joined them, settling around the table. "Work?"

Jeffrey climbed into Jake's lap, resting his head on Jake's chest, and a warm buzz of happiness flashed inside. "High Water changes."

"Summer planning meeting," Petra explained.

"Adjustments to our routine, living arrangements, that sort of thing." Kevin placed a cup of tea in front of Tansy then settled into his chair.

A small hand slipped up to Jake's face. Jeffrey cuddled in, patting his cheek softly. Trusting that he was safe.

Trusting that he was loved.

Trust. Beautiful and precious.

Trust...and love. They really did go hand in hand.

THE GATHERING WASN'T what she'd expected to deal with right after getting home, but it was a good idea, Tansy decided. If she'd settled into the couch she might have gotten all tangled up again in mentally rehashing the day before, and nothing good could come from that.

She picked up her tea and took a sip, preparing for what might come next. "Changes?"

"It's important that we keep our goals in mind," Declan offered seriously.

"Oh, hang on. You need this." Jinx brought Tansy a box.

Everyone stared expectantly as Tansy picked up the black case with its stream of silver stars down the middle. "It's pretty."

"Open it," Jinx demanded impatiently. "Jake bought it for you."

"Jake did?" She met his eyes then lowered her voice. "Is it safe to open in public?"

He chuckled. "Very safe."

Eagerly, she popped off the top to reveal a hardcover black journal with a scattering of silver and gold stars over the surface. The journal part screamed Jake. The stars were definitely more her style.

"Beautiful yet practical." Tansy smiled at him. "Thank you."

"Open it." Jinx again. The girl nearly bounced in her seat.

Tansy raised a brow but did as commanded. Instead of the fresh clean blank pages she expected—

"Someone wrote in here already. I see..."

She stalled out. The first page was blank, but the second page displayed Petra's familiar handwriting, and it started with *The best friends own a piece of your heart forever.*

"Pretty journals are the worst." Petra leaned forward as she offered an explanation. "It's like you don't want to actually use them in case you make a mistake or mess up. So we decided we'd get things started for you."

No way did Tansy want to rush through reading the message from Petra. Or the one on the next page from her sister Rose. Or the one after that signed by her Grandma Sonora.

Tansy flipped slowly through the pages, stealing the barest glimpse of messages of love and acceptance from all the people in her life who meant the world to her. Everyone at the table. Messages from her family.

Smile firmly in place, her lips quivered a little as emotion struck.

She flipped to a page that held a few sketches and paused. She laid the book open on the table. "What's this?"

"Possible renovations to the main house," Jake explained.

Tansy met his gaze. "More renos?"

"We made some good plans when we dreamed about High Water," Aiden said. "The living quarters for each of us Skye brothers out under the art studio, for example. But we forgot that life changes, and our needs would change as well. We're not three bachelors setting up rooms anymore."

Tansy eyed the drawings closer, her jaw hanging open as she mentally rearranged the rooms and figured out what it meant. "Is this an addition past my bedroom?"

Jake adjusted Jeffrey slightly. The kid's eyes were half-lidded. He'd probably had a terrible sleep after the hell of the past few weeks.

Oh. *Oh.*

"A room for Jeffrey," Tansy guessed.

"Yes, and a small living space so you have privacy even when there are female ranch hands around." Jake cleared his throat, looking slightly sheepish. "So *we* have privacy."

Tansy laughed quietly, so as not to startle Jeffrey. "For a quiet, private guy, you really are doing this thing between us right out there in the open."

"When you're in love, you do stupid shit," Jake drawled.

"Or so I hear," Tansy teased.

They grinned at each other.

She was so damn tempted to do the final thing. The part she'd tried to spit out last night before getting loopy on drugs, but consent mattered. While getting a family living space tossed at her in front of all of High Water might seem a big tell, she wanted one thing to be only them.

"You good with the idea?" Declan asked.

"It's a great idea," Tansy returned firmly, peering closer at the pages. "Don't bother to put a kitchen in there, though."

"Just a space for a kettle and a snack fridge," Jake suggested.

"Perfect." Tansy glanced around at the family gathered at the table. Because that's what they were. Just as much family by choice as the Fields were. "Because *this* is my kitchen." She gestured to the counters and ovens behind her. "My domain. My *precious*...." She offered the last in a nasally, teasing tone.

The instant smiles in reaction were perfect.

The next hour was spent with actual planning, not only for the renovations to the house. Kevin and Logan good naturedly argued over which of them should move into Jake's former space, i.e., both insisting the other should take it. Logan won the battle, which meant Kevin rolled his eyes a lot but headed out willingly with Declan and Logan to move his things into the apartment.

Tansy fought exhaustion then snickered as Petra leaned in close and glared at her. "That's a pretty face."

"That's my *you will do as you're told* face. Naptime. As you've heard, you're off official cooking duty for at least a week."

"I *want* to cook, though." Although not at this exact moment.

"Trust me." Aiden slid in beside Petra. "You will be called upon a lot to help. But you're sous chef, not executive chef."

Now was not the time to explain that meant more work, not less. "Fine. I'll cut and chop as ordered."

"Right now, you'll count zzzzs in your bed," Petra ordered.

"Yes, Mom." Tansy wiggled her way upright, accepting the crutches Jake handed her. "You plan to tuck me in?"

"Absolutely." Jake hesitated. "There's something we need to do first."

"Sure." Tansy eyed her leg cast. "As long as it doesn't involve dancing."

He held his hand to her. "No Tansy Dance Scale tonight."

Aiden winked. Petra grinned. Even Declan looked as if he knew what was up, but Jake ignored the rest of the room and guided Tansy toward the bedrooms.

She wobbled when he led her to the right instead of the left. "Okay?"

"I want to check in on Jeffrey," Jake offered.

Jinx had taken him away during the meeting and tucked him in for his own nap. "He's probably asleep." Tansy peeked in the door then hummed softly. "You're not asleep."

Jeffrey sat upright on the mattress they'd temporarily placed in the corner of Jinx's room so he wouldn't be alone.

He looked nervous, and Tansy hurried to his side the best she could. "Hey, bucko. You should be sleeping."

He glanced past her to Jake. "I have something for you."

It took some coordinating, but Jake helped, and in the end Tansy sat on the mattress beside a very wiggly Jeffrey.

Jake settled on the other side, an accepting smile in place. "Go ahead," he encouraged.

Jeffrey took a big breath then slid his hand under his pillow. He pulled out a shiny silver and gold bracelet that was strangely familiar—

"Oh. I found that before." Tansy frowned. "Wait, I found that a long time ago and forgot about it." She glanced at Jake, but he was smiling reassuringly at Jeffrey. "I don't know who it belongs to."

"I do," Jake said quietly. "Go on, Jeffrey."

"I didn't steal it." Jeffrey wrinkled his nose. "I mean, I *did* steal it, but I didn't give it to her. It's yours. I wanted to give it back."

Tansy's brain buzzed. "I found that—*Sheesh*, the day the girls discovered Logan. It was under the couch. What with one thing and another, I put it somewhere safe then forgot about it."

"It was in your bathroom." Jeffrey looked ready to cry. "It's yours."

"Oh, sweetie. Thank you. I'm glad you gave it back. Come here." She opened her arms and Jeffrey wormed in tight. She glanced at Jake, hoping for a few more clues. "You said you know who the bracelet belongs to?"

"It was my mom's," Jake offered softly.

Wow. "How did it get under the couch?"

"Not sure, but that part doesn't matter. Jeffrey made a choice to do what's right, and that's what's important." Jake leaned in and peered at Jeffrey. "Good job, buddy. It's not easy to do what's right, but you did it. I'm proud of you."

The tear factory turned up to high. Tansy felt a little weepy herself.

"Hey, I don't mind a little tears, but I do need your help. So if you can, let's do the next thing, okay, Jeffrey?" Jake clapped his hands softly.

Jeffrey wiggled free, wiping at his face with the backs of his hands. "'Kay."

"Like we practiced," Jake prompted.

The little guy nodded vigorously then turned to Tansy. "Jake says he's my daddy now."

Oh God. Tansy held it together by a thread. "Yes, he is. And he loves you very much."

Because being loved had made all the difference to her, and it would to Jeffrey as well.

The little guy waved the fist that held the bracelet. "This is a mommy bracelet."

Her heart leapt, pounding against her ribcage.

Jeffrey opened his palm, offering the trinket like a sacrifice. "It's for you."

"Perfect." With zero hesitation, Tansy picked it up and held it to her chest. She swallowed around the knot in her throat. "Because I love you and want to be your mommy."

The three way hug that followed was perfectly awkward and very tear-filled. Tansy wouldn't have wanted it any other way.

When Jeffrey finally settled down, eyelids reluctantly closing in sleep, Jake picked Tansy up and they stole into her —*their*—bedroom.

Jake paused by the door. "I'm sorry for throwing that at you unannounced. When he showed me the bracelet, he was worried Melissa did what she did because he'd hidden it from her. I had to tell him about being his dad, and then he begged to know if you were his mom and—"

"Marry me." Tansy tossed it out, interrupting Jake's monologue, leaning on her crutches as she grinned at this man who was now impulsive in all the right ways.

Jake's jaw dropped.

"Marry me," she repeated. "I'd get down on one knee, but I might not get back up again very quickly."

His grin bloomed. "I'd say you should have wined and dined me first, but you pretty much do that every night."

"I have a ring for you," Tansy informed him.

He gaped at her. "Get out."

It felt amazing to be able to say it. "I. Planned. Ahead."

"You're beyond amazing." Jake curled himself around her. "Where's my ring?"

"Where's my answer first?"

A moment later, Tansy was resting in Jake's lap on the edge of the bed. He stroked his knuckles over her cheek, love in his eyes as he examined her face. "I wanted to learn how to be more like you. So in love with life and the people around you. So full of joy and passion. I never dreamed how contagious it would be—exposure to full-on *life at maximum* is addictive. But it's not only your spontaneity, it's your heart. You give so much. You love with every fiber of your being."

Tansy kissed him gently. "Marry me," she said again.

"I would be honoured to be yours in every way possible.

But you've already got me, heart and soul." Jake pulled away when she would have kissed him again. "My ring?"

She laughed. "Side table. It's in the candle tin with the pink mandala."

He wiggled far enough away to lean over and pull the drawer open and nab the tin. His arms around her, she helped open it, then pulled out the worn silver ring she'd been saving for the right moment.

Jake swallowed hard. "That's a family ring."

"It was my original grandfather's. I never met him, but Grandma Sonora said Greg was the best of men. She fell head over heels in love with him at eighteen, and even though she's in love with Ashton now, she said love doesn't die when a person leaves us. It's precious and forever, and when I told her I loved you, she said she wanted us to have it."

Jake closed his fingers around hers. "I'm honoured," he repeated. "And I'm thrilled to be welcomed into the Fields family. A family made by choice."

"And love." Tansy slid the ring onto his finger. "So much love."

"Definitely that."

He twisted them to the mattress and slipped off her sweater. She pulled his shirt over his head, and eventually they finished getting naked, although the kissing and touching and laughing made it take a long time.

Also the cast, but they had no trouble getting creative to deal with that issue.

When he'd already brought her up once and Tansy was breathless from keeping quiet, Jake rolled over her and slid them together intimately.

He paused. "We're readjusting the renovation. Our bedroom is going to be on an outside wall where you can make all the noise you want."

"Deal," Tansy agreed instantly. She caught him around the shoulders and kissed him until they were both seeing stars.

"I love you," he whispered as they tipped over into pleasure.

"I love you too."

As they lay cuddling on the bed later, Tansy sighed happily. "You know, you were right. Spontaneity is fun, but so is planning ahead."

"You can plan right now?" Jake asked. "I need to up my game."

She laughed. "Trust me, your game is great."

He hummed. "Trust me, I love you. Spontaneous or preplanned, we got this."

EPILOGUE

Sydney Jeremiah. Child prodigy, near genius, sarcastic as fuck, with an evil sense of humour that somehow tickled Declan's funny bone in ways he never expected.

He swore she was trying to drive him out of his goddamn mind.

It wasn't the fact that she was smarter than him by umpteen degrees. Or even that she kept putting herself into fucked up and dangerous situations by offering medical services to cranky bastards who lived in remote-as-hell places. Her bravery annoyed him but also turned him on.

That? *That* was the issue.

She only had to glance his direction, and he was ready to fuck her into tomorrow.

Barely over five foot three with curves that would not end. Deep red hair that shone with golden highlights as it lay over his pillow. Her silvery eyes flashed fire as he adjusted his hips and drove them together again, pleasure rippling up his spine until it blasted the base of his skull.

It was only supposed to be sex. Hot, sweaty, dirty sex that left them both satisfied and boneless. No obligations, no expectations.

They'd fallen into bed the first night they'd met at Rough Cut pub, nearly a year ago. A quick release of urgent need and mutual attraction that had turned into booty calls and clandestine meetings all over High Water and Heart Falls. Somehow they'd kept it secret from her best friends and his brothers, although how, Declan had no idea.

Now as he leaned on an elbow, free hand slipping between their bodies to slick over her clit, the need to get her off before he lost control was the only thing on his mind.

After, though? When he lay there with barely enough energy to move and she was happily pulling her clothes back on, that's when it hit again.

Dissatisfaction.

Not with the sex—hell, no—but with the rest of it. The secrets and the idea that it was *only* sex. As fucked up and strange as it was for him to feel that way.

Sydney stood, tucking her shirt into her pants and pulling her hair over the collar of her neat medical shirt. "I'm pleased to confirm you don't have a concussion."

Declan grunted his amusement. "You figure that out while fucking me?"

"No. I knew before. The fucking was a bonus." Sydney leaned over him, one hand pressed to his chest as she looked him over carefully. "Your brother did make me promise to haunt you and make sure you didn't overdo it after the accident."

Another grunt escaped Declan. "Like you need permission to annoy me."

She smiled sweetly. "Hydrate well today, and no riding for

another few days." When he would have protested, she held up a hand. "You don't have a concussion, but you did get hit hard enough to go unconscious. Humour me. If you don't feel like humouring me, do it anyway. I have zero problems telling everyone at High Water you can't ride for a month."

He swore at her softly.

"Right? I can be such a bitch." Sydney put a knee to the bed and leaned in close enough to press their lips together, and suddenly all he could think of was getting her back into bed for another round.

But she moved like lightning and slipped away, waving evilly before vanishing. Leaving him with thoughts that kept circling back to what in the hell was wrong with him.

Sexiest woman in all of Heart Falls was down for a quiet, no-holds-barred affair, and he was...

Declan folded his hands under his head and stared at the ceiling.

Don't sugarcoat it, love. You want more.

He heard the comment in his wife's voice even though Sadie had been gone for four years now. He didn't talk to ghosts, but sure as shit, he knew she'd give him hell if she was able.

It still hurt, thinking about Sadie being gone, but his subconscious, or his id, or whatever the hell they called the part of the brain that wouldn't let a person blow smoke up their own ass was calling the shots right now.

It was time.

He'd been grieving for Sadie, and nothing had interrupted that pain but the plans for High Water. Then he'd still been grieving but ready for sex, and Sydney had jumped in with both feet.

He didn't think he'd ever fully be done grieving for Sadie,

but superficial sex, even spectacular superficial sex, wasn't enough anymore.

Which meant he had some figuring out to do. Sydney was everything Declan had ever wanted in a woman. He liked them smart, he liked them sexy, and he liked them stubborn.

Now to convince her she wanted him too.

❧

New York Times Bestselling Author Vivian Arend
invites you to Heart Falls. These contemporary ranchers live in
a tiny town in central Alberta, tucked into the rolling foothills.
Enjoy the ride as they each find their happily-ever-afters.

❧

The Skyes of Heart Falls
A Cowboy's Bride
A Cowboy's Trust
A Cowboy's Claim

The Stones of Heart Falls
A Rancher's Heart
A Rancher's Song
A Rancher's Bride
A Rancher's Love
A Rancher's Vow

The Coleman's of Heart Falls
The Cowgirl's Forever Love
The Cowgirl's Secret Love
The Cowgirl's Chosen Love

❧

305

ABOUT THE AUTHOR

New York Times and *USA Today* bestselling author Vivian Arend loves to share the products of her over-active imagination with her readers. She writes contemporary, western, and light-hearted paranormal romances. The stories are humorous yet emotional, usually with a large cast of family or friends, and a guaranteed happily-ever-after. Vivian lives in British Columbia, Canada, with her husband of many years— her inspiration for every hero and a willing companion for all sorts of adventures.

www.vivianarend.com